Bluefin
Blues

Also by Paul Kemprecos

Bluefin Blues

Paul Kemprecos

St. Martin's Press ⁑ New York

Library of Congress Cataloging-in-Publication Data

Kemprecos, Paul.
    Bluefin blues / Paul Kemprecos.
        p.   cm.
    ISBN 0-312-16787-3
    I. Title.
    PS3561.E4224B58   1997
    813'.54—dc21   97-19601
                             CIP

First Edition: November 1997
10 9 8 7 6 5 4 3 2 1

For my wife, Christi,
who still makes the sun shine

Acknowledgments

I'd like to express my grateful appreciation to Alex Carlson for giving me his detailed overview of the bluefin tuna fishery in exchange for a cup of coffee at Larry's PX; Walter Williams, who generously shared his time to guide me through the finer points of finding and harpooning giant bluefin tuna; Molly Benjamin for filling me in on bluefin regulatory issues; Brenda Sullivan for explaining the impact regulations have on the fishermen; and Andy McGeoch for his technical expertise. I'm also grateful to Douglas Whynott, whose book *Giant Bluefin* I used as a background source. Any deviations from the factual are mine alone.

Those whom the gods wish to destroy, they first make insane.

—EURIPIDES

Bluefin
Blues

One

CAPT. HAL WEBBER didn't like the fog that enclosed his boat. Not one damned bit. He took a tentative sniff of the heavy, wet air like the basset hound he resembled and wrinkled his sun-mottled nose.

"Stinks," he muttered.

In three decades as a fisherman Webber had used that nose a lot. The other charterboat captains who worked Cape Cod Bay had heard, more often than they cared to remember, that a good sniffer was the secret to a long and healthy career at sea.

The new electronic gadgetry mounted in front of him on the *Osprey*'s console could do wonders, but it paled next to an educated proboscis, in his view. Inhaling a lungful to demonstrate, Webber would declare that an experienced nose could detect a brewing storm, fetch a whiff of schooling fish, or point the direction home like a compass needle.

More important, it could smell trouble, the way it was doing now.

To start with, there was the way the fog materialized. Most daytime fogs give you plenty of warning, appearing as a furry cloud bank that rolls across the surface of the sea. This fog seemed to rise from the depths like foul vapors from a swamp, its pale tendrils quickly weaving a thicket that shut out sound and light. Webber stared morosely through the wheelhouse window thinking the color was off too. Not gray-white like a normal fog. This one was *piss*-colored.

Earlier that morning Webber had brought his thirty-six-foot sports fisherman to a point about a mile west of Billingsgate Shoal. The shoal used to be the island home of a thriving fishing community before it sank beneath the waves, like Atlantis. The waters of Cape Cod Bay were glassy smooth except for a puckering of the water that indicated schooling fish a hundred feet off the port bow. Terns swooped down in quick, jerky dartings to feed on baitfish driven to the surface madly trying to escape the snapping jaws of hungry blues.

The party boat had been over a real honey-hole. The fishfinder screen was covered with blips, indicating hits at every level. Then without warning the temperature dropped at least ten degrees. The atmosphere took on a rank odor, like the kelpy exhalations of drowned men. The little computer-generated fish vanished off the finder's video screen. The seas began to heave in great oily mounds.

That's when Webber moved the *Osprey* to calmer waters nearer Billingsgate. He had barely dropped anchor when the fog caught them. The rising sun should have burned off the mists. Instead, the radiant heat hiked the humidity to steambath levels, and the anemic rays of filtered sunlight gave the fog its unhealthy yellow pallor.

Webber heard a commotion on the deck. Joel Rankin, one of the quartet of New York stockbrokers who'd chartered the *Osprey,* had pulled in a sea robin. The sea robin must have been named by a jokester. The saltwater version of the red-breasted herald of spring bears no resemblance to its feathered namesake. The sea robin is all spikes, gaping mouth, angry pop-eyes, and big bat-wing fins.

Rankin's previous encounters with *any* kind of fish all had taken place in seafood restaurants. He couldn't have known that sea robins are vocal. When he tried to pull the fish off the hook, it puffed up, opened its maw and croaked at him. Rankin

2

recoiled in horror, flung his catch onto the deck, and dropped the rod and reel with a clatter.

"*Careful* now," Webber called, stepping out of the pilothouse. "Spikes on that little fella will go right through your hand."

Rankin backed away from the flopping sea robin. "Goddamn fish *barked* at me."

Rankin's friends had been watching the drama. A stockbroker nicknamed Norman because he looked like the barfly character on *Cheers,* guffawed. "Hey, Joel, you having that monster stuffed and mounted?"

Dave Hanson, the *Osprey*'s young first mate, grinned and picked the sea robin off the deck with a gloved hand. The skinny, towhead youth was still in high school but he had been around boats since he could walk. He carefully removed the hook and tossed the fish over the side.

The stockbrokers let out a chorus of aws.

"Man, I'm exhausted after fighting that monster," Rankin said. "This calls for a beer."

"Sun's not over the yardarm," one of his friends said.

"What the hell's a *yardarm?*" Rankin answered. He went forward and pulled a cold Heineken from the cooler, popped the top, and chugged down half the can. "Beer break," someone said. The others stuck their fishing rods into metal holding sockets and joined Rankin at the cooler.

Webber cocked his head, trying to listen above the laughter and fizzing beer cans. The corners of his mouth drooped into a puzzled frown. He had felt a tremor in the air from the low-end vibration of an engine.

No mistake. A boat was moving in the fog.

He cupped his good ear and tried to get a direction fix. Diffused by the fog, the sound came from every direction at once. Webber slowly moved his head back and forth like a radar antenna homing in on a blip. He froze. His razor-sharp gray eyes peered out from under the visor of his tan cap and tried to probe the impenetrable wall of fog off to the starboard.

His brain processed the data like a computer, comparing the evidence of his senses with the stored experiences of more than thirty years at sea. Big boat. Inboard power. Moving fast. Too *damned* fast. You'd have to be crazy to move at more than a crawl in this visibility. Hell, the *Osprey* wasn't the only fishing boat sitting out the fog. Webber had caught glimpses of other ghostly outlines in the mist.

Webber called out to his mate.

"Hey, Dave, pull in those lines," he said evenly. "I'm going to start the motor."

The sentence was barely out of his mouth when he heard the throb of an engine more clearly than before.

Guuurrr.

The mate picked up on the sound. Like Webber moments earlier, he looked around in an effort to pinpoint it.

"Do it *now*, Dave. We might have to move in a hurry."

Hearing the urgency in Webber's voice, the mate grabbed the nearest rod from its socket. He rapidly rewound the line onto the reel, his hand a blur. Satisfied that the kid was on track, Webber went forward and punched the starter. The *Osprey*'s motor kicked into life with a throaty gargle. Webber grabbed an aerosol canister with a plastic trumpet attached to it and stepped back onto the deck.

The stockbroker named Norman wiped the foam off his upper lip and looked at the aerosol Klaxon. "What's going on, Cap'n?"

"This spot's gone sour," Webber replied nonchalantly. "While you folks drink your breakfast, we're going to look for a new honey-hole. Cover your ears, boys," he warned. He pointed the horn into the fog off the starboard and pressed the button.

Haawnk!

The blast was loud enough to be heard for a mile. As the Klaxon's echoes faded, Webber listened.

Guuurrr.

There was no indication that the other boat had slowed its speed. More worrisome, it sounded even closer.

Webber set his jaw and let the Klaxon blast again, this time for a good ten seconds. Then he listened, his leathery features stitched into a tight-lipped expression of intense concentration.

The pitch of the approaching engines was unchanged; the boat was keeping a steady speed.

"Shit," Webber murmured.

Seconds later a new sound sent shivers up his spine.

Shush-shush.

The boat was so close he could hear its bow cleaving the water. Tiny wavelets gently slapped the *Osprey*'s hull and set it to rocking.

The Klaxon might as well be a fart in a hurricane for all the good it was doing. He put the horn aside, helped Dave reel in the last line, and started toward the pilothouse.

The stockbrokers sensed something was amiss. They had stopped laughing and stood, beer cans clutched in their hands, looking off the *Osprey*'s right.

Webber followed their gaze.

At first he saw nothing. Then his eye caught a movement. He saw thin dark lines several feet above the water, formed in an inverted V by the stainless-steel framework of a boat's pulpit. The metal bow extension seemed to hang suspended in space for an instant. Then the knife edge of the white bow it was attached to blasted out of the fog into the clear. A second later the boat's spotting tower came into view.

Tuna boat, Webber thought. He calculated that the boat was doing twenty or thirty knots in conditions that called for no faster than five. Christ, what was wrong? The bastards *had* to see the *Osprey* sitting dead in the water. The boat would be on them in seconds at that speed.

Webber had a couple of choices, and neither was any good. He could stay where he was and hope the other boat would cut throttle and change course. Or he could get the *Osprey* moving and risk having the boat veer right into him. The decision was made for him. There was no doubt that the boat was headed straight for the *Osprey*.

Webber dashed into the pilothouse and gunned the throttle. The propeller blades bit into the water, the engine roared, and blue exhaust smoke filled the air. After what seemed like hours the bow lifted and the *Osprey* lurched forward.

Too late.

The boat was on them.

The stockbrokers scrambled in every direction. David had frozen into position, transfixed by the oncoming disaster. Not until the pulpit's metal framework was over his head did the first mate react. He ducked under the curve of the hull just before the boat slammed into the *Osprey.*

There was an earsplitting crunch and the groan of wood against wood, followed by an explosion of splinters. The starboard rail disintegrated. Webber was thrown to the deck. He staggered to his feet and tried to walk. The *Osprey* was moving when it was rammed. It lurched violently under the sliding impact and lifted from the water at a crazy angle. Webber was catapulted like a missile from a siege machine. Arms flailing, he splashed into the water. He went down several feet before he clawed his way to the surface, gasping for breath.

The *Osprey* was about twenty feet away. Its bow was high in the air and the stern was partially underwater. The starboard side looked as if it had encountered a buzz saw. There was no sign of anyone in the boat. Webber only caught a glimpse of the *Osprey.* His knee-high rubber boots had filled with water and were dragging him under. He took a deep gulp of air, doubled over, and pulled off one boot. The second boot was harder to remove, but after some strenuous tugging, it too came free.

He bobbed to the surface and snagged a flotation vest that was drifting by. He managed somehow to slip his arms through the holes. With his head out of the water, Webber spun slowly around looking for David or the passengers. He sputtered angrily.

"Goddamn hit-and-run!"

It was supposed to be a yell, but the feeble sound that escaped his throat sounded more like the croak of a sea robin. By then, the big white boat had merged with the fog and its outlines blurred. It was hard to see anything with all the purple-blue exhaust fumes in the air and the seawater that stung his eyes. Painted on the transom in big black letters that stood out clearly against the white was the boat's name:

Lady Pamela.

He watched until the boat disappeared and the rumble of its engine was barely audible. With a heavy heart, he started to swim toward the mangled wreck of the *Osprey* to look for David and his passengers. With each weary armstroke he cursed himself for not acting at the first faint whiff of disaster. The next time his nose told him trouble was in the air, he vowed, he would move a hell of a lot faster.

Two

AT THE TENDER age of twenty-two Coast Guard seaman first class Frankie Mello was experiencing an epiphany. He was painfully discovering he no longer had the stamina for debauchery he had possessed at twenty-one.

Mello would have given up the contents of his stomach hours ago if not for the cool sea air that whipped his face as the forty-four-foot patrol boat moved easily through the water. Tightening his grip on the wheel, he sucked in a deep breath, carefully, as if his ribs were brittle and might break, and let it out slowly, ridding his lungs of tequila vapor. He drank from a scalding mug of black coffee that washed away the coppery taste in his mouth, taking small sips so as not to start a roiling in his gut.

Yesterday on his birthday his friends at the Provincetown Coast Guard station got him trashed. They primed the pump at the Governor Bradford's bar, then made the rounds. The outing had gotten totally out of control after somebody suggested they do shots of Cuervo.

A hand rested on his shoulder. "You doing okay, Frankie?" Petty Officer Eddy Eldridge's ruddy, round face wore an expression of concern.

"Yeah, thanks, I'm okay."

"Coulda fooled me. You look like shit."

"No big surprise. I *feel* like shit."

"You need a break from the helm?"

"Nah." Mello managed a painful grin. "My Coast Guard training will pull me through."

Eldridge tightened his lips in a skeptical smirk.

"Seriously, Eddy," Mello reassured him, "I'm fine. This is the best place for me to be, out here in the fresh air and sunshine."

Eldridge nodded. "Sorry I had to pull you out of the sack for a crummy safety patrol. If'd been up to me, I woulda let you sleep it off. But then I'd have to tell the chief. He wouldn't have been too happy. Schedule's all screwed up after that mess off Billingsgate."

"Guess yesterday was a good day to visit my folks in New Bedford. Guys told me what happened while I was away."

"Coulda been worse if it hadn't been for that EMT out there fishing with his kid. He got right on the radio, called in a Mayday. Then he pulled everybody out of the water and started first aid until we could get a boat and chopper on scene."

Mello nibbled at a plain donut. "One of the guys died, I heard."

"Yeah. Hell of a note. New Yorker goes on his first fishing trip. His pals got banged up, one of them real bad. Medevac took them to Mass General. Skipper and mate were okay."

"Guy running that tuna boat's in deep shit."

"They gotta find him first." Eldridge shook his head. "That was a five-knot fog, and that's pushing it. Any faster with that visibility, you'd have to be crazy or stupid."

Mello nodded in agreement as the boat passed Wood End Light and moved into the open waters of Cape Cod Bay. It was the time of year when the color of the bay shifts away from green and more toward sapphire on the color spectrum. The morning light had the honeyed tint that it gets on the edge of fall. The bay was busy with a mix of commercial and pleasure craft, and whale-watching boats on their way to Stellwagen Bank. There were sails in every direction.

On Eldridge's orders, Mello steered toward the Cape Cod Canal on the other side of the bay. For a landmark he used the tall smokestack at the canal electric power plant.

The patrol was uneventful until they reached the center of the bay, where traffic had thinned out. Eldridge raised his binoculars to his eyes and focused on a distant object. After a moment he lowered the glasses.

"There's a boat about a half mile away," he said, pointing. "Let's check the guy out."

Mello swung the bow around and after a few minutes Eldridge took another look. "She's got a spotting tower and pulpit."

"Tuna boat?" Mello said.

"Yeah. Seems to be drifting. Let's get closer."

The forty-four-footer cut the distance in half. Eldridge, who was squinting through the glasses, said, "Uh-oh."

"What's uh-oh?"

"Take a look. I'll steer." Eldridge handed the binocs over.

Mello studied the vessel through the glasses. It was a wide-beamed, sturdy-looking boat with a wooden hull. There was something else.

"There's a big gash up by the bow," he said, lowering the glasses.

Eldridge had been writing down the boat's registration number. "Take us around so we can check out the name."

Mello wheeled the patrol boat in a lazy circle that took them behind the tuna boat. The name on the transom was *Lady Pamela.*

"What the hell's he doing?" said a crewman named Joe Perry, who had come into the cockpit. It was a good question. The tuna boat just sat there. No anchors were out. It was drifting slightly, pushed by the northwest breeze, its tall spotting platform swinging to and fro in a small arc.

Eldridge studied the boat from one end to the other. Nothing moved. He picked up the radio microphone and called on Channel 16, the emergency hailing channel.

"Come in, *Lady Pamela.* This is the Coast Guard off your stern. Come in on Channel 22, please."

He flicked the channel selector over. There was only the

slight crackle of static. Eldridge tried the hailing channel again, putting some impatience into his voice. "*Lady Pamela,* this is the Coast Guard. We're right behind you. Come *in.*"

No answer.

"Guess we're going to have to pay a house call." Eldridge barked into the microphone, "*Lady Pamela,* stand by for boarding."

Eddy turned to Joe Perry. "Take the helm, Joe. C'mon, Frankie, maybe they'll have some tequila on board."

Mello gave Eddy a dark look. "Something's weird. You don't leave a boat just sitting out here in the middle of the bay."

Eldridge chuckled. "You want to pack your Beretta?"

Mello shrugged. "Just seems strange, that's all."

Eldridge told the helmsman to come around on the tuna boat's port. The crew hung fenders over the side and got lines ready. Joe carefully edged the patrol boat in. It was a little tricky because of the tuna boat's drifting. When the two boats were a few feet apart, Eldridge jumped onto the deck quickly, followed by Mello.

"Tie us off, Frankie. I'll check inside."

Mello was cleating the bowline when he heard Eldridge yell from the pilothouse.

"Holy shit! Frankie, get in here."

Mello stepped into the pilothouse and saw that the boat was not entirely deserted. He saw, too, why no one had answered the radio call. He stared in disbelief until finally, the rank smell of drying blood and the buzz of flies in the enclosed space got to him.

Mello had manfully held on to the contents of his stomach all morning. Now the bile began to rise in his throat. Stirred to action, he dashed from the pilothouse, leaned over the side, and tossed his cookies into the sea.

Three

SAM HELD THE hook high over his head as if he were inviting the world to take a look. Except for a few shreds of bait clinging to the barb, the hook was bare. He grunted profoundly.

"Don't need the US government to tell me fishing has gone to hell in a teakettle," he muttered.

I stopped coiling nylon trawl line into a plastic tub and stared in disbelief. My fishing partner is a good Methodist who would rather *die* than swear. His use of the coarser designation for Hades was about as strong as his language gets. Goes to show how low a fisherman's morals will sink when the fishing is lousy and the feds restrict what you *do* catch.

We had left the pier at four that morning. By eleven o'clock we'd caught barely enough fish to fill a sardine can. After a short discussion, we decided to try a spot nearer to shore. We were coursing along, 360-horsepower Detroit diesel kicking the forty-eight-foot steel hull through the waves at a brisk clip, when *klunk!* It felt as if we'd driven into a pothole.

Sam cut speed to an idle and we coasted to a wallowing stop. He went below to check for damage. I scanned the water but didn't see anything bigger than a few clumps of seaweed.

"No leaks," he said, coming up. He gazed out over the ocean. "Musta been a floating log."

"I dunno, Sam. I think I saw a great white whale with a peg-legged man hanging on to its side just before we heard the bang."

Sam stared at me for a few seconds. He shook his head.

"I'd say that was a *whale* of a story," he said, unsmiling.

Yankee humor. It was as close as Sam ever got to wise-cracking. Sam had been a bit moody. I was happy to see my smart-alecky ways were rubbing off.

He got the boat moving again. At cruising speed the *Mildred D.* began to shake like a wet puppy. The tremors came at regular intervals, fading and starting up again. Sam slowed the boat to a crawl. He listened a few minutes and grimaced.

"Three hundred years ago they'd have hanged her as a witch."

"Who's that, Sam?"

"Millie."

"Somehow I never pictured your sweet wife on a broom-stick."

He sighed and pushed his duckbill cap back so the un-tanned white band of forehead showed just above his frosty eyebrows. "Millie and I had a row last night. Says I've been working too hard. She's worried about my ticker acting up. I told her I have to fish longer to make a decent catch because the fishing's so poor. She told me I was being an old fool."

I had wrongly chalked up Sam's grumpiness to the lack of fish. Domestic discord simply didn't exist within the walls of his house. If Sam and Mildred could put their marriage to music, they'd have a symphony by Mozart. Ann Landers would go out of business if everybody had a marriage like theirs.

"You're saying Millie put a *hex* on you?"

Sam admired Millie's spunk and grinned in spite of himself. "Bad fish day. Now boat trouble."

"Still kind of a reach, Sam. We've had crummy days before this."

"Maybe. Don't know if I ever told you this, Soc, but Millie's ancestors were from Salem."

"I'm a believer. Too bad I forgot my rabbit's foot. Guess we're through fishing for today."

"We were through before we *started*," he said. He pulled his cap low over his eyes, goosed the engine, and swung the wheel around, pointing the *Millie D.* back to port. He kept the boat at low speed so the hull vibration wouldn't shake the bolts loose.

Before long we passed from the ocean into the harbor through a wide cut in the barrier beach and followed the channel markers to the fish pier. Judging the drift exactly, Sam brought the boat alongside the bulkhead, leaving a space barely wide enough to slip a codfish scale into. Sam is getting a little stiff in the joints, and on land he tends to scuttle along like a crab, but on the water he can make a boat move as gracefully as a swan.

We unloaded our catch, which hardly took a minute, moved the trawler over to the jog next to the fish pier, washed down the deck, hosed out the fish box and gathered our gear. Sam was fretting that repairs were going to be expensive. They'd have to haul the boat out of the water, and who knows what they'd find. His guess was a bent driveshaft.

Sam loved the *Millie D.* almost as much as its namesake. To put his mind somewhat at ease, I said, "Tell you what, Sam. Why don't you call up your bride and see if she's had lunch. Take her to that A and W root beer place she likes so well. While you're making Mildred happy, I'll get my scuba gear and take a look under the boat."

He pondered that. Sam's tight as a tick. Spending money on lunch was a weighty decision.

"Sure you don't need me around, Soc?"

"No problem."

Sam was looking tuckered out lately. It might have been age finally catching up with him, combined with the crummy catches that were putting us in the hole financially. Whatever it was, it worried me.

I told him I'd call him later. My scuba equipment was in my pickup truck. I'd left it there after a guy who said he was a treasure hunter hired me to help him find an old schooner. He had

14

top-notch electronic gear, but I should have figured he was no Mel Fisher when he forgot to tighten the clamps on a new outboard motor. It fell off his boat and sank in forty feet of water. The next day he left town. I never dove on the schooner, but I did find his outboard. He never paid me for the work. He must have been in a big hurry because he left his equipment behind. My guess was he hadn't paid for that either and it was only a matter of time before the bank would come looking for it.

I zipped up my wet suit, pulled my air tank on, and slipped into the oily waters of the cove. Moments later, I was under the barnacled hull of the *Mildred D*. It only took a few minutes to discover Sam was right about the bent driveshaft. I was examining the propeller for damage when the clanging began. Sound travels four and a half times faster in water than it does in air, which is how a humpback whale can make a date over hundreds of miles without using the telephone. My head felt as if it were stuck in an iron bucket that was being whacked with a pipe. It did no good to cover my ears. I skidded out from under the boat and kicked to the surface. I pulled the face mask down under my chin and looked over at the fish pier. A fish-packer named Lance was hammering like a blacksmith at a forge on one of the steel ladders that runs down the side of the pier. He saw my head bobbing and gave me a friendly wave.

I swam over to the ladder and handed up my tank, weight belt and fins. Then I heaved myself onto the loading platform and yanked the hood and mask off my head.

"What the hell's going on, Lance?"

Lance was a tall blond kid who wore swept-back ski glasses. "You've got a call. Guy said it was important."

He went into the office and came out with a cordless telephone. I stuck the phone in my ear and said hello. It was hard to be sure because the Boston Pops was playing the "Anvil Chorus" in my skull, but I think somebody was saying my name.

"Mr. Aristotle Socarides? My name is Ansel Forbes. I'm with the law firm of Forbes and Farnham. We'd like to retain your services as a private investigator."

Lance's hammering must have warped my hearing. "Sorry, I've got water in my ears. You *did* say Forbes and Farnham?"

"You've heard of us." It was more a statement than a question.

"Yes, Mr. Forbes, I've heard of your firm." Forbes and Farnham was one of the biggest and oldest law firms in Boston.

"I was hoping we could discuss this matter over lunch. I'm at the beach grill. You know where it is, of course."

I squinted south from the fish pier along the shore. "I can practically see it from where I'm standing."

"How soon can you join me?"

"How about fifteen minutes?"

"I'll be waiting. Looking forward to meeting you."

As I got out of my wet suit and changed into dry clothes, I recalled what I'd heard about Forbes and Farnham from my days as a Boston cop. Not every legal firm can say that its initials are an "expletive deleted" in the halls of justice: prosecutors call it "Effen' F." One bruised and bloodied district attorney told me that taking on an F 'n' F client was like climbing into the ring with a whole team of five-hundred-pound gorillas in pinstriped suits.

My legal clients tend more toward underpaid public defenders looking for a bargain-basement PI. I was wondering why a high-powered law firm like Forbes and Farnham would call me.

After putting my scuba gear in the truck, I started off along the beach. The beach grill is only a couple of hundred yards from the fish pier. As Einstein proved, everything is relative. The stroll along the water's edge took only a few minutes, but it would turn out to be one of the longest walks of my life.

Four

THE WIDE WOODEN deck attached to the one-story restaurant building was crowded with people bulking up under the shade of the big umbrellas. From the red-hot glow of their faces, it was clear most had spent the morning imitating slices of toast on the beach. A man wearing a tie waved at me. I went over and asked if he was Forbes. He stood and flashed a pearly smile, pulled out a latticework metal chair, and squeezed my hand in a strong grip, all in one single fluid motion. Forbes had two inches over me, which must have put his lean frame at about six three.

"Thank you for seeing me on such short notice, Mr. Socarides."

"You're in luck. My partner and I had some boat trouble, otherwise I'd still be out fishing."

"Not a serious problem, I hope."

"Nothing a little counter-witchcraft can't help."

"Pardon me?"

"Fisherman's joke, Mr. Forbes."

"I see," he said, although he clearly didn't. "Well, let me tell you why I called. I'd like you to talk to one of our clients if you don't mind." Forbes glanced at his watch. "He won't be available for at least an hour. In the meantime, perhaps you'll allow me to buy you lunch." He picked up the menu. "I recommend the Scotch salmon salad."

"Thanks, but I've been looking *at* fish or *for* them since five A.M." I ordered a Black Angus burger and a Pete's Wicked Summer Brew. Forbes noticed my Red Sox ball cap. I follow the eighteen-legged disaster that is our Olde Town Team the way people watch a jumper perched on the ledge of a ten-story building. You don't really want to witness the unfolding tragedy, but it draws you nonetheless. We exchanged canny strategies for altering the curse that had started when the Sox traded Babe Ruth to the Yankees. Forbes said I would have to come to the company box at Fenway Park. I don't think he really envisioned the two of us sucking down Buds and devouring Fenway franks elbow to elbow, but it was nice of him to make the gesture even if he didn't mean it.

The waitress who brought our food was a pretty, young blond woman who said she was a poli-sci major at Ohio State. Her family has owned a summer house in town since before she was born. While Forbes charmed the information out of her, I gave him a quick study.

Forbes wasn't the stuffy Back Bay lawyer I'd expected. He had an adolescent's unlined face that didn't go with the silver of his hair, which was carefully combed and parted slightly to the middle in a 1920ish mode. He had an air of dissolution about him, like an uninvited guest at a Gatsby party. I noticed the redness of the eyes when he removed his sunglasses. The quickness with which he gulped down his martini and ordered another. The slightly muted loudness of the tie. The careless way he had taken his tan Armani suit jacket off and draped it over another chair.

Apparently Forbes had been sizing me up as well. He washed down a forkful of salmon with gin and vermouth and said, "You're not exactly what I expected, Mr. Socarides."

I thought he was talking about the manly fragrance of old fish and engine fuel that wafted downwind from me. Or the tattered workshirt and cutoffs. The other sea grill customers looked as if they had stepped out of the L.L. Bean summer catalog.

"Funny, I was just thinking the same thing about you."

"I have the advantage, though," Forbes said with a Reynard-the-fox smile. He pulled a manila folder from an alligator-skin briefcase next to his chair and slid out a sheet of paper, which he placed on the table in front of him. A photo was clipped to it.

"This gentleman looks strangely familiar."

He slid the picture over. The dark brown hair was cut shorter then it is now and hadn't been tinged with streaks of gray. The face was lean in the jaw and hadn't yet been weather-beaten by the sea. It was before the Zapata mustache and the gold earring.

"I'd say this was taken about the time I was going into the police academy," I said.

"It's the best we could do in the short time our in-house snoops had to work up a CV on you. You've had quite a background. Marine in Vietnam. Boston police department. Now a private investigator."

"That's me. A professional tough guy. You forgot the commercial diving."

"The diving is here."

"How about the fishing? It's what I do mostly."

He ran his finger down the page. "You've been fishing seven years."

"Six, actually."

Forbes took a Waterman fountain pen out of his shirt pocket and made an adjustment to my resumé. "I'll have to talk to our background checkers. It says *seven* years here."

"Don't fire anyone. Most of my first year playing *Captains Courageous* was spent chopping frozen bait and pulling fishhooks out of my thumbs."

He scanned the folder. "A fisherman who studied the classics at Boston University."

I don't often get a chance to show off the results of the money my family wasted on college tuition. I said, " 'What is this Athens, of which all men speak?' " I repeated the phrase in ancient Greek.

19

Forbes raised an eyebrow, pawed through his memory for a moment, and said, " 'They bow to no man and are no man's slaves.' I just know the English version. Aeschylus, I believe."

There was more to Forbes than just a slick city lawyer with a few rough edges.

"Aeschylus it is. It's from *The Persians.*"

"I was a Merit Scholar in ancient Greek drama at Andover."

"Which means you went on to Harvard."

"The only one at F 'n' F who *hasn't* gone to Harvard is the head janitor. He's taking English courses through the college extension, so who knows?" He smiled. "I hope you don't mind. We do a check on all prospective employees."

"You could have saved yourself a lot of trouble and expense. Talk to the regulars at Elsie's coffee shop about me and you'd get an earful. Some of it might even be true."

"Fair's fair, Mr. Socarides. What can I tell you about Forbes and Farnham?"

"Call me Soc, it saves wear and tear on the tongue. I've always wondered, how did your founder avoid getting tarred and feathered by the Sons of Liberty back in Revolutionary times?"

He pushed the folder aside. "Easy. Great-great-granddaddy Ansel Forbes would hire out to *any*body. Whether you were a British redcoat who'd killed patriots in the Boston Massacre, or a patriot who destroyed Crown property at the Tea Party."

"Another question. F 'n' F can hire its pick of Boston investigators. Why does an old law firm with a hundred and twenty-five lawyers want me on its payroll?"

"One hundred and *forty* lawyers to be accurate. You came recommended."

It wasn't the first time a potential client found me through the "old cop" network. I tossed out the names of a couple ex-Boston cops, a guy named Shaughnessy who runs his own detective agency in Boston, and J. W. Jackson, who does some detecting on Martha's Vineyard when he's not fishing or cooking bluefish.

Forbes shook his head. "I wasn't told who gave us your name. Only that you had the right qualifications."

"Brilliance, cleverness, or the fact I work cheap?"

"None of the above, I'm afraid. Our client wants you because you're a fisherman."

I jerked my thumb toward the nearby harbor. A half dozen fishing boats swung at anchor off the beach beyond the cabanas. "Any one of those guys is a better fisherman than I am. With fishing the way it is, they'd be glad for the work."

"Not every fisherman is a detective. This is a very unusual case, Soc."

"It might help if you told me about it."

"I apologize. This isn't the way I normally do business. Let me go back a bit. You must have heard about the tragic boating incident in Cape Cod Bay a couple of weeks ago."

"Fishermen are the biggest gossips in the world. There was a lot of talk along the shore. The way I heard it, a tunaboat slammed into a charter."

"Then you know one person was killed in the crash, and another died under suspicious circumstances."

Lawyerspeak is even less revealing than coptalk. "I would say being found dead on a runaway boat with a tuna harpoon sticking out of you is a suspicious circumstance, yes."

"The men who died, do you know anything about them?"

"Only that one was a tourist, from New York. The guy on the tuna boat was Japanese, a bluefin buyer, I think."

"Right on both counts."

"Glad to hear that. My news sources at the fish pier can be long on rumor and short on facts. Where do you fit in, Ansel?"

"I'm basically a highly paid gofer. The pinstripers on Beacon Hill who do the heavy lifting keep me around because I'm the last Forbes who can claim a direct line of descent from ol' Ansel. They told me to come to the Cape, buy you lunch, and set you up to meet the client."

I looked around. "I'm ready when he is."

"Good, I'll take you to him." Forbes folded his napkin, paid the bill, then led the way along paths lined with red and white impatiens to one of the silver-shingled "cottages" built on a low hill overlooking the harbor. He stopped at a two-story, gambrel-roofed house, unlocked the front door, and we went in.

"The firm maintains a suite here," Forbes said. "Make yourself comfortable while I get us a couple of drinks."

The suite was decorated in Cape Cod neo-seaside-colonial. The plush chairs and sofa had scallop designs on them, and primitive seascapes hung on the walls. The light streaming in through the French doors bounced off the high polish of the dark hardwood floor.

I walked onto the deck. There was a good view of the tennis courts and the blue harbor just beyond. Forbes came out a minute later and handed me a bottle of Chimay, a Belgian brew. Forbes was drinking another martini.

"I just made a call. Our client is almost ready, if you don't mind."

We went back inside and through the living room to a large parlor. Sixteen upholstered straight-back chairs were arranged in four rows facing a trestle table. On the table was a TV set with a screen big enough for a drive-in movie. Two small floodlights on tripods were set up, one at each end of the table, flanking the TV. On top of the TV was a camera with the lens barrel aimed at the first row of chairs.

"This is our seminar room," Forbes said.

"Nice." I looked around. There were just the two of us. "You *did* say I'd be meeting a client."

"He should be with you momentarily." Forbes picked up the TV remote and punched the on button. A fuzzy white pattern danced on the screen. "Would you mind sitting there, in one of those middle chairs."

I plunked myself into the front row.

Forbes switched on the floodlights. "Sorry about these. It shouldn't be too hot in here with the air-conditioning. The idea is not to look directly at the lights. They'll make you blink." He attached a small clip-on microphone to the front of my shirt and glanced at his watch again. "I'll leave you alone with the client."

Forbes apologized for taking my half-full beer. He said I was welcome to more in the refrigerator, after the interview. He came out of the kitchen with a china teapot and cup and set them on a small table where I could reach them. He would wait for me at the sea grill, he said. He pulled the gold drapes shut, then he left. I was alone.

I stared at the screen, arms folded, waiting for something to happen.

Zany lines of color danced on the TV screen. Squawks and sizzles came out of the speaker.

Then a peculiar thing happened: the television set called my name.

Five

"Mr. Socarides," the TV said. "Please move slightly to the left."

Television sets must be getting smarter since I bought my ten-dollar black-and-white RCA at a yard sale. I shifted to the next chair.

"How's that?"

After a moment the voice said, "Thank you." Polite too.

The screen flickered and I was looking at swimming goldfish. They were big fish with long whiskers, lacy fins, and black-and-white piebald splotches on their scales. Not the glass-bowl-type goldfish that kids overfeed to death.

The fish disappeared and rippling, light-splintered water took their place for a minute. Then that scene vanished. Next came a miniature waterfall and the pleasant gurgle of a rushing stream under a high-arching bridge. Dissolve. Go to a rock covered with pale green lichen. It lay in a bed of fine white sand that had been raked into pleasing wavy line patterns.

The goldfish reappeared and swam around. "Hello, fish," I said.

"Are you enjoying my garden, Mr. Socarides?" the voice

said, pronouncing my name in quick time, as if the vowels burned its tongue.

"Yes, very much, thank you."

The fish disappeared. The face of an old man took their place. He stared out at me from under wild, untrimmed brows. The skin on his broad face was as wrinkled as an old apple. He wore a dark blue business suit and a conservative polka-dot red tie.

"I am most honored." He smiled and inclined a head, covered with thick hair the color of new snow. "Allow me to introduce myself. I am Hashimoto Takaido." The slight bow again. "Thank you for agreeing to meet with so little advance warning."

"My pleasure."

The smile broadened into a toothy grin. "Please allow me to welcome you to my home, Mr. Socarides. I asked the gentleman behind the camera to show you my garden. Perhaps it will help you to know me since I could not come from Tokyo to talk to you in person. My most humble apologies."

"No problem."

I have been known to talk in more than one sentence at a time. Sometimes even two. But I don't often find myself in a luxury seaside suite having a telelink conversation with Tokyo.

"Thank you for your kind indulgence," Mr. Takaido said. "Please excuse my poor English."

I know Cape Cod natives who speak with a heavier accent. His English was practically flawless. I told him so.

"You are very kind. I worked with the Americans after the war."

I did a quick mental computation. Figure Takaido was probably at least twenty to get a job with the American occupation. Add on fifty years since 1945 and he had to be in his seventies.

"I'm told you are a fisherman, Mr. Socarides."

"I like to think so. The fish don't always cooperate. I have a lot to learn."

"Ah," he said with that self-effacing smile. "Skill comes with patience. My family is still mastering our craft and we have been in the fishing business for three hundred years."

"Three hundred years is a very long time."

"We had considered it only the beginning. My only son was to take over the business. He died two years ago." His unwavering smile failed to disguise the sadness in his words. "It is sometimes difficult for people to understand why this is so important, for the son to carry on the family tradition."

Takaido had hit a raw nerve. My parents run a family-owned business they built using years of their lives as bricks and hours of hard work for mortar. As eldest son, I should have taken over for the folks as they got older. Instead, I left them in the lurch. I had removed myself from their mind and body and left it to my siblings to take my place. I said, "I understand completely. I'm very sorry to hear about your son."

The head bow again. "You are very kind. My grandson Akito was to take my son's place in the family business." He paused and glanced around as if searching for something in the darkness beyond the lights that illuminated his face. "Akito loved my garden. When he was very young, he would frighten the fish in play. In time he came to know that each piece here is necessary. When something is missing, the harmony of the whole is disrupted."

I'm old enough to remember when Zen was a big fad, although to this day I can't describe the sound of one hand clapping. My guess was that Takaido didn't go through all the trouble of making a long-distance connection just to talk about rocks and water.

"It might help if you started at the beginning, Mr. Takaido."

"Please excuse my rudeness. It is not our way to talk business immediately." He brought a teacup to his lips. "Your meeting with our legal representative, was it satisfactory?"

"Yes, I spoke to Mr. Forbes."

"In Japan we often use a go-between in delicate transactions. He speaks to both parties. If there are obstacles, he finds ways around them. Or ends the negotiations. I am very happy to see that you have overcome the first obstacle. You have agreed to talk."

"Mr. Forbes said you might be in need of my services. He didn't go into detail."

"That is my doing. I wished to speak to you directly. To see your face. It was necessary if we were to have *haragei.*" He paused. "What we call the 'art of the belly.' A meeting of minds without words."

I pondered the explanation. "Is that the same as a gut feeling?"

"Yes. We distrust words alone. They cannot be relied on to show what is in a man's heart." Takaido took another sip of tea. "I mentioned my grandson."

"Akito. The one who liked your garden."

"Yes. He had grown to be a young man. Our company ships bluefin tuna from the United States to Japan. He was working in your country to learn about the tuna industry when he was killed."

A switch clicked on in my brain. Was Takaido's grandson the tuna buyer who had been killed with a harpoon?

"Mr. Forbes mentioned him," I said cautiously.

"His death has brought disharmony to our family. It cannot be restored until those responsible are found."

"The police will find out who did it, Mr. Takaido."

"We appreciate the efforts of the authorities. But our family would like to work with someone we have *uchi* with."

I gave him a blank look.

He sighed an old man's sigh. "Excuse me. There is no end to my lack of manners. *Uchi* means 'within.' When our company makes a contractual agreement, you become part of our family, so to speak. It goes back to the days of the samurai."

"I'm flattered, Mr. Takaido, but you don't really know me."

"We know you are a fisherman. That you are one of us in spirit."

"I don't have the resources of a large private investigatory firm. I work by myself."

"Proclaiming one's unworthiness is a Japanese trait," he said, amusement in his voice.

"I just want you to know what you're getting for your money."

He pondered my answer for a few seconds. "You fish alone, Mr. Socarides?"

"No, I work with one other person."

"Would you catch more fish if your boat carried many fishermen?"

I thought about the way Sam and I functioned as a team, with him handling the boat, and me doing the grunt work.

"No," I said finally. "More crewmen would just get in the way. It might even be dangerous on a slippery deck with the hooks and gaffs flying around."

Takaido spread his hands and smiled. He had done some skillful angling himself. He'd used a simple analogy to get me to take the bait. Now all he had to do was reel me in. He did it so gently I hardly felt the barb in my mouth.

"Our family would regard it a great honor if you would consider our wish to put this upsetting matter to rest. Our debt of gratitude would have no limits."

Usually the first word out of a potential client's mouth is "Whatsitgonnacostme?" This gentle old guy was grieving over the death of his beloved grandson. I had the chance to make him happy. Restore his family's harmony. And earn a few yen to help Sam and me get by the lean times we'd been having.

Still, I wasn't sure. Takaido wasn't the only one who had the art of the belly. *My* gut was telling me not to jump in too fast.

"I'm interested in taking the case, Mr. Takaido. I don't like to make snap decisions."

"I understand completely. Prudence is the mark of a wise man, Mr. Socarides."

"Let me think it over. I'll get back to you through your attorneys."

"Of course. I have no wish to pressure you. I am grateful for your time." He raised his cup to his lips. "It is my expectation that you will find favor in our family's request. In our country it is traditional to seal a bargain with tea."

I took the hint, poured myself some tea, and held the cup up where he could see it.

"I'll get back to you as soon as I can, Mr. Takaido."

His eyes bore into mine as if we were physically in the same room. "A great shame has been placed against our family. Remove this stain and we would be forever in your debt."

I drank the tea.

He smiled once more and raised his hand in signal. The picture vanished. I stared at the fuzzy screen.

"Weird," I whispered.

I clicked the set off with the remote, went into the kitchen, and emptied the tea into the sink. With a fresh Chimay in hand, I went out onto the deck and let the breeze clear my head. Tokyo was gone. Out there was the blue Atlantic with nothing between me and Portugal but three thousand miles of ocean. From the tennis courts came the *pok pok* of a ball being batted back and forth. I thought about the strange conversation I'd just had. "Weird," I repeated.

I finished my beer, left the cottage and walked back to the beach grill. Forbes was at our lunch table. I noticed he was drinking coffee.

I had made up my mind on the three-minute walk. Sam and I needed boat repair money. It was as simple as that.

I slid out a chair and sat down. "I'll take the case."

Forbes put a finger to his temple like a nightclub psychic. "I was betting you would."

From his shirt pocket he pulled a folding cell phone. "I just got a call from Boston. They talked to Japan. Takaido says you'll do fine. Said to give you whatever you wanted." He handed over an envelope. "This is our contract. We've based the fee on Boston rates for private investigators, plus some. It's quite generous. Don't be afraid to bill us for any expenses. Want a drink?"

I had a buzz on from the Chimay. "No thanks, I've got to talk to my partner about our boat and I need to do it with a clear head."

"Oh, yes, the repairs. Not serious, I trust?"

"We'll know better after Fletcher's boatyard gives her a CAT scan. I'm not optimistic. On the good side, if the boat's hauled out, I'll have time to work on this case."

"We're very pleased." He glanced at his watch. "Well, I must be going. The company plane is picking me up shortly."

We shook hands and I headed back to the fish pier along the beach, taking my time. What I knew about Japanese culture could be summed up in the mouthful of sushi I'd spit out a couple of years before in a Japanese restaurant. I took consolation in the fact that ignorance has never bothered me before when I had taken a case.

A couple of things *did* bother me, though.

Takaido wasn't the only one who disliked disharmony. I have a sharp sense for incongruities. It's what got me through Vietnam, and later, it saved my butt on the mean streets of Boston. In the Mekong I learned that a bent piece of grass could be just that, a bent piece of grass. It could just as easily be the mark of a VC land mine. In Boston, the unnatural quiet in a crack house could mean someone was napping or lurking behind a door with a lead surprise.

A instant before Takaido's face disappeared from the TV screen, something had gone out of kilter. The snowy-haired grandpapa-san who'd been practically groveling at my feet vanished. Takaido's thick brows would have covered his eyes if they weren't already largely hidden by folds of flesh. Yet when he said the word "shame," it was with a look so hard that it got past the hooded eyelids, flew around the world, bounced off a couple of satellites, and squeezed into a cable without its hot intensity diminished a single degree. It was what Evil-Eye Fleagle used to call a "triple whammy." It only lasted a second. Then it was gone and I was looking at the grieving grandfather once more.

There was something else.

Takaido had done all the right things. He had mined a deep vein of guilt in me that goes back to the fact I'd broken off from a family business and still feel lousy about it. He'd invoked our common bond as fellow fishermen. He'd exploited my warped sense of honor. And he'd sweetened the deal with offers of largess at a time when I could really use the money.

It was almost as if he knew me better than I knew myself.

Six

State Police Lieutenant Leo Boyle was about to pontificate. I knew this was going to happen because he had leaned back in his swivel chair, locked his hands behind his head, and announced, "I don't mean to pontificate . . ."

"But," I said helpfully.

"My job isn't fun anymore."

"Some people might wonder how a homicide detective's job could *ever* be described as *fun,* Leo. What's the problem? Not enough murders amid the peaceful sand dunes of ole Cape Cod?"

Boyle snapped forward like the springer in a mousetrap. He was a tall, big-boned man, and the move would have scared the hell out of somebody who hadn't seen it before. He pointed a thick finger at me.

"*Wrong,* my friend. Dead wrong."

On the drive to the district attorney's office in the Barnstable county complex, I had vowed that I wouldn't let Boyle sucker me into one of his dumb debates. The fact that it was inevitable was small consolation. Open your mouth in a yawn and Boyle would jump in feet first. The good news was that

Boyle's dialogues were one-sided. All I had to do was sit there and nod my head.

I nodded my head.

"It's not the *quantity* of the murders that disturbs me so much as the *quality* of the perps."

"For some reason I've never thought that people who stabbed, shot, or chopped their fellow human beings into pieces were what you'd call 'quality folks,' Leo."

"I'm *surprised* at you, Socarides. You've lost your appreciation for the finer points of homicide since you left the Boston PD."

I nodded.

"You're obviously not a student of history. Tell me," he went on, "what do you think of when you hear the words *Cape Cod?*"

"Beaches. Lighthouses. Saltwater taffy that pulls your fillings out. Fried clams. Too much traffic in the summertime."

"And you'd be right. But a lot of people don't realize this place has its darker side." He yanked a thick scrapbook out of his desk drawer and flipped it open. "There haven't been a lot of murders, but they've been bizarre. Look at this. Guy in 1772 acquitted of killing his four shipmates. In the 1800s, you've got a religious nut inviting his neighbors in to watch him put a knife through his four-year-old daughter's heart. She was supposed to rise from the dead the next morning."

"You mean she *didn't?*"

"Not that morning or *any* morning. Look here. You've got a nurse who poisoned thirty-one people. What do you think of that?"

"I think you're giving me indigestion."

He slammed the scrapbook shut. I said a prayer of thanks. "The difference between then and today is—"

"Class," I chipped in. I was used to playing Greek chorus to Leo's declamations.

"Right." He tapped the scrapbook. "These guys, and ladies too, had class. When they dispatched someone, it was done with whaddya call it, beau geste. That the term?"

"Close enough, Leo."

"What kind of crapola do I have to deal with these days?"

Since I knew the answer, I gave it to him. "*No*-class."

"You've got it. Guy beats up on his wife or girlfriend. She takes out a restraining order. Hell, she can't bust *his* balls. We're talking *manhood* here. He grabs a gun or the nearest blunt object and kills her. *That's* what I have to deal with. Fucking hormones. Whatever happened to premeditation?"

He was getting heated up. It was hard to know whether Boyle was more disturbed about the murders or the fact that they lacked class. His line of discourse gave me both a headache and an opening.

"What about this thing with the Japanese guy? Does that fit in with your definition of a class act?"

He snapped his fingers. "Funny you should bring that up."

"I'm a regular Henny Youngman when it comes to murder."

"No, funny *peculiar*. Just got a fax this morning. They're sending somebody over."

"Somebody over from where?"

"Tokyo." He rummaged through the stacks of paper covering his desk. "Damn, must be in another office." He came across a brown eight-by-eleven envelope and tossed it to me. "Be my guest."

I opened the envelope and slid out the color photos inside. They were pictures of a Asian man, in his late twenties or early thirties, taken from various angles. He was lying in the pilothouse of a boat, crumpled on his side, the long metal shaft of a harpoon protruding from between his shoulder blades. He wore black slacks and a long-sleeved shirt that was more crimson than it was white.

After studying the pictures a few minutes I handed them back to Leo.

"Class?"

"Dunno," Leo said, scratching his head with a forefinger. "Maybe just bizarre."

"Run it by me. I'll give you the benefit of my astounding powers of ratiocination. Without charge, I may add."

Leo's wide mouth curled down at the corners. "Nothing like I've ever seen. Tunaboat comes out of the fog."

"They call them stick boats."

"Huh?"

"The tunaboats. They're called *stick* boats."

"How come, cause they stick the fish with a harpoon?"

"I've always heard it was because of the way the super-structure, the pulpit and spotting tower stick out from the boat."

"I like my theory better. Anyhow, this stick boat slams into a charterboat. Kills one guy and injures the others. Coast Guard finds the tunaboat the next day. It's run out of fuel. On autopilot. This guy is on it. Sushi kebab. Just the way you see him. Looks like he crawled into the pilothouse after somebody nailed him on the deck."

"How'd the boat get out there on its own?"

"Coast Guard said somebody put it on full throttle and locked the wheel."

"What about the boat? Japanese guy own it?"

"Hell, no, he's just a tuna buyer. Comes and goes. Boat's owned by a guy named Charlie Snow. Heard of him?"

"Nope. Snow's an old Cape Cod name. Phone book's full of them. So where was Mr. Snow while his boat roamed the high seas like the Flying Dutchman?"

"He says he was at his sister's place. Claims the murder victim must have taken his boat without permission." Boyle shrugged.

"What was the financial picture with Snow's boat?" I asked. "Did he have a mortgage?"

"A hefty one."

"Insurance?"

"Insured to the hilt. If he'd lost the boat, he could have paid off the mortgage and got himself a new one. What's your interest in this, if you don't mind my asking?"

"Not at all." I told him about the interview with Takaido.

"Hmmm. First the fax from Tokyo, now you show up on my doorstep. Something more here I should know about?"

"Maybe. I'll let you know if I hear anything. Any suspects?"

"Call me stubborn. I keep coming back to Snow. He and this guy Akito didn't get along. They had a big dust-off the day of the incident."

34

"That's interesting. What were they arguing about?"

"Price of fish from what I heard. Some of these fishermen get ten or twenty thousand bucks for one lousy fish. Is *that* right?"

"It's what they say."

"Christ, I'll stick to Chicken of the Sea, ninety-nine cents a can on sale at the A and P."

"Fingerprints?"

"Sure. Snow's prints are all over the boat and the murder weapon. But what the hell, it's his boat, his harpoon."

"Where's the boat now?"

"Over on the northside. Sesuit Harbor. They got it repaired and back in the water. Snow's lawyer finagled it—Henry Daggett, who used to be an assistant DA, wife's father was on the bench. Daggett knows all the judges. They always ask how his wife and kids are. I was just thinking, that's pretty wild, Soc, getting hired on TV like one of those dating services."

"It's a first for me. Akito Takaido must have meant a lot to his grandfather."

"I guess. But you got the name wrong."

"Huh? What do you mean, Leo?"

"Akito. His last name is *Mishima,* not Takaido."

"Can't be. Akito's father was Takaido's son."

Boyle handed over a sheet of paper. "Right here in the death certificate. *Mishima.*"

It was there in black and white. Akito Mishima. I gave the certificate back to Boyle, shaking my head.

"Maybe something got lost in the translation."

"That cop Tokyo is sending might be able to help. Tell you what, pal, I'll give you a buzz when he gets here."

I stood up to go. "Thanks, Leo. I appreciate it. What's next from your office?"

"We're checking around to see if Snow's alibi has got legs. I've got one of those feelings. What about you?"

"Like the experts say, start with the corpse."

"Where'd you hear that?"

"Maybe I saw it on *Law and Order.* I want to know more about young Akito whatever-his-name is. I'll keep you posted."

We shook hands and I left the converted white clapboard house where Boyle had his office. The day was bright, but opaque clouds were casting shadows in my mind. The misunderstanding over Akito's name was an incongruity. Like a broken piece of grass.

Now that I had his name right, I asked myself, Who *was* Akito Mishima?

Maybe I'd find the answer at Sesuit Harbor.

Seven

ON A MAP Cape Cod looks like a big curving arm frozen in the final phase of a mighty uppercut. I've always thought of it as a defiant gesture, a slender strip of sand taking a swing at the mighty Atlantic, and getting away with it.

The clenched fist is at Provincetown, the Cape Cod Canal is the shoulder. Sesuit Harbor is about where the biceps would be. It starts as a narrow creek that meanders through velvety marshes and widens into a V that flows into Cape Cod Bay. The bay side on the north shore is still mostly windy roads, low-slung cottages, and hushed villages, the way the Cape used to be before the big-money boys arrived with platoons of lawyers and engineers to build the malls and megastores that are turning a nifty piece of real estate into Anywhere, USA.

They told me at the harbormaster's office that he was at town hall. His assistant was outside a corrugated-metal shed washing down the patrol boat on its trailer. His name was Brad. He was a stocky, black-haired guy with a beard. I gave him my business card and said I'd been hired by Akito's family to look into things. He didn't seem surprised to talk to a private investigator. Few people are these days. People hire PIs to dig up dirt on their date before they'll go out to a movie. In a way I can't blame them.

Brad put the hose aside and pulled a pack of Marlboros out of his shirt pocket. After several wet-fingered tries, he got a soggy butt going. "Damn shame about Akito. He was a good kid."

"Sounds as if you liked him."

"It was hard *not* to." Brad chuckled at some remembered joke. "He was a real character. Skinny guy with thick glasses. Very funny. He loved American stuff. Big Macs. T-shirts. Cigarettes. He was always bumming butts from me. Crazy about American TV. I think he'd seen every episode of *Gilligan's Island*. He could quote lines." He shuddered. "That harpoon and all, hell of a way to go if you ask me."

"When did he start showing up at the harbor?"

"At the *start of* the summer, which is unusual."

"How so?"

"Most of the dealers have a Japanese technician working with them, but they come at the end of summer, early fall, when the fish are top quality and fetch top dollar. Akito arrived around June. He rented a place not far from here."

"How'd he get along with the other folks around the harbor?"

"Pretty good for the most part. The guy was a real politician. He had an incredible memory for names. He'd high-five you, shake your hand as if he were running for selectman. He hung around the little snack bar a lot. Always buying people doughnuts." He shook his head sadly at the thought of the lost bounty. Judging from the size of Brad's gut, he'd had more than one honey-glazed in his time.

"I heard he had some problems with the tuna fishermen."

Brad started to coil the wash-down hose. "His job sometimes put him in a tough position."

The phone rang in the shed. Brad went inside to answer it and came back a few minutes later.

"Sorry. Someone calling to see if there's a slip open. Where were we?"

"You were explaining why some people might not like Akito."

"Well, it's not complicated. Say you've caught a big bluefin. Figure it'll run five hundred pounds trimmed down. You're coming off the bay all excited, thinking, 'Maybe this is the big one. Thirty, forty bucks a pound.'"

"Fifteen to twenty thousand dollars. Not a bad day's work for one fish."

"I'd take it for half a *year's* work. Like I said, you're thinking how you can do a lot with that money. Pay down the mortgage. Kid's college fund. New cabinets for the kitchen. Maybe use it toward a new boat. All that stuff's running through your head. But everything depends on the grade of the meat on that fish. The Japanese won't pay the big bucks unless it's real fatty the way they like it. The stuff we think is top grade they call trash."

"So Akito was the guy who'd tell you whether the fish was gold or garbage."

"That's right. He'd be waiting on the dock. It was really something to watch him. He'd take a core sample, test it, make the initial bid to the fisherman before the fish gets air-shipped to Japan."

"Which means his word carried a lot of weight."

"You bet. He tells a guy, 'So sorry, this tuna doesn't have enough fat,' then offers you ten bucks a pound for a fish you think is worth three times that—it's not gonna make you a friend."

"So the price drops from fifteen to five thousand. For that kind of money you could still get some nice kitchen cabinets and buy groceries to fill them."

"Sure, but you can go a long time without seeing a bluefin. I should know. I used to go tunafishing before I settled for a weekly paycheck." He waved his hand toward the harbor. "Meantime, you've got to pay for fuel. Dock fees. If you've got a spotter plane, the pilot takes a thirty-percent cut. You've got to make a year's paycheck in a couple of months. With the government quotas, you could be shut down in a matter of days."

"Why wouldn't a fisherman try to find a dealer who'd give him the best price?"

"That's happened. Some of the fishermen have gotten together and sell fish directly to Japan. Pretty amazing when you consider how independent these guys are. The fish go to the auction house in Japan. You can send it over on consignment, take a piece of what they get at the auction, or take a flat fee at the dock. There are a bunch of wholesalers around, on the Cape and in Boston. They buy the fish, process it, and airfreight it to Japan."

"Akito couldn't have been the only buyer, then?"

"He wasn't, but he had money to throw around. He went to all the dealers and fishermen and said he'd top whatever the other companies paid. Most people started going through him."

"Sounds like Akito could make or break your day."

"Hell, with the money some guys have tied up in their boats, Akito could make or break their *life.*"

"Yet most of the fishermen thought he was okay."

"I'd say so. The smarter ones saw working with Akito as a chance to learn how the Japanese did things. As long as they figured he was giving them a fair price, they were happy."

"What about the ones who weren't happy?"

"There's a lot of conflict in the bluefin fishery. No one's *really* happy with the way things are." Brad looked toward the end of the floating piers where a grove of metal towers jutted above the marina. "You've got a few hotheads in every group."

"Anybody in particular?"

"Maybe you should talk to the cops about that."

"I just did. The State Police told me about the argument Akito had with Charlie Snow. If there's anything you know it would help."

"It's no secret," Brad said with a shrug. "Everybody in the harbor heard them. Charlie came in from fishing all pumped up. Caught himself an eight-hundred-pounder. Figured it to be an A-1 grade. Akito didn't agree. Said the meat was bruised and low in fat. Charlie went through the roof. Said Akito had been shortchanging him right along. Even called Akito's company in Japan to complain. Said Akito had been playing favorites, giving better prices to the other fishermen. Charlie said Akito had put the kibosh on him, that he was trying to drive him out of business."

"Why would Akito discriminate against Charlie?"

"Charlie's kind of a big mouth and he's taken some pretty unpopular stands."

"Did Charlie get anywhere calling Akito's company?"

"Guy he talked to was real polite, was what I heard, but he told Charlie it was all up to Akito. Then Akito got pissed off after he heard Charlie had called his home office. I'd never seen him like that."

"Maybe he didn't like Charlie going over his head."

"He really lost his cool." Brad laughed. "He forgot how to speak English a couple of times. It would have been funny if he weren't so upset."

"What happened to the fish?"

"Charlie was fuming after he called Tokyo. He said he'd lose his shirt before he went crawling back to Akito. He loaded that fish in the back of his truck and drove it straight to the market in the village. Lots of people had tuna on the barbecue that week. Charlie took a beating on the price."

The phone rang again. A few minutes later Brad came out of the shed shaking his head. He apologized and said it was a clerk at town hall who didn't understand something on a report.

"When was the last time you talked to Akito?"

"Just after he had the argument with Charlie. The kid was still pretty upset. His hands were shaking, he was so mad. I told him to forget it, that it was just the way Charlie was. Akito said he understood, but that his company had gone through a lot of trouble to get him over here. He said Charlie shouldn't have called the company. It could bring shame to him if the people back home thought he was cheating fishermen."

"Did he say anything else?"

"It was mostly small talk. He calmed down eventually and asked me where to buy stuff to take back to the people in Japan. Skateboards, jeans, things that would cost a fortune over there."

"Then he was going home soon?"

"He didn't say so, but I expect that's what he had in mind. The fishermen have been pushing their quotas. Everyone was expecting the government to shut down the fishery pretty soon."

"Did he ever talk about his grandfather? Guy named Takaido?"

"Not that I remember. He was pretty closemouthed about his family. I guess that's the way the Japanese are. He talked about his company, though. I get the idea Golden Sun has been around awhile."

"Three hundred years."

"God, that's older than the USA."

"One more question. What kind of a guy is Charlie Snow?"

Brad puckered his mouth in thought. "Charlie's a piece of work. But look, I have to deal with the guy, so I shouldn't be talking about him. This is a small harbor. Stuff gets around. Maybe you should judge for yourself. His boat's over there. You may want to wait though. Charlie might not be in the mood to talk."

The telephone jangled again. Brad excused himself and went to answer it. I waited awhile, then poked my head into the shed and waved my thanks.

I strolled past the two big metal buildings that serve the marina. The old clipper-ship boatyard the Shiverick boys ran here is long gone. There's a charter sailboat that comes up from the Florida Keys every year, a marine service that takes care of the fishing and pleasure boats tied up at the slips that line both shores. There are no nightspots or posh waterside restaurants. Only an unimposing yacht club and a snack bar by the fuel dock.

I bought a Coke and sat at a picnic table overlooking the breakwater at the harbor entrance. A Boston Whaler with a family on board cruised slowly toward the bay between the stone riprap walls that flank the channel. I watched the Whaler fade into the blue haze and let my thoughts wander. I was thinking how hard it was to bring a dead man back to life, even in a metaphoric sense. It was like that old Japanese movie

Rashomon, which used to play in the art houses. Every witness to the crime tells a different story.

So far, I had heard that Akito was personable, fair, and trustworthy. Practically an Eagle Scout. He liked *Gilligan's Island,* but that's still no reason to kill him.

I finished my Coke and walked along the edge of the harbor back toward where my truck was parked. Someone was shouting. I thought a couple of guys from passing boats were yelling to each other over the sounds of their motors. But these voices were raised in anger. The shouts were coming from the end of the floating dock where the tunaboats were tied up. I headed that way.

The last time there had been a hot argument at the harbor somebody ended up dead. I didn't really expect lightning to strike twice. But you never know.

Eight

AT THE END of the dock where the tuna fleet was lined up, bows facing into the harbor, a barrel-chested man stood in the stern of a white-hulled workboat. He was maybe six two, probably in his late fifties judging from the reddish-gray hawk's nest that stuck out from under his cap. Middle age had fleshed the jowls of his ruddy, weather-seamed face, but it had done little to soften a body that looked as if it had been assembled in a refrigerator plant. A nonstop stream of curses flowed from his mouth, widened to a raging river, and washed over a younger man who stood a few yards away on the dock.

"You screw around with me again, Powell, and you'll be eating your dinners with a straw!" the big man thundered. His thick finger jabbed the air as if he were trying to poke holes in it.

Several fishermen warily watched from a prudent distance. I leaned up against a piling and did the same.

If the man named Powell worried about the promise of radical dental work, he didn't show it. He stood his ground defiantly, hands on his hips, legs wide apart.

"For Christ sakes, simmer down, Charlie," he shot back. "My guy was only doing his job."

Charlie puffed up around the neck like an enraged adder. "He shouldn't be flying if he's that blind. You know the rules. Someone's on a fish, you stay the hell away from them."

"I didn't see your name on that tuna. Once it went under, it was fair game."

"God damn it, do I have to draw you a *picture?* We were on *top* of that fish. I was all set to stick him. The only reason he dove was because your plane put a shadow on him."

"Hell, *you're* the one who drove him down. Bluefin are skittish."

"Don't tell *me* about bluefin. I was sticking them while you were still filling your diapers."

"You went in under my spotter plane, Charlie. He was circling over that tuna."

"Bullshit! I saw that fish first. Your spotter saw me heading for it and beat me to him."

"That's just the way it looked to you, Charlie."

"Damn *right* that's the way it looked. You horn in like that again and you'll buy yourself a raftful of trouble."

Powell smirked. "What are you going to do, Charlie, stick *me* with a harpoon?"

Charlie's complexion went from a medium cranberry shade to a deep beach-plum purple. He made a low sound in his throat.

"You son of a bitch," he said. No yell this time, only a hiss and a toothy smile that was pure menace. The quiet tone made him look bigger and meaner. He put a booted foot on the transom, ready to launch himself onto the dock like a building wave.

It must have dawned on Powell that his comment had been unwise, ill-timed, and possibly fatal. His face went bone white and he clenched his fists at his sides. He was younger than Charlie, not that much shorter, and looked to be in pretty good shape. All that might gain him ten seconds before Charlie flattened him like a steamroller.

You could feel the violence in the air the way the atmospheric pressure drops just before a storm. The tension had ratcheted higher with each escalation in the decibel level. The

45

fishermen who'd been watching sensed the change. They nervously shuffled their feet, ready to bolt for cover at any second.

I was about ready to join them when the cabin door opened and a woman stepped out onto the deck. She was dressed in jeans and a denim shirt. But nothing, not even the fish scales clinging to her sun-bleached work clothes, could have distracted from her striking looks, the alabaster skin and dark hair that glinted with amber highlights like the shadows in a Rembrandt.

"Charlie," she called in a voice that was soft as it was strong. Not waiting for a reply she stepped around in front of him and put her hands on his shoulders. She whispered in his ear and lightly brushed the white stubble on his chin with her slim fingertips. At her touch he seemed to melt. A boyish grin replaced the frown chiseled into his jaw. I've heard of people being turned to mush. Charlie had gone from a raging bull to a bowl of beef goulash.

It's usually a mistake to make snap judgments about people. No chance of miscalculation here. Charlie was a man in love. He skewered Powell with his eyes. Then he put his muscular arm around the woman and guided her toward the cabin. Before they went inside, she glanced over at Powell and gave him a look of cold fury.

The fishermen who'd been watching went back to their chores. A strange peace descended on the harbor. The only sounds were the gulls' cries, the tinny slap of halyards against aluminum masts, and the buzz from a passing outboard motorboat. I let out the breath I'd been holding for the last three minutes.

Powell had the dazed look of someone who'd had an eighteen-wheel trailer truck swerve away at the last second. All that adrenaline was pumping through his body with no place to go. He came out of his trance, looked around, and saw me.

I had been studying the boat. It was about forty feet long, with a heavy-timbered wooden hull. It was wide in the beam, but the builder had managed to avoid a tubby look by incorporating pretty lines and an upturned bow into the design. The boat was at least twenty years old, but every square inch of exposed surface was newly painted and the brightwork and metal fittings gleamed like polished silverware. Painted on the transom was the name *Lady Pamela.*

I pointed at the boat. "Was that Charlie Snow?"

Powell unclenched his fists and massaged the circulation back into his hands. He glared at the closed door.

"Yeah, that's Charlie Snow." His voice was hoarse, as if he'd been thinking about Charlie's big hands wrapped around his throat.

I grinned to lighten the mood. "It's probably not a good time to talk to him."

Powell snorted. "Not unless you've got a death wish."

"He seemed pretty upset."

"*That's* certainly an understatement."

"I'll wait till he's in a better mood."

"Good luck. Charlie's had a lot of problems lately and he's not dealing with them very well. Anything I can help you with?"

"Maybe. Are you a tuna fisherman?"

He glanced back at the boat and laughed ruefully. "Charlie doesn't think so."

Powell did seem more like an ad for J. Crew than someone who harpooned half-ton fish. He had movie-star good looks and an easy smile. His dark brown hair was razor cut, his poplin chinos were sharply creased, and his blue oxford dress shirt didn't have a wrinkle in it. Even his Docksides were polished. So I was being a little disingenuous when I said, "Why would he think something like that?"

"Charlie's been fishing for bluefin so long he thinks he *started* the bluefin fishery. As far as he's concerned, that bay out there is his own special pond, stocked with his fish. He says guys like me aren't serious. That we're dilettantes, in it for fun."

"Is that true?"

Powell had been self-absorbed, staring absentmindedly at the cabin door, now closed. He regarded me with a curious gaze.

"You sure ask a lot of questions."

"I'm inquisitive by nature." I handed him my business card. "And by occupation."

He read the card. "A private investigator?"

"I'm talking to people who knew Akito Mishima. His family wants to know more about his death."

Powell gave me a hard look. "His *family?*" he said as if I had just told him the sky was falling. "Why did they hire an investigator? Don't they trust the police?"

"Trust doesn't come into it. If the cops learn something, they'll keep it to themselves until they can use it. They don't report what they find directly to the family. I will. Maybe it's a Japanese thing."

The friendly smile returned. "Is your name *really* Aristotle?"

"It's a long story. Most people call me 'Soc.' "

"Then Soc it is." He studied the business card and knitted his brow. "You may be right about it being a Japanese thing. Why don't you come aboard my boat and we'll talk about it over a cup of coffee."

I followed him along the dock. I was glad he knew what I meant about a Japanese thing, because I sure as hell didn't.

Nine

THE *BLUESDUSTER* WAS a Hatteras, a sleek fiberglass craft that looks as if it's moving when it's standing still. The long bow had been modified with the addition of a pulpit, and a tall spotting platform extended above the cabin.

Powell called the cabin a "salon." The furnishings were plush, the floor covered with wall-to-wall carpeting, the windows tinted.

"Nice," I said, noting the microwave oven and the television set.

"I was fortunate to pick her up at a good price," Powell said. "They'll go up to seven hundred thousand new. The twin diesels can suck down four hundred dollars a day in fuel. But she'll cruise at twenty knots, and you need a fast boat so you can get to a fish in a hurry when the plane spots it. She'd be an expensive toy if all I wanted her for was a plaything, which is what Charlie calls her."

I settled into a comfortable sofa and tried not to think about the warped floorboards and yard-sale furniture at my house. Powell brought over a coffeepot and two mugs. I stared up at the beige acrylic "mouse-fur" ceiling. "Now I know why they call these 'fur boats,' " I said.

He flashed his Hollywood smile. "There's no rule that says you have to go to sea in a scow. The *Bluesduster* was built for speed *and* comfort."

A boat can say a lot about the person who owns it. The *Lady Pamela* and the *Bluesduster* were both around forty-five feet long, bigger than most of the other tunaboats, which seemed to average about thirty-five feet. Powell's boat was expensive and flashy. Charlie Snow's was solid-built and heavy. It was the difference between a racehorse and a Clydesdale.

"I'm curious," I said. "What *really* happened between you and Charlie? I only heard the condensed *Reader's Digest* version a little while ago. It sounded as if you were ready to cross pulpits out there in the bay."

Powell scoffed at the suggestion. "Charlie likes to exaggerate. We both had harpooners out, but we were nowhere as close as he'd have you believe. Besides, Charlie would never risk banging up his beloved *Lady Pamela.* You couldn't get Charlie to agree in a hundred years, but the truth is, we saw that fish first."

"Charlie said he was on the fish before your spotter saw it."

Powell's brow darkened. "That's the way it looked to him from his boat. My pilot spotted the fish and called it in to us. We're faster, but Charlie was closer to the tuna and his boat still has some life in her. We got there at about the same time."

"Maybe you should try flipping a coin when the call is that close."

"You may be right. But here's where Charlie and I differ. He thinks that once he's on a fish, it's got his name on it. I say that when it dives, it's a new game. The fish can come up two hundred yards away. Hell, I've lost tuna the same way to other guys. Bluefin swim up to fifty-five miles an hour. In a few seconds they can cover a lot of ground."

"How big *was* the fish?"

"Damned if I know. When Charlie saw he wasn't going to make it, he gunned his throttle. The engine noise drove the damned thing deeper." Powell laughed. "It's probably *still* diving."

"I thought Charlie said your plane made it dive."

"Again, that's the way he saw it. Look, it's like that bumper sticker: 'Shit happens.' It was no hard feelings for me. I was planning to apologize. You know the rest."

"So Charlie doesn't use a plane?"

"Hell no! In fact he wants planes banned from the sky entirely. Charlie's made a lot of enemies with his position. Some people don't like the fact that he's hooked up with Audubon and the other conservation groups that are trying to cut our quotas. Charlie justifies it because he thinks planes are wrecking the fishery."

"Are they?"

"The tuna fishery has changed a lot since the old days. You'd find everything from 'Moonies' to cokeheads running boats. The problem with Charlie is that he doesn't like to admit this is a business now. You use whatever tools you can. Charlie sometimes goes on about the good ol' days when every fisherman was a gentleman. Do you know much about bluefin tuna fishery?"

"Mostly that one good fish can make your day."

"That's what everyone thinks. The fifty-thousand-dollar fishes we're all supposed to be pulling in. How they'll pay seventy-five dollars an ounce for bluefin in the Tokyo sushi bars."

"They *don't* pay that much?"

Powell smiled. "Sure, of course they do. They say the Japanese 'eat with their eyes.' That means they'll pay top dollar to have that nice little sliver of *maguro* served up on a white plate. But getting the fish onto that plate is a complicated and expensive process. People don't talk about the fish you never see, the ones you never catch. They don't have to deal with the heavy-handed government regulations that don't make sense. The bluefin fishery is a lot more complicated than people realize."

"In what way?"

"Basically, you're dealing with a fish that can run anywhere between the size of a football to a half a ton. Depending on what license you hold, you can catch that fish in a net, by rod and reel, by trolling a rig, or by harpooning. The harpoon-only people consider themselves the elite. They're allowed an unlimited number of fish a day."

51

"Why wouldn't *every*one have a harpoon license?"

"Very few people make good in it. You have to be highly skilled, and it's got a small quota. Once it's filled, they're done for the year, which means they can be out of business as early as July when the best fish are starting to come through. I work it both ways. I've got a harpoon-only license for a smaller boat, the thirty-five-footer tied up alongside this one. Then I've got a general-category license that allows me to catch one fish a day from the *Bluesduster.* When the season ends for one boat, I can keep on going. That's something else Charlie holds against me."

"You're right, it *is* complicated."

"That's only the *beginning.* Say you've chased your fish from Maine to New York and finally caught it. You haul it in fast, then you gut and dress it, ice it down right away. You've got to take care of the fish. The Japanese pay a lot of money for it and they have a right to be fussy. You call the dealer or the company manager on the cell phone. It's got to go through four gradings. You bring it to shore where the grader is waiting."

"Someone like Akito?"

He nodded. "The Japanese call the graders 'technicians.' It can take years to become one. The grader takes a cut as big as your hand from the tail, looks at the fat content, color, and oil. They like the small giants—three hundred pounds or so. They want the meat fat and they want it oily. If it's all red meat, the fish is sold domestically. But say the fish is good enough to go to Japan, you've got a couple of choices. You can ship it on consignment and see what they'll pay for it in Japan. It's great if you can get two Japanese dealers fighting over a fish. You can take the money right at the dock. But you might get ten bucks for what you think is a thirty-dollar-pound fish."

"Or vice versa."

"That's right. If it passes muster, the fish is chilled overnight—to give it better color. The next day it's airfreighted to Japan. They like a smaller fish in Tokyo. If it is five hundred pounds or more, it goes to Sapporo. The price can go from practically zip to fifty or sixty dollars a pound for a real cream puff, but that's rare."

"A five-hundred-pounder even at the low end of that scale would bring five thousand dollars. That's not a bad day's pay."

"I'd be the first to agree. Normally a good fish runs you around twenty dollars a pound. Anything in the teens is good. But the price depends on the yen and the dollar. If the seiners flood the market, the price can drop. There was a food-poisoning scare in Japan once and the price went down to two to three dollars a pound. There's a grace period even after they buy the fish. If they find something wrong with it, they can cut back on the price. They even have a judge and jury."

"So what you're saying is that it's not as easy to get rich at this as everyone thinks."

"Don't get me wrong. You can make a good deal of money in this business. But you have to hustle. You'd think the competition Charlie complains about was something new. On top of our philosophic differences, Charlie and I disagree on methods. There are the spotter planes, of course. And he doesn't like the idea that I use an electric harpoon and he doesn't."

"It seemed a little more personal than just a disagreement over fishing methods."

Powell opened his mouth a little, as if I had known something I wasn't supposed to.

When he saw it was only a shot in the dark, he said, "It *is* personal. At least with him. Charlie can't forget that he was once the teacher and I was the student."

"Charlie taught you how to fish?"

"Uh-huh. I worked for him when I first came into the fleet. When I left Charlie about a year ago, his whole attitude changed. He accused me of picking his brain dry just so I could go into competition against him."

"You'll have to admit it could look that way."

"It's not just the competition. Charlie's got plenty of other competitors. Everything was okay with Charlie as long as he was top dog. When I decided to run my own operation, that changed the equation. Charlie and I became *equals* as well as competitors."

"So you're a relative newcomer to the tuna fishery?"

"That's an understatement. I got my MBA when it was the thing to do. Sloan."

Sloan is the graduate business school at MIT. "I'm impressed."

"Don't be. My father got his engineering degree at the Institute, so the family had an in. I didn't have his brains for science. I did an internship at one of the big wholesalers at the Boston fish pier. I liked the grittiness of the whole scene and worked there full-time when I got out of college. But I got sick of crunching numbers in a very short while and wondered if I could make a go at fishing. Most of it seemed like factory work. Throwing the net in, dragging it up. Not very inspiring or romantic."

"It isn't. Take it from me."

He cocked his head quizzically. "You sound like you're speaking from experience."

"When I'm not asking people rude questions, I work on a line trawler."

"Wow! A private detective who *fishes.* Will wonders never cease."

"Obviously you thought tunafishing wasn't like factory work."

"Hell no! It had a mystique. Like the harpooners on the old whale ships. It was the difference between hunting and farming. The way the fish are airfreighted to the other side of the world. The idea that what you catch will go for incredible amounts in Japan. I did a lot of poking around, decided to come down here because it wasn't the big-time operation you see in big ports, like Gloucester."

"That's when you went to work for Charlie?"

"He was looking for a deck grunt. I fit the bill. Trouble with Charlie is, he thinks he invented this business. If you want to be picky about it, you could say that Charlie's just taking advantage of what others have done. The seiners actually opened the overseas market. One day back in the late seventies a limousine pulled up to the docks and six Japanese guys in suits and hats got out with their checkbooks. Price had been two dollars a pound for years. In no time it went sky-high. Charlie can't take the credit for that."

"Does his resentment have anything to do with the fact you're a college guy?"

"That's part of it. The fact is, there are more college-educated tuna fishermen than you'd find in the dragger fleet. He probably expected me to fail. He resents the fact that I've been successful. Two boats. New gear. He thinks I'm one of these rich guys who's nothing but a trophy-hunter, a sportsman who gets it both ways, fishes for fun and sells the fish he catches. Ironically, Charlie and I are more alike than he'd admit."

I raised an eyebrow.

"We both fish for a *living*," Powell continued. "And bluefin is our livelihood. We're not the millionaires some people think we are. The average yearly catch is ten fish. That's not going to make you rich. I burn up anywhere from a hundred to four hundred bucks a day in fuel. Repairs can be in the thousands. I'll admit I've got a little dough in trust funds, but I'm a serious tunaman. Okay, this is a sweet boat. Just because you like to fish in comfort doesn't mean you're not serious."

"Charlie obviously doesn't see it that way."

"I've tried to patch things up, but he'd have none of it. Once I even suggested that we go into business together. You need every bit of clout you can get dealing with the Japanese market. I could give him that. I studied Japanese when I was in college. I've got some knowledge of Japanese culture and customs. With his skill as a fisherman, we would have made a good team."

"Charlie didn't go for it?"

"Wouldn't *hear* of it." Powell chuckled. "Well. So *that's* how a private detective works. You've got me to tell you my life story. I thought you were interested in Akito."

"I am. I'm also interested in Charlie. It looked to me after seeing the fireworks on the dock that you seemed to be in a good position to tell me about him."

"You know, Charlie Snow isn't the only one who's been having troubles. C'mon, I'll show you something."

We went below. Powell took a harpoon shaft off the wall.

"This is an electronic harpoon. The line goes in from the power source to the harpoon. It's insulated except for bare wire up near the point. The spotter hits the power button just before the harpooner throws. A bell goes off as a signal. The harpoon stuns the tuna, so it's essentially dead when you haul it on board. You need a good poke to knock out a big fish like that. Look at this insulation."

There was a square chunk taken out of the plastic covering the power cable.

"This doesn't look like wear and tear," I said.

"I always check the cables before I go out. It's not a good idea to be holding a hot line while you're leaning up against a metal railing, standing in wet rubber boots."

"Any idea who'd do something like this?"

"Yeah. Somebody who knew what he was doing."

"You think it's tied in with Akito's murder?"

"Got me. I thought *you* were the private detective," Powell said with a grin.

"Thanks for the reminder. Okay, then, back to Akito. I'm trying to retrace his steps back to the time he was killed. When did you see him last?"

"Around dusk that night. Akito came by the harbor. We talked awhile."

"Do you remember what you talked about?"

"He'd had a donnybrook with Charlie that afternoon over the price of a fish. Akito was really upset. Said he was going to talk to Charlie."

"Did he?"

"I don't think so. Charlie was gone by then."

"His boat was still in its slip?"

"You can see how close our boats are. I walked right by it. Didn't see anybody on it."

"That reminds me. Who was that dark-haired woman on Charlie's boat?"

"That's Pam. Charlie's wife."

I didn't do a good job of hiding my surprise because Powell said, "The age difference between them is twenty years, in case you're curious."

"She's a very pretty lady."

"More than pretty. She's a damn good fisherman."

There were footsteps on the deck. A man stepped into the

56

cabin. He must have been nearly seven feet tall, but if he weighed more than 175 pounds I would have been surprised. He had dirty-blond hair down to his neck and a droopy mustache that accented his dour expression.

Powell greeted him. "Hi, Shorty. Meet Soc. Shorty is my harpooner. One of the best."

We shook hands.

"Nice to meet you," I said, and turned back to Powell. "Thanks for the help, and the coffee."

"Anytime. Come by again."

I was halfway out the salon door when I heard Powell ask, "What's Spinner doing?"

"He checked out the plane and headed over to Smugglers for some R and R."

I stopped and said, "Did you say *Spinner?*"

"Yeah," Shorty said. "Pilot who spots tuna for us."

"Not Spinner Malloy?"

They exchanged surprised glances.

"That's right," Powell said. "Do you know him?"

"Yeah, if it's the same guy, we were in Vietnam together."

"Small world," Powell said with a shake of his head. "He's a good pilot. In fact he's the one Charlie Snow says drove his fish down."

"You said he's over at Smugglers?"

"I just left him there," Shorty said. "Bikers' bar on the south side."

"Thanks, I know the place."

On the walk to my truck I tallied what I had learned at the harbor. In short, Akito was a prince. Charlie Snow was a hothead. They had argued. Charlie had a young wife who looked like a dancer from the Bolshoi Ballet. Powell had had an interesting reaction when I commented on how pretty Pam Snow was. The best Powell could do was tell me what a great fisherman she was. He was either hormone dead or homosexual. My guess was that he didn't want me to think that he noticed her.

Crazy case. I didn't think it could get any crazier until I heard Spinner Malloy's name.

Ten

SMUGGLERS WAS A low-slung, dirt-colored building on a back road near Nantucket Sound. The bar was as dark as a cave except for the red neon glare from the Budweiser sign. A couple of big, slow-moving ceiling fans kept the air moving in yeasty eddies, but they couldn't clear away the memories of whiskey dreams, promises unfilled, and hangovers in the making that lurked in the shadows.

The place was almost empty. Chairs were stacked on the table. It was too early for lunch and the hard-core drinkers were still waking up and wondering who'd used their mouths for ashtrays. A couple of pimply-faced skinny guys in black jeans and T-shirts were playing eight ball as if they knew how to hold a pool cue.

The bartender was slightly smaller than a haystack and from his size, I guessed he did double duty as the bouncer. Right now, he was bouncing off the walls.

"No credit!" he boomed at his only customer. "No frigging credit! I give you another drink on the cuff and the boss will have my ass in a sling."

It was like hearing the opening notes of a dimly remembered song. When the chorus came, I could almost say the words by heart because I'd heard them many times in other gin mills.

"Simmer down, Tony. We're not talking a big deal here. I'm working out a payback program."

Tony wiped the bar top as if he were trying to push it into the floor.

"Payback with *what,* your good looks?"

"Thanks, Tony, but I know, as incredibly handsome as I am, you don't mean it about my good looks."

"You're right," Tony rumbled, "I *don't* mean it."

"Now you've wounded me; you have truly hurt me."

"Keep busting my balls and I'll *really* wound you."

"I'm very insulted that you would even *joke* about physical action."

"I'm *not* joking," Tony growled.

"In that case, we will do this like the gentlemen we are. My seconds will call on you in the morning to make arrangements for our duel. You have the choice of weapons."

"You don't *have* any seconds. You don't even have any *firsts.*"

"Then it will have to be my thirds. Good, that's done. Since one of us will soon die in mortal combat, what say we drink to that."

The bartender slapped the bar top and whooped with laughter. It was obvious he'd played this game before. "Christ, you are a royal pain in the ass." He reached into his pocket, threw down three dollars, quickly took the money back, and rang it up. "I'll buy you a frigging drink. Even give myself a quarter tip, okay? Just don't bother me again."

"You are a peach, Tony. A prince among men. Tell you what, for being so understanding, I'm going to give you a ride in my chopper as soon as I get it in the air."

"Jeezus," Tony said, "you'd never get me in that crate."

"There, you've hurt me again. Better make that a double."

The bartender shook his head and poured a tall shot of Scotch.

"The next one's on me," I said, easing onto a stool.

Spinner Malloy slowly turned, removed the thin cigar from his clenched teeth, and grinned.

"As I live and breathe," he whispered reverently. "It's the Golden Greek." He wrapped his arms around me. The heat from the lit end of the cigar was dangerously near my ear. "God, Soc, you look great! Tony, do you know who this guy is? This is my man. Rambo. The Terror of the Rice Paddies. We're old war comrades. Go back a long way."

Tony glared at me as if I were another freeloader until I put a ten-dollar bill down on the bar and ordered a beer and a drink for Spinner in the well. Tony went to fill a mug.

With his thin mustache and dissipated good looks Spinner had always reminded me of what Errol Flynn might have turned into if he hadn't screwed and drank himself to death. Spinner's dark red hair had gone almost entirely to silver, and his face had lost the battle with sun, booze, and cocaine. But his mocking grin and twinkling eyes still lurked amid the ruins.

"What the hell you doing in a dump like this, Soc? That's okay, Tony knows it's a dump."

"I ran into Shorty. He mentioned a pilot named Spinner. When he said you were hanging out in a bar, I knew he was talking about Spinner 'the Sinner' Malloy."

"Hah. Did you hear that, Tony? Hey, Soc, tell this man why they call me Spinner."

Tony came over to deliver the beer and shook my hand. "It's not hard to figure out where the Sinner part came from."

"All lies," Spinner said. "Tell Tony the exciting stuff. Like what happens when the tail stabilizer gets shot off your chopper."

"You pay your bar bill?" Tony said with a straight face.

"Ha ha, big guy. Not even close. Tell him, Soc."

"The tail rotor counters the centrifugal force from the main rotor," I said.

"Chrissakes, tell him in English what that means, Soc."

What it meant was that the first time I laid eyes on Spinner he was descending from the heavens in a deafening clatter of flying metal and shredded treetops. The sound and fury was sweeter than a chorus of angels. My unit been pinned down for hours by a bunch of VC who must have had an ammunition factory with them. The first chopper that found us in the morning fog made it safely down, but the pilot was killed the second the runners hit the ground. Then Spinner arrived in a second helicopter. He was hovering above the treetops when his chopper's tail rotor disintegrated in a hail of fire. The helicopter began to spin wildly around its main rotor and came down through the trees like a giant whirligig. In no time it had torn itself to pieces.

"What it means is that Spinner invented the first Weedwacker," I said.

Spinner pounded my back and laughed until tears came to his eyes. "Goddamn, how long has it been, Soc?"

"I was trying to remember on the drive over. Five years. I was in the Keys to do some bonefishing. You were flying a sight-seeing operation down in Marathon."

"Yeah, that's right. Jeezus, what a good memory. Good thing I don't owe you money."

"You do."

"You sure? How much?"

"Forget it. Still flying *Annabelle?*"

"Old eggbeater's in P-town."

"Provincetown? What are you doing up here? I thought you *hated* the North?"

"I needed a change, Soc. I was doing okay summers, with the German tourists and all. A buddy said I could do big tourista business in P-town. Chance to get away from the heat and the mosquitoes."

"When did you go from tourists to tuna?"

"Barely got the old girl in the air." Spinner shook his head. "Mechanical problems like you wouldn't believe. By the time I got her going again, tourist season would be half over. I'd shelled out major shekels coming North. The tuna-spotting thing came up. Potential for big bucks. I'm working for four different boats."

"You should be doing pretty well."

"Helps pay the rent."

I wondered if it paid for more than that. Spinner would be

getting big bucks spotting tuna, but he couldn't pay his bar bill. Familiar story. He'd made a lot of money through the years. Spinner used to have a heavy cocaine habit, and a lot of what he's made he stuck up his nose.

"So *Annabelle*'s back in the air?"

"Naw. Chopper's too noisy for spotting, scares away the fish. Lucky I'd kept my fixed-wing license up-to-date. I'm leasing a plane. Soon as the season ends, I get *Annabelle* in shape, pay off my bar bill, then I'll put her on a flatbed and head south. Much as I like old Cape Cod, I want to be back in the Keys when the winter winds blow off the ocean. That's me. What about you?"

"I'm still fishing. I do a little private cop work on the side. That's how I met Shorty. I was talking to Powell, poking around on this Akito Mishima thing."

"Yikes, man. That was spooky." Spinner shuddered and crossed himself like a repentant sinner. "Figure it out?"

"Not yet. You ever have any dealings with Akito? Or a fisherman, Charlie Snow?"

"Never met either one of them. I'm pretty much apart from the whole thing. Tunaboats tell me when they're going out, I meet them over the water, we talk on the radio. Otherwise, I stay away from those guys. They're all crazy. Hey, speaking of crazy, look who's here."

Shorty was coming in the door. He had to duck his head. He looked at me and grinned. "See you found him."

"I was just telling Soc here how you tuna guys all got elevators that don't go to the top floor."

Shorty ordered a beer and said, "No argument there. The whole business is insane when you think of it. Buncha guys who think they're God's gift to fishing chasing around a fish people used to throw away 'cause nobody wanted it." He sipped the beer and wiped the foam off his mustache. "And the spotter pilots are crazier than anyone."

"No argument there, either," Spinner said.

"Is Frank Powell an exception?" I said. "He seems to think of himself as more of a businessman than a fisherman."

"Yeah, you got it right," Shorty said. "Frank talks about

stuff like 'units' and 'consumers.' Bluefin's pretty much just a product to him. But he really knows how to make money."

"He told me he spoke Japanese."

"Yeah, he's into all that stuff. He even went over to Japan this year."

"He didn't mention that," I said.

"Yeah, he wanted to see the big market in Tokyo where all our *units* go. Talked to the head honchos at Golden Sun. They gave him a tour of the Tsukiji fish market."

"Interesting. You been working for Powell long?"

"This is my first season."

"Did Frank tell you about his discussion with Charlie Snow?"

"Yeah, Frank said Charlie wanted to rip him a new asshole. Guess I can't blame Charlie. Things did get a little tight out there. But Charlie's living in the past, and he hasn't changed with the industry."

"Charlie said your spotter plane buzzed him."

"Look, Soc," said Spinner, "things can get real wild out there. People don't see a *fish,* they see dollar signs. You've got to realize the pilots work on a percentage basis. No fish, no dinero. Spotting is tough. If there are ripples in the water, it's hard to see. You've got three or four planes circling over fish at five hundred feet, banking, looking out the windows. They don't pay attention to flying. I've had a few close calls. Maybe this guy thought I was buzzing him. Mostly I'm trying to stay alive."

"I've got a lot of respect for Charlie, but he's his own worst enemy," Shorty said. "He reminds me of some of the tough old-timers back home in Maine."

"Tell Soc how the best harpooners come from Maine," Spinner said, anxious to get the spotlight off himself.

"What do you need to be a good harpooner, in addition to coming from Maine?"

"Harpooning is an art and a science. You try to get behind the fish. Sometimes the tuna will roll and you can see its white belly. You've got to have a good eye. You try to avoid hitting the belly because it's the most valuable meat. You'll lose money if it's damaged."

"Hey, Soc," Spinner interrupted, "you ever see any of the other guys from Nam?"

We talked for a while about comrades lost and living, nurses we'd loved, and officers we'd hated. Some people find it cathartic to relive war stories. That's never been the case with me. It's why I stopped going to Nam vets' meetings. I didn't need a bunch of long-haired guys in cammy outfits and combat boots bringing up names of places I'd rather forget.

The bar was getting claustrophobic. I told Spinner I had to go, that we'd get together again soon. We exchanged telephone numbers and slapped each other on the back a couple more times. Then I was out into the bright sunny day. I stood in the gravel parking lot letting the sunlight toast my face, sucking in big gulpfuls of the sweet sea-blown air. The skinny pool players came out, hopped on their Harleys, and roared off in a fusillade of exhaust pops.

It's been a long time since a backfire could make me try to dig a foxhole in the tarmac with my fingernails. But some things you can never get out of your system. You don't even know they're still there until you start hyperventilating for no apparent reason, which was what I was doing in the bar.

Seeing Spinner had brought it all back. The suffocating heat, the rank smell of fear, the stinging insects, and the cries of the wounded. After Spinner's helicopter crashed, I gave up hope. Then I saw a figure crawl out of the wreckage of the second chopper. He dashed for the grounded medevac and pushed the dead pilot out of his seat. Before long the rotors started whirling. The flames and smoke from the crashed chopper gave us the cover we needed. I yelled at what was left of my company, and we crawled, ran, and limped to the chopper, dragging the wounded with us. The overloaded medevac struggled into the air. I think Spinner got it off the ground through sheer willpower.

The leap back through time with Spinner had left me neither here nor there. I needed someone to yank me back to the present. I knew just the person who could do it.

64

Eleven

THE OCEANUS MARINE theme park is a concrete monolith that sits on several acres of blacktop covering what used to be a lovely but not commercially valuable marsh. The developers who built Oceanus knew visitors to the seashore would be eager to pay to see things that swim in the water. At Oceanus you can see penguins, sea lions, belugas, and dolphins, all brought in from far away. You can see piranhas from the Amazon and electric eels from the South Seas. Just don't ask to see a codfish from Cape Cod.

The centerpiece at Oceanus is a big oval pool with bleachers on three sides and a two-story administration building at the open end. The bleachers were empty when I arrived. An attendant said Sally Carlin was in her office taking a break before the next show. I walked to the edge of the pool and scanned the green surface of the water. All was still except for a few ripples on the far side about fifty feet away.

It was a good safety margin if I moved fast. I started around the pool, keeping a cautious eye on the water. Nothing stirred. Halfway around the pool I broke into a brisk walk. At the curve I tensed for a sprint to the office building.

The water exploded.

A gunmetal gray projectile shot upward like a Polaris missile. It reached its apogee, arched in a glistening blur, then crashed back into the pool in an ungraceful belly flop. A geyser erupted. Shards of water rained down on my head. A wave washed over the edge, crested against my kneecaps, and ebbed into my Reeboks. I couldn't have been more soaked if I had walked into a raging surf.

The waggling gray head that poked out of the water opened its mouth in a clownish grin and made a sound like a saw cutting into brass. Then it gave out a steamy *whoof!* and disappeared in a flurry of flukes and foam. Another wave washed over my sneakers.

Every perverted combination of swear words I knew sputtered from my mouth. Even a few epithets in the language of my ancestors. None of it made me any drier. I headed for the office building, trying to ignore the *squeep, squeep* sound as I walked.

Sally was behind her desk, I must have looked like the ghost of a long-lost sailor who'd crawled from the bottom of the sea.

Her gentian-tinged blue eyes widened, *"Uh*-oh. Puff got you again."

"Sorry to drip on your rug. I could use a towel."

Sally got a towel out of a closet and I dried my hair with it. "Soc, I'm *so* sorry."

"Faked me out completely," I ranted. "He usually comes across the pool like a torpedo. He was *waiting* for me this time. Cut me off at the pass. Got me just as I let my guard down." I rubbed my face dry. "It's uncanny. How does that overgrown sardine know when I'm here?"

"Puff is *not* a fish. We've been through this before."

I rubbed the back of my neck dry. "No, he's a *menace.* He's a warm-blooded mammal who's just too damned smart for his own good."

"I'll talk to Puff, make him apologize."

I wrung a pint of water out of the front of my T-shirt. Sally got another towel and patted my chest with it.

"No use. Puff has apologized to me before. He's not sincere."

66

"I don't know what else I can do. He's much too big to spank."

"It wouldn't do any good. Tell you what," I said magnanimously. "I won't bring charges against your fiendish finny friend if you let me take you to lunch."

She looked at her watch and frowned. "I've got a show to do."

"I checked the schedule board. It isn't for another hour. We've got time to grab a quick bite."

She hesitated. "You're awfully wet."

"Maybe you can find some dry clothes for me."

"I don't know."

Our dancing around a simple luncheon invitation had nothing to do with lack of time or my being waterlogged. It had everything to do with common sense. Which Sally possesses in abundant amounts. Sally and I have been lovers and friends. She thinks love should grow and blossom like a flower. I've neglected to give it the sunshine and water it needs to grow. The result has been more like a stunted weed.

I said, "I promise not to whine about your demented dolphin."

"Well . . . in that case . . . you can't go anywhere like that. I'll be right back."

Sally returned to her office after a few minutes carrying a pair of tan shorts and a sky-colored polo shirt that had the word OCEANUS as part of a stylized logo on the breast.

"I've always liked to see couples dress alike," I said, coming out of the bathroom where I'd changed.

She draped my wet clothes on a chair and grinned slyly. "Those shorts are awfully tight. Have you gained weight?"

"I'll try not to split them. Does Mademoiselle prefer Le King de Burger or Monsieur McDonald's?"

"Neither," she said, smiling brightly. "I just talked to Mike. He said he'd do the next show for me. That way we won't have to hurry."

"I thought Mike had retired to muscle beach by now." Mike had once had designs on Sally's affections, and I tend to act like a lovesick adolescent at the mention of his name.

"Don't be childish. Mike's a dear."

"Tell the dear boy thanks. My chariot awaits without."

I drove to a restaurant that has a deck overlooking Hyannis harbor. We used to come here often and knew the menu by heart.

"The usual cholesterol overload?" I asked.

"Fried clams, french fries, and onion rings would be very naughty."

"And?"

"And very nice," she added.

Over lunch we watched the island ferries come and go and made small talk. Mostly I watched Sally, enjoying the way sunlight glinted in red highlights off her chestnut hair; the play of shadows around her high cheekbones and full mouth. It is almost unfair for someone so bright to be so lovely as well.

"I'm sorry about Puff's bad behavior," Sally said, squeezing a lime into her glass of cranberry juice. "Frankly, I'm surprised he recognized you."

Sally was making a point. I hadn't called her in weeks. No reason. Just me.

"I think Mike showed Puff my picture when he was giving him mugging lessons."

"I think you'd better go back to detective school, Mr. Sherlock."

"Speaking of school, how are things going with you?"

Sally had been studying part-time for an advanced degree. She wanted to get away from the dolphin pool at Oceanus. She used to think working the dolphin tank was a way to study creatures she loved. She realized later that there was more showbiz than science in training dolphins to jump through hoops.

"It's been going fine. I'm going to pick up a few credits doing some survey work."

"What kind of survey?"

"For the tuna fishermen's association. They need some scientific data. I'm going to try to help them."

"That's a coincidence. I'm doing some tuna research myself."

I gave Sally a condensed version of the Akito case, from

Ansel Forbes's call to Charlie Snow's tantrum at the tunaboat dock.

"I should have known you'd be involved with something like this," she said with a smile. "You're drawn to conflict like a moth to a flame."

"I'm just helping an old man who's mourning the death of a favored grandson. Maybe you can help. What's going on in the tuna business that would be worth killing someone over?"

"Take your pick. I've never seen a fishery that's so contentious. There's just layer after layer of competing interests. When the tuna fishermen aren't fighting the National Marine Fisheries Service, the conservation groups, and the scientists over quotas, they're arguing among themselves. The commercial people don't like the so-called sport fishermen. The harpooners don't like the seiners. The harpooners are toe-to-toe. Some harpoon boats want the first part of the season closed so they'll get a better price later when the fish are more fatty. Others don't. It even comes right down to the kind of harpoons they're using—electrical or traditional. The only thing any of the fishermen *agree* on is that the U.S. piece of the tuna pie is too small, and other countries are getting an unfair break."

"Don't forget the spotter-plane controversy."

"We could devote a whole lunch to that."

"Which all goes to beg the question, what's a nice girl like you doing out there where the harpoons are flying?"

"You probably know that every year in Madrid the International Commission on the Conservation of Atlantic Tuna takes the latest stock assessment and divides the bluefin pie up by country. In the U.S. the NMFS is responsible for seeing everybody gets a bite of the pie."

"Only some people want a bigger bite than others."

"That's right. The whole thing balances on stock assessments. The conservationists say the stocks are dangerously low. The fishermen say the assessments are unrealistic. There's even disagreement between the scientists who go out in the field and those who use 'bioeconomic' computer models to make their projections."

"You still haven't told me where you figure in on this."

"Some of the spotter pilots say they have seen huge schools of bluefin that extend for miles, with thousands of fish in them. I've been hired to go up in a plane and see if I can document their sightings scientifically with photos and statistics. The tuna fishermen will use the information to make their case in Washington and Madrid. While I'm getting paid to count fins, I can also gather data for my master's thesis, which, coincidentally, has to do with the conflict between empirical observation and scientific assessment methods."

"Here's to the sweet smell of conflict and job security," I said. We clinked glasses.

"Tell me more about Pam Snow," Sally said. "She sounds interesting."

"She's more than that. She's beautiful. Dark hair and white skin. You could put her in the chorus of the Bolshoi and nobody would raise an eyebrow."

Which is what Sally did, arching it to tell me I had gone overboard when I described Pam.

"Well. A tuna fisherman who looks like Pavlova."

"Maybe I exaggerated a little. But it's still strange seeing a woman in her situation."

"Working on a tunaboat or being married to a gruff old man?"

"Both, maybe."

"Well, why do *you* fish?"

"When I left the police department without a full pension, I was looking for a way to pay the rent and keep the fridge filled with feta."

"There was more to it than that, if I recall."

"Sure there is. I wanted to do something that was so demanding I could focus all my attention and energy into it. I wanted the sea breezes to blow away painful old memories. When you're bone cold and so tired you could sleep on your feet, things fall into the proper perspective."

"You must have blown away those memories by now."

"Most of them." I was thinking of how my reunion with Spinner had set the hands of the clock back decades.

"Yet you always go back to fishing. There must be more."

70

I thought about it. "Yeah, I guess there is. I used to talk to an old Nova Scotia doryman when I started hanging out at the fish pier. He was in his nineties, tougher than a barnacle. He'd shake his head and wonder why he'd ever do anything as dangerous as fishing the Grand Banks for so little reward. But his eyes almost misted over when he talked about the first day of fishing, with dozens of schooners ready to set sail for the grounds. Sure, there's a romantic side to all this, when the ocean is at her best anyway. I won't always feel that way, but it suits me now."

"Isn't it possible a woman might fish for the same reasons?"

"Very possible. How about point two? The spring-and-autumn marriage?"

"That's no mystery. Older men can be more caring. They've done it all, so they're not running around trying to prove to the world that they're a superstud when it comes to bed or business. Aside from that, there could be a very simple reason why they are together."

"She's looking for her father? He's looking for the fountain of youth?"

Sally's blue eyes flared with anger. "You're much too smart to go around spouting psychobabble. Did it ever occur to you that these two people are married because they *love* each other? Why does everything have to have a hidden meaning for you?"

Sometimes I hated these chats with Sally. She attributes perfectly normal motives to people while I'm looking for sinister ones. I didn't have the chance to come up with a glib face-saving answer. Sally looked at her watch and said, "Uh-oh, I've got to get moving."

We didn't say much on the short drive to Oceanus. I walked her to the park's back entrance.

"Soc, I was thinking about what you told me," she said, putting her hand on the doorknob. "Maybe you should talk to the sister."

"Charlie Snow's sister?"

Sally nodded. "Point one. Didn't you say his alibi rests entirely on her word?"

"She says he was at her house all night."

71

"Point two. Did she say *she* was there all night?"

"I don't know."

"Sometimes men have a tendency not to listen. They hear what they want to hear. Sorry for sounding sexist."

"Apology accepted. I'm listening very hard right now to what you're saying."

"Point three. If *she* wasn't there all night, Charlie could have left the house."

"Sometimes the way your mind works scares me."

"It's the same thing I said a minute ago. *Your* mind works more than it *has* to. You tend to complicate things needlessly. Don't try to figure out whether a person is lying or not. It's practically impossible. It's far easier to assume they're telling you the truth. All you have to do is listen and ask yourself whether they're telling you *every*thing."

"Amazing. Did you learn that working with dolphins?"

"Maybe. You tend to think in basics in the dolphin pool. I want Puff to perform. He wants a fish. What does Charlie's sister want?"

"A fish?"

"No, she wants to protect her brother and not have to lie about it, because maybe he *did* kill that man. Simple as one-two-three."

"I'll remember that," I said, not exactly sure what I was remembering. "Thanks."

"You're welcome. Maybe I'll see you at the protest rally."

"What rally is that?"

"The tunaboat association is organizing a protest. Tomorrow at two P.M. outside the federal building in Hyannis. Lunch was fun. Bye-bye."

She gave me a quick kiss on the lips and disappeared into the park. I stood there and tried to figure out the *real* reason Sally had mentioned the rally. Sally was right, I decided after a minute; I waste too much time searching for auguries. As I drove off and joined the line of slow-moving summer traffic, I decided that Sally was also right about something else. Charlie's sister. I found a pay phone outside a gas station and called Leo Boyle.

"How airtight is Charlie Snow's alibi?" I asked.

"He says he went out to a bar and had some drinks. We checked. The bartender knows Charlie. He said he was there when he says. Then he want over to his sister's house. Says he had more to drink and passed out for the night."

"What's the sister say?"

"Same. Charlie was loaded. He wanted to drive. She made him lie down and he conked out."

"Where was Charlie's wife, Pam?"

"Home. Says she got a call from the sister saying Charlie was there sleeping it off."

"Good indirect backup alibi."

Boyle responded with an unhappy grunt.

"Quick question. What was the time of death for Akito?"

"The ME says around three A.M. A striper fisherman talked to Akito around eleven the night before. He must have come back to the harbor later."

"Why was Akito at the harbor so late?"

"Guy says he had the feeling he was waiting for someone."

"Did anyone see Charlie's boat leave the harbor?"

"Nope. But a neighbor says she heard the sound of an engine not long after the time of death."

I asked for the name and address of Charlie Snow's sister.

"No problem. But you may be wasting your time. We already talked to her. She swears Charlie was at her house all night."

"I'll bet you didn't ask her if *she* was home all night."

"Yeah. No. I don't know. God, I'll have to check. That's a hellofa good point, Soc. God you're a genius."

"Not really, Leo. It's as simple as one-two-three."

Twelve

GRETCHEN SNOW LIVED in a neighborhood that was no longer fashionable and may never have been. The single-story cottage of pizza-house green was in one of the old summer settlements that dot the Cape. Some of the blue-collar havens that once echoed with hard-edged accents from the factory cities around Boston have evolved into neat year-round settlements. Gretchen's hadn't.

Most of the miniature houses in the subdivision had a sad, neglected air. The brown shingles on Gretchen's place curled like ingrown toenails. The lawn was mowed for a foot on either side of the walkway, but the burnt-out grassy strips only called attention to the cracks and splits in the half-buried flagstones. The shutters had been touched up without sanding, and the black paint had blistered.

The FOR SALE sign out front may have had something to do with the lame attempt to increase the dump's marketability. The sign gave me an idea. I drove past the house, noting that the driveway was empty, and parked on a quiet side street. I keep a plastic Hefty bag filled with thrift-shop offerings in my truck. I changed into a pair of tan chinos that weren't any more wrinkled than a dried apricot, and a blue dress shirt cut in a style that's going to come back someday. I slipped on a navy blazer with a crest over the heart and drove back to the cottage.

The driveway was still empty. I went up to the door anyway because it's the kind of thing professional snoops do. No one answered my knock. I tried again, louder.

"She isn't home."

The voice came from an elfin man in the front yard of the house next door. I went over and asked if he had any idea where Ms. Snow was.

"Went out about an hour ago. Store probably."

I told him I was a real estate agent, using the company name on the FOR SALE sign.

The small, sharp eyes in the wizened face stared at my beat-up '76 GMC truck.

"I didn't think the real estate business was so slow," he said.

"Oh, *that.*" I brushed imaginary dust off the seat of my pants. "My Mercedes is in the garage and one of our workmen said I could use his pickup. I didn't want to hurt his feelings." I chuckled sympathetically. "He really loves that old wreck."

The little man shook his head and turned his attention back to Gretchen's house. "Going to have a hell of a job unloading that place the way it is."

"Y'know, I was thinking the same thing," I said, puffing out my cheeks. "Places like this are a tough sell with the hand-kerchief lots and old septic systems." I glanced at his house. "Now if the property looked like *yours . . .*"

"Lot of time and money went into this house," he said, sounding like a proud father.

Most of that money must have been spent at roadside stands. I counted three bathtub shrines to St. Mary, a flock of wooden ducks with swirling windmill wings, a couple of shiny silver globes on fluted pedestals, and a family of pink flamingos. Two flags, one Irish, the other Italian, fluttered from a flagpole.

The house and yard were picture-perfect neat, though, grass as green as AstroTurf and each blade no longer than an inch, new paint on the trim and shutters, and a blacktop driveway still wet where it had been washed down. An RV with Florida tags was parked in the drive.

"It's obvious you've put a great deal into your house," I said without exaggeration.

"It was a cottage originally. Just like that one. We bought it in the fifties, added on as the money allowed. Kitchen space, garage. You could do a lot back then before all the regulations."

The man's name was Cosmo Orsini. He'd had a little masonry company in Revere. Now he spent his time between his cottage and a trailer park outside of Tampa. His skin had the leathery look that comes from year-round sun, and the tip of the nose that occupied most of his face had scars in it from skin-cancer treatment, which was probably why he wore the wide-brimmed panama hat.

"I like your pink flamingos," I said. "I've got one in my yard, but the paint isn't as bright."

We exchanged the family history of our birds like a couple of collectors discussing our holdings of fine crystal china.

Glancing back at Gretchen's house, I said, "Wonder if she'll be coming back anytime soon."

"More than likely. She has to get ready for work. Shift starts at five o'clock."

I looked at my watch and frowned. "I've got an appointment. Maybe I can catch her later at work. We must have that information at the office."

"It's the Buccaneer out on Route 28. The place that looks like a pirate ship. Little pricey because of the atmosphere. Not bad with a senior discount."

"She works nights, then."

"Mostly. We go to bed early. But I get up couple of times to take a leak. Like clockwork. Three-thirty A.M. Prostate. She rolls in just as I'm taking my second pee of the night."

I wanted to ask Cosmo if he remembered Charlie Snow coming or going two weeks before. It wasn't the kind of thing a real estate man should be interested in. I put the question aside, thanked him for his time, and drove off to the Buccaneer.

The restaurant was a short drive from Gretchen's house. I turned in at the sign of the Jolly Roger. The Buccaneer was actually only the Hollywood facade of a two-masted ship that had been built onto an ordinary restaurant building on the edge of a creek.

The hostess who greeted me wore a puffy-sleeved white shirt and black shorts with the hems cut into pointed tatters. She had a stuffed parrot on her shoulder and a plastic cutlass in a scabbard. She said, "Yo-ho-ho."

"Yo-ho-ho yourself."

She smiled and said the Captain Kidd dining room wasn't open yet, but I could go out onto the Long John Silver deck or into Blackbeard's Bistro and Lounge.

"Actually, I came by to see if my little girl left her Winnie-the-Pooh pocketbook here last night. It's a little red plastic thing. I think our waitress's name was Gretchen."

"Are you sure? Gretchen's our bartender."

"My mistake. In any event, we were sitting over there at that big table."

The hostess said she would check with lost and found. She came back a minute later shaking her head.

"You wouldn't believe the stuff people leave. No Winnie. How about a Kermit the Frog?"

"Thanks, she's got one."

"Sorry. I'll ask the waitress who had that station when she comes in. Can you come back later?"

"Gee, I've promised the kids miniature golf. Maybe I can drop by tomorrow."

"No problem. I'll check with her tonight."

"Thanks. By the way, what time do you close here?"

"We stop serving around ten o'clock. Depends how busy we are. The last dinner customer leaves around eleven or twelve, usually. Bar stays open until one."

I went into Blackbeard's Bistro. The bartender was a college kid who laid a yo-ho on me and recommended a rum specialty drink they called a Muzzle-Loader. The fried clams from lunch had finally settled down and I didn't want to stir them up. Besides, I needed a clear head. I settled for a Rolling Rock.

As my eyes roved over the fake skeletons and treasure chests, I pondered where Gretchen figured in this case. Sally had advised me not to take Gretchen's story at face value, to make sure she was home *all* night long to back up her brother's alibi. Yet I had just learned she worked the night shift. I wondered if the cops were aware she might have been working the night she was supposedly baby-sitting her drunken brother. I called Boyle's office from a pay phone near the bar.

"Leo, did you know Charlie Snow's sister works nights?"

Boyle let the wind out of my sails. "Way ahead of you, Soc. She tends bar at that restaurant, funny one that's supposed to look like a boat."

"I'm there now."

"You get around, don't you? We checked already. The night her brother was over at her house she had off."

I thanked Boyle and went back to the bar. Gretchen went off her shift when the Buccaneer bar closed at 1 A.M. On nights she worked, according to her busybody neighbor Cosmo, she came home at 3:30 A.M. Like clockwork, Cosmo said. Just like his bladder. If she wasn't home for two and a half hours, she must be someplace else.

It was probably irrelevant because she didn't work the night Charlie crumped out at her place, but you never know in this business. Sometimes you pull at a thread and unravel a whole sweater. I ordered another Rolling Rock and nursed it until Gretchen came on duty. I knew it was Gretchen because she was the only woman bartender and she had a name badge pinned to her pirate blouse. Gretchen was a handsome, buxom woman in her forties. She had Nordic features and could have stepped out of a Wagner opera, except for the pirate outfit.

Blackbeard's Bistro was getting busy. I drained the foam from my beer mug and headed out. I'd be back soon enough.

Thirteen

KOJAK, THE SEVENTEEN-POUND black Maine coon cat who lives with me, was waiting outside the converted boathouse I call home. He herded me into the kitchen where he went through the whole starving-kitty routine. Pitiful glances. Drooping head. He deserved an Oscar, but settled for an extra dollop of 9 Lives special supper. With the important stuff out of the way, I called Sam. The estimate to replace the bent shaft was three thousand dollars. I said I was expecting money and to go ahead and order the work. Sam doesn't like operating on the margin. I told him it was either fix the boat or swim to the fishing grounds. That settled it. Sam can't swim.

Later changing into shorts and a T-shirt I sat at the kitchen table and scribbled some notes for the case report I'd do when I presented F 'n' F with a bill. By then my stomach was growling. Rolling Rock is no substitute for solid food. I couldn't decide between a grilled tuna-melt sandwich or a chili dog, so I did both. Poor man's surf 'n' turf. I washed dinner down with a glass of retsina wine that tasted almost as good as aged turpentine.

After I cleaned up in the kitchen, I turned on the TV and watched the millionaire gentlemen of the Red Sox prove once again that money can buy talent but not winners. I dozed off on the couch and woke up near midnight with a bad back and a furry tongue. I got back into my real estate man outfit and put some strong coffee in a thermos. The cool night air coming off the bay helped revive me as I crunched across the clamshell driveway to the pickup. I stopped by a Christy's convenience store and bought a bag of Smartfood and a couple of six-packs of Mountain Dew.

The big parking lot behind the Buccaneer was well lighted except for an angle of darkness near the edge of the creek. Around 12:30 A.M. I backed the pickup into the shadows, drank my coffee, and watched the back door of the restaurant.

The southwest breeze coming across the marsh from Nantucket Sound brought with it the smell of sea salt, goldenrod, cattails, and rich, dark sulfuric mud. The chirp of insects had a tired edge to it. Summer was fading, and autumn waited in the wings like an eager understudy.

Before long the back door opened and what looked like the cast for the *Pirates of Penzance* began to straggle out. At ten past one Gretchen emerged. She was still in her uniform. She paused to light up a cigarette, then walked over to a faded blue Toyota. I let a couple of cars get between us leaving the parking lot. Gretchen didn't go right, which would have taken her home. She turned left instead. After going about two miles, the Toyota pulled into one of the motels on the Route 28 commercial strip.

She parked next to a silver Dodge van and quickly walked to the only unit that had a light on in the window. The door opened before she got there. A stocky man was framed in the light. She slipped inside and he quickly closed the door. The light stayed on about five minutes before the curtained window went dark. I read the letters painted on the side of the van: COBBLER'S ELVES CLEANING SERVICE. It was 1:25. I pulled a can of Mountain Dew out of the cooler and ripped open the bag of Smartfood cheddar-flavored popcorn.

The bag was long empty by 3:15 A.M. when the door opened. Gretchen and the man came out and went into a hot clinch. She got into the Toyota and he got behind the wheel of the van. They drove away from the motel in opposite directions. I followed him along Route 28 to an office building about three miles from the motel. He parked in front and went inside. Stakeout number three.

The caffeine high from the Mountain Dew must have faded because I dozed off. A thud awakened me. It was the door of the van slamming shut. I blinked my eyes fully open and yawned. The sky was gray going to pink in the east where the sun was coming up. Five o'clock. The van started out of the parking lot with me tagging some distance back. I followed it along Route 28, then down a series of back roads that led to an old but well-tended subdivision just south of the Mid-Cape Highway. The van turned into the driveway of a gray-shingled Cape Cod house. The driver got out and went up the walk, stretching his arms. He was a thick-set, olive-skinned man with dark, thinning hair.

I pulled in front of the house and got out of the truck. Noticing the name on the mailbox, I said, "Excuse me, Mr. Souza?"

The corners of his mouth turned down in a what-the-hell-do-you-want look. I didn't blame him. It was a little early to be getting a visit from an unshaven, puffy-eyed guy in rumpled clothes.

"Yeah?" he said warily.

"Are you the head elf?" I said, glancing toward the van.

"Huh?" he said, puzzled. Then he laughed. "Oh, yeah. That's my kid's idea. He heard the story about the cobbler and the elves, little guys who used to stay up all night making shoes."

"Cute kid, Mr. Souza."

"Smart too." He yawned. "What can I do for you? Looking for some cleaning?"

I had my ID ready, the card that shows I'm duly licensed as a private investigator by the Commonwealth of Massachusetts. Normally it gets me the same reaction as proof of membership in a price club. Souza's guilty conscience gave him a good reason to be impressed. He looked at the license. "Shit! My wife hire you?"

"I've never met your wife, Mr. Souza. But from what I saw

at the No-Tell Motel a little while ago, she might be in the market for a detective."

"Hey, I don't know what you're talking about. I was doing a cleaning job for the motel. Ask the owners if you don't believe me."

"Yo-ho-ho."

"Huh?"

"Maybe I should ask Gretchen Snow."

"Look, mister . . ." His eyes narrowed in suspicion. "Wait a minute, if you're not working for my wife, who *are* you working for?"

"Somebody who's interested in Gretchen Snow. If you've got the right answers, we forget the whole thing. Video, tapes."

"Jeezus, you've got *video?*"

"It's amazing where you can hide a camera and a microphone these days. The quality is terrific. All the details. Some of the stuff we've shown in divorce court looks like professional porn."

He ran his hand over his balding head as if he were wiping down a bowling ball.

"Aw, shit. Look, I've got a family—"

"Of course. That's why we're willing to wipe the slate clean if you cooperate."

It only took him a second's glance at his house to decide his part-time squeeze was expendable. "What kind of information would you want on Gretchen?"

"You see her every night?"

He hesitated. "Most nights that I'm working."

"Let me guess. You kiss your wife and kid good-bye, go off on a cleaning job, give the elves a motel break around midnight, then head back to work."

"Yeah," he mumbled, "something like that. I work alone."

"Why don't you go to her house? It would save a lot of dough on motel bills."

"Gretchen's got this neighbor, nosy old guy. I don't think he ever sleeps. I get the room for doing some work at the motel."

The story spilled out. Souza had been running the cleaning

82

business for three years. He used to take a late-night break at the Buccaneer. That's where he met Gretchen. His wife was pregnant and for some reason not always "in the mood." The assignation between the elf and the pirate started with a few smooches in the parking lot, then, hormones being what they are, heated up in the van. When a shelf loaded with cleaning bottles collapsed on them during a particularly torrid moment, he made the deal with the motel owner.

"Think real hard. Two weeks ago. A Tuesday night. Did you see Gretchen then?"

"I'll have to check." He opened a battered calendar book he'd been carrying. "Yeah," he said a few seconds later. "I was cleaning a bank branch."

"Gretchen had the night off."

He looked at the book again. "That's right. But we met at the motel anyhow."

"So Gretchen was with you the usual time, from about one o'clock to three-thirty?"

"That's right. Look, I don't want you to think I'm cheating my clients. I get the job done. I got a reputation to uphold."

"I'm sure you have. Thanks for your time." I started back to my truck.

"That's *all*. That's all you want?" he said, as if he'd been cheated. I gave him a case of the smarts as a good-bye present.

"Not quite. When you tell Gretchen it's all over, don't say you've talked to me. Just say you feel like a slimeball cheating on your wife and kids."

I'm a real Ann Landers at heart, but I wasn't hopeful. Guys like Souza never learn. He mumbled his thanks and hurried into his house. With him went Charlie Snow's alibi.

Gretchen was at her love nest between the hours of one-thirty and three-thirty. Akito was killed around three. It was more than enough time for Snow to get to the harbor, skewer Akito, and go back to Gretchen's place. I made a mental note to ask Cosmo Orsini if he'd seen Charlie leaving Gretchen's house.

I got back in the Jimmy and drove home. The sun was a ball of orange fire above the distant dunes of the barrier beach. I had some cranberry juice to get the stale taste of Mountain Dew out of my mouth. I stripped down to my underwear, kicked Kojak off my pillow, and crawled under the sheets.

Nice job, Socarides, I said as I closed my eyes. Still got the old touch. Less than forty-eight hours and you did what the cops couldn't do, crack the alibi of the major suspect. I was thinking how much fun it was going to be to pop this one on Boyle. It might even stop him from pontificating for a while. I couldn't have known that Boyle had his own bag of surprises.

Fourteen

THE TELEPHONE RANG, and when I answered it, Boyle's sharp-edged cop voice ripped through my wooden-headed wake-up fumblings like a noisy buzz saw.

"Good morning, Mr. Socarides," he said with annoying cheeriness, "glad to find you at home."

I leaned close to the window next to my bed for a breath of fresh air and mumbled, "What's up, Leo?"

"I've got something for you on the Akito case."

"That's a coincidence, Leo. I've got something for *you* too."

"Aren't we just wonderful. You got time to swing by my office this morning?"

I blinked at the clock on the nightstand through sticky-lidded eyes and said I'd see him around eleven. After a scalding shower and a shave my mental state went from semiconscious to walking comatose. Ten minutes later I was at Elsie's coffee shop where I ordered coffee and a bagel. Elsie's coffee ranges from dishwater to jet fuel. She was serving the high-octane rocket-fuel stuff today. I took one sip of the molasses-colored brew and my eyelids snapped open like runaway window shades. The bagel was like petrified wood. I tapped the counter with it. Even dunking it in the muscular coffee didn't soften it. Sam came in. He'd seen my truck outside.

"How's the coffee today?" he said warily.

"It will do a good job of cleaning out your sinuses."

"Uh-oh. She made the Rust-Oleum. I think I'll have the orange juice."

He watched me trying to penetrate the bagel crust with a steak knife. "Careful you don't cut yourself, Soc. Shoulda ordered a doughnut, at least you can gnaw away at 'em."

I held the bagel to my eye like a monocle. "Maybe Elsie could sell these things to a skeet-shooting club."

"Too tough. Pellets'd bounce right off."

"Guess you're right." I noticed that Sam didn't look as glum as the last time I saw him. In fact he was smiling.

"You look pretty chipper today. Did Miss Millie make her special quahog pie for dinner last night?"

"Better," he said with a guilty glance over his shoulder. "Darndest thing, Soc. I just dropped by the boatyard to talk to Ed Fletcher about payment and all. He was about to call me. Seems someone made a big mistake on the boat estimate."

"What kind of mistake?"

"The finest kind," he said, grinning. "Instead of three thousand, it's going to be more like one thousand!"

I put the bent steak knife aside. "That's some mistake, Sam. Sure it wasn't just for the parts?"

"Nope. The whole terwilliger."

"How could they make an error like that?"

"Asked Fletcher the same thing. He just said it happened. He'd have the work done in two days at most."

"Hold on, didn't Fletcher tell you he was weeks behind in his work?"

"Guess he found time to slot us in. Maybe our luck is changing, Soc. It's like somebody waved a magic wand over the whole thing."

I picked up the bagel. "I wish somebody would wave a magic wand over this bagel."

Sam winked. "Wouldn't do any good, Soc."

* * *

86

The receptionist at the DA's office said Lieutenant Boyle was expecting me and to go right in. A man was sitting in a chair in front of Leo's desk. Leo wasted no time making an introduction.

"Soc, thanks for coming by. I'd like you to meet Assistant Inspector Horishi Kashiba from the Japanese National Police Agency in Tokyo. Inspector, this is Aristotle Socarides, the private investigator I was telling you about."

I don't know what the well-dressed Tokyo cop wears these days, but I'd bet it wasn't red snakeskin boots, jeans, and a Hawaiian shirt with purple angel fish swimming in a sea of melted butter. The ball cap on his head had the letters NYPD on it.

Kashiba stood up as if he had springs in his legs, the top of his head coming to about my chin, and pumped my hand in a knuckle-crunching grip. He had a boyish, good-natured face that was mostly smile from the nose down. "Hi. Pleasure to meet you-all," he said, sounding as if he meant it. "I'd appreciate it if you called me Rick."

"The inspector drove up from New York last night," Boyle said, waving me into another chair. "He's attached to the Japanese delegation at the UN. We've been talking about this tuna guy case."

"Want my opinion," Rick said, blinking through thick-rimmed glasses, "the whole thing is *meshuga.*"

"Sorry," I said with a shrug. "The only Japanese I know is what I learned from the *Shogun* TV series."

Rick laughed and slapped me on the shoulder. "You don't get out much, do you, Soc? That's not Japanese. It's *Yiddish.* Means 'crazy.' "

"Oh, *that* meshuga."

Despite my off-the-cuff reaction I was really confused. I had narrowed Rick's American accent to coming somewhere between Charleston and Roanoke. Now he was talking as if he'd grown up in the shadow of the Brooklyn Bridge.

"We were just going over this stuff, Soc," Boyle said. "I want you to take a real close look."

Boyle handed me a pile of eight-by-ten color glossies marked with the medical examiner's stamp. I thumbed through a few photos that showed Akito lying faceup on the medical examiner's table in various stages of dissection, from the initial chest incision to the Y-shaped stitches. Next came some shots with Akito lying on his stomach. I blinked.

The harpoon had made a ragged hole between his shoulder blades. But the wound was almost lost in a swirl of violent reds and greens. Every square inch of skin between his neck and buttocks was covered with tattooing. This was no casual tattoo. It had been etched into the epidermis over many hours, and whoever handled the needle knew what he was doing. You could have lit a cigarette with the hot flames shooting from the nostrils of the dragon's crimson head. The translucent wings that extended to the shoulders looked as if they could start flapping at any time. A thick, scaly tail curled around the struggling figure of a Japanese warrior.

I whistled in amazement.

"What do you think?" said Boyle.

"I think there's more skin art here than you'd see at a Hell's Angel's picnic." I handed the pictures back.

"You ever see anything like that?"

I had, but couldn't remember where right away. Then it dawned on me. "Sure. Movie I saw years ago. Robert Mitchum was a PI who went back to Japan to do a favor for a buddy."

"That was an awesome flick," Rick chimed in. "Mitchum was great, but Takakura Ken made it happen. Ken's like Clint Eastwood in Japan."

"Christ, you two sound like Siskel and Ebert," Boyle said. "What the hell are you talking about?"

"The movie," I said. "Came out in the seventies, I think. It was called *The Yakuza,* about the Japanese gangster clans. Some of the bad guys in the movie had tattoos like this. There was something else I remember. Yakuza guys would chop off a finger if they broke their promise to the clans."

Boyle was being cute. He had one more photo, alternatingly holding it at arm's length, then up close where he squinted at it. He passed it over to me. It was a picture of Akito's hand. The top joint of the pinky was missing. The amputation looked newly healed. I looked up from the photo. They were both staring at me. Boyle was tight-lipped. Rick had a bemused expression.

"*Uh*-oh," I said, glancing at the photo again. "Akito was a *bad* guy?"

"Damned straight," Rick said.

Boyle snorted like a draft horse. "See, Inspector, I *told* you my pal here was smarter than a hockey puck."

They were having a little too much fun at my expense. "I'd appreciate it if you gentlemen would cut the comedy and take it from the top. Even a hockey puck needs a little shove to get going."

Rick slipped the ball cap off his head, twirled it a few times on his finger, then hung it on the pointed toe of his boot.

"Akito was with the Red Dragons. It's one of the biggest Yakuza gangs in Japan. The official name is the Takaido-Gumi."

I was having a case of the thicks. It took a second for the announcement to penetrate my skull. "Takaido," I said finally. "As in *Hashimoto* Takaido? That nice old Japanese gentleman who hired me to look into Akito's murder?"

Rick winked and clicked his tongue.

"That nice old gentleman is the Red Dragon's head honcho. The big enchilada. The *tutti con tutti.* The Mafia mensch."

"Boss of bosses," Boyle said with just a little too much glee. "Like the godfather."

Rick made a dismissive gesture. "Naw, I'd say Takaido is more a combination of Al Capone and Genghis Khan."

My throat felt as if somebody had poured sand down it.

Boyle was practically giddy with joy. I couldn't blame him for being happy being involved in something like this after all the homicides with no class that he had had to handle. But I would have liked it if he hadn't been so jovial at my expense.

"Rick here is an expert on the Japanese mob. He was just telling me that the Red Dragons make John Gotti's organization look like the Dead End Kids," Boyle said. "Five hundred groups. Maybe ten thousand people. They're into *every*thing. Gambling, prostitution, drugs, porn, you name it. It's organized in a big cartel, like Sony or Mitsubishi."

"It's *bigger* than Sony or Mitsubishi," Rick said.

"Maybe I should have asked for their prospectus," I said.

"I've got one if you want to see it, Soc. No kidding. It shows their legitimate businesses."

"I'll put it on my required reading list. Is the Golden Sun fish company one of the legit enterprises? I'm kinda curious since they're the ones signing my paycheck and I'd like to know what to tell the IRS."

"Golden Sun is the prize heifer," Rick said. "The gang started hundreds of years ago as a fishermen's association. The old feudalistic system was going down the tube. The samurai were out of control. Fishermen didn't have the master's protection anymore, so they formed a secret ninja society to keep the samurai off their backs. Called it the Red Dragon. Golden Sun was the original fishing group. They're semi-legit. No money laundering. Books are all up-and-up. No strong-arm stuff."

"That certainly makes me feel warm all over," I said, rubbing my eyes. "Excuse me for reacting like I've just been kicked in the chops. We've had organized-crime guys involved in rum-running and dope smuggling going back to Prohibition here on quaint little old Cape Cod, and if you looked hard enough, you could find a motel or restaurant owned by a straw corporation for the Mafia. But we don't get many Yakuza types, dead or alive."

Rick leaned back in his chair and locked his hands behind the bowl-cut black mop that framed his face.

"Can't blame you for kvetching," he said, blinking from behind his glasses. "I'll lay out the whole schmear."

"I'd appreciate that," I said.

"Here's the megillah in a nutshell. Takaido runs his organization like a business. No guys in tight suits hanging around a social club like you see in the Sicilian mob. His upper management works real jobs, preferably legal ones. It's a way of learning the business and keeping the cops off your butt."

"So Akito actually *was* a tuna grader?"

"Sure. He was working for Golden Sun as a technician, guy

90

who grades tuna. It's a big, important job. You have to put in your time to learn it."

"I think I hear a *but* in there."

"You do. A *big* one. Akito had gotten his ass in a wringer back home. He shot a guy from a rival gang over a woman. Things were hotter'n spit on a skillet. Cops were looking for him too. Takaido needed time to bribe officials and mend fences with the clans. Takaido stashed Akito here until it was safe for him to return."

"Takaido went through a lot of trouble."

"Akito was the fair-haired boy. He was being groomed to take over the organization."

"That's another thing," I said. "Takaido said Akito was a *grandson.* If that's the case, why are their last names different?"

Rick looked at me over the top of his glasses.

"Well, now, you got a brain after all. The reason their names are different is because Akito was Takaido's nephew."

"I still don't get it. He called Akito his grandson when I talked to him."

"Sure, Takaido is the *oyabun.* Means 'head of the family.' The patriarch. Everyone refers to him as 'grandfather' same as they call the mob boss the godfather in this country. Takaido's real son was the meanest mo-thah this side of the Ginza. Got killed in a gang shoot-out."

"So you're figuring this thing with Akito was a mob hit."

Rick shook his head. "*Uh*-uh. That hound just won't hunt. Doesn't fit the pattern. My contacts back in Japan are as clueless as anyone. I can't figure it. Leo said you were working on the case. I wondered if you'd come up with anything."

Boyle stirred. "Hey, Soc, didn't you say on the phone that you had something new you wanted to tell me?"

I'd been all set to brag about how I'd cracked Charlie Snow's alibi. Now I wasn't so sure I wanted to. "Yeah, I thought I did, Leo, but it turned out to be nothing."

"Tell me about it anyway," Boyle said, bending over to inspect a photo. "Maybe there's something there that will strike a chord."

I glanced over at Rick, panic in my eyes, gave him a barely imperceptible shake of the head, and silently mouthed the word *no*.

Rick was a fast study. He looked at his watch. "Nearly lunchtime. Any place around here I can get some real Cape Cod seafood?"

I saw my chance and grabbed it.

"Sounds like a great idea. I didn't have breakfast," I said truthfully.

"No sweat, you can tell me what you have over lunch," Boyle said, starting to get out of his chair. "There's a seafood restaurant across the street."

"Good deal," Rick said, plonking his cap back on. "Hey, I was wondering, we near the Kennedy compound?"

"The *Kennedy* compound?" Boyle said.

"Yeah, man, you know. Hyannis Port. Camelot. The summer White House. Maybe we can work it in before we eat. It's something I can write about for the folks back home."

Boyle screwed his mouth up in a doubtful pucker. "It's on the other side of the Cape," he said. "Traffic's going to be a hell of a mess."

"If it's too much of a *schlepp* . . ." Rick said.

Boyle sat down and ruffled some papers on his desk. "Look, why don't you two play Kennedy groupies. I'll send out for a sandwich."

I didn't think Leo would change his mind, but I got out of the office as fast as I could, and Rick followed me. Boyle had always been up-front with me, and I didn't like holding back on him.

Of course, that was before I knew I was working as a point man for one of the biggest mob gangs in Japan.

Fifteen

"GOT SOMEBODY I want you to meet," Rick said on the walk to the parking lot behind the DA's office. He led the way to a red Mustang convertible with the top down. A woman was sitting on the passenger side.

"Hey, Robin," Rick said. "This is my buddy, Soc. He's a private investigator."

The woman looked up from the Harlequin paperback she was reading. She had a wide brown face and cheekbones as round and red as apples. Her shiny black hair was parted in the middle and tied down in a ropy braid. She showed me a set of teeth that were as big and white as piano keys, then went back to her book.

"Ever work with a psychic, Soc? Robin's one of the best in the business. Picked her up in Providence on the drive from New York. Watch this. I haven't told Robin *any*thing about the case." Rick had borrowed the autopsy pictures and he passed the envelope holding them to Robin. "What do you see, Robin?"

Without lifting her eyes from the page she rested a plump hand on the envelope.

"Water," she said.

"Billy-be-damned," Rick said. He turned to me. "Guy in these pictures was murdered on the water, right?"

Robin gave an embarrassed shrug of her wide shoulders. "No. I *want* water. I'm thirsty. Hungry too."

Robin decided she could put aside her thirst and hunger after she heard we were going to the Kennedy compound. As a precaution we stopped and picked up a bottle of Evian for Robin and a couple of Dr Peppers for us. Rick popped a Garth Brooks tape in the player. I asked if he had any Jimmy Buffett. None of that candy-assed phony-island stuff, he said, and cranked up the volume until the speakers buzzed.

On the way across the Cape, Robin said she was half-Polish and half-Inuit, an Eskimo, born in Alaska. Her father was in the navy, and when he got transferred to Newport, the family came with him. She lived in Pawtucket outside of Providence. She had a good business carving authentic soapstone walruses she sent to Anchorage for sale.

Robin had gotten into the psychic business by accident. The retarded teenaged son of a Federal Hill family had wandered off. Robin told the police they'd find the kid near the river. She'd been delivering walruses and had seen the kid throwing stones into the water. The family didn't speak English well and spread the word she'd seen the boy in a vision. She'd had a pretty good batting average since then. Mostly she pointed the cops to water, where lost kids and dead bodies seem to wind up anyway. Robin likes the work. She meets a lot of nice people, she said, and usually sells a walrus or two.

Hyannis Port has its own little post office, but it's more a neighborhood of big seaside houses than it is a village. The Kennedy compound is surrounded by a tall stockade fence so all you can see from the outside are roofs.

"Which house is Jack's?" Robin asked, straining her neck to look over the fence.

I was wondering whether I'd stumbled into some parallel universe. I was still reeling with the news that I was on the payroll of the Japanese mob. Now I was casing the Kennedy compound with a Kyoto cowboy and an Eskimo psychic. Picking

94

houses at random, I said, "That one's Jack's. That's Bobby and Ethel's. That's Teddy's."

"Oh, Bobby's. Oh, Ethel's. Oh, Teddy's," Robin said.

At this rate we'd run out of Kennedys before Robin ran out of ohs. She calmed down after I took her picture in front of the Hyannis Port Yacht Club sign.

It was early afternoon when we got to the little clam shack on the harbor around the corner from Leo's office. Rick and I took the styrofoam containers of fish and chips to the edge of the pier. Robin said she would have a picnic on the beach while we talked.

Rick dipped a fry into the tartar sauce. "Lieutenant Boyle doesn't know what he's missing."

"Thanks for getting me off the hook back there in Leo's office. He tuned out when you mentioned the Kennedy compound. He used to be a town cop. He did guard duty there when JFK was in town. It was exciting stuff for a young guy. He was there the last weekend Kennedy was on the Cape before he went to Dallas and doesn't like to go back."

"You were looking at me like a possum up a tree. Figured maybe you had a reason you didn't want to talk to him."

"You figured right."

Rick scraped up the last of his fish with a plastic fork and carefully wiped his hands and mouth with a Handi-Dri. Then he leaned back against a piling, arms folded. He had exchanged his regular glasses for narrow-framed punk shades. His eyes probed me from behind the dark lenses.

"Mind filling me in on the big secret?"

"I will if you tell me where you learned redneck talk."

He sighed heavily. "Guess most folks expect a Japanese detective to sound like Mr. Moto."

"Maybe they simply don't expect to hear Jed Clampett."

"Well, it's not that complicated, Soc. You need a college education and fluent English to get anywhere as a cop in Japan. I decided the best place to learn how to talk 'Merican was in the USA. I spent two years down at Johns Hopkins in Baltimore. Studied American police work with a minor in anthropology. Did a lot of field studies for my master's in the Deep South.

Lived with the locals. Nice people, but the only reason most of 'em hook up to the power line so's they can watch *Hee Haw* on TV. Anyhow, that's where I picked up the *Deliverance* shtick."

"That's another thing. When did they start speaking Yiddish down in cracker country?"

Rick tapped the visor of his NYPD cap. "Picked it up the same place I got this. I worked down in New York with an old homicide detective named Rosenweig. He's the one who nicknamed me Rick. Said it was close enough to Horishi. Go figure."

"How'd you go from bubbas to *bubkes?*"

"Long story. I cut my teeth with the Metropolitan Police Department in Tokyo. I worked the Tsukiji fish market. You've got seventy thousand people in one small area. Even got its own police force. The MPD patrols the perimeter. That's how I got to know Golden Sun. Later worked the Fukuokawa prefecture, lots of gangs there. Went to Tokyo University, law department. I was an up-and-coming star before I got tainted."

"Tainted?"

"Yeah. I moonlighted with the Baltimore Police Department while I was doing advanced study at Johns Hopkins. When I got back to Japan, my career was in the shithouse. I'd been scarred by my exposure to American police methods. You've heard that Japanese saying 'The nail that sticks out will be hammered.' I stuck out and I got hammered. Brass figures anybody who thinks there's *anything* good about American police work is a cowboy. The National Police Agency had the UN opening in New York. I felt like Brer Rabbit and Brer Fox. *Puleeze* don't throw me in that there brier patch. Hell, I was *dying* to come here. I worked with the NYPD on a few cases. Leo said you used to be a city cop too."

"Burnout compounded by city hall politics. I arrested a kid with connections. It was a case of drop the charges or quit. I quit."

Rick shook his head. "How did someone with city street smarts manage to do a nudnick thing stepping into a cow pie like this?"

"Y'know something, Rick, I've been wondering the same cotton-pickin' thing myself."

I told him about my lunch with Forbes and my TV talk with Takaido. He asked me to go over Takaido's exact words a couple of times. When I was finished, he let out a long, low whistle.

"Congratulations, Soc. Hardly anyone's seen Takaido in the flesh, so to speak, over the last couple of years. Some people have even wondered if he's alive. Kinda like Howard Hughes."

"He's alive, believe me, and he isn't hiding in Vegas letting his fingernails grow long."

"I *do* believe you. And it worries the hell out of me. You still haven't said what cards you were holding back in Boyle's office."

"After I heard you say who I was working for, I wasn't sure if I wanted to tell Leo I'd busted Charlie Snow's alibi."

"*Whoo*-ee. That sure complicates things."

"That was my gut feeling. I wanted to talk to you first about my options. What do you suppose will happen if I tell Takaido that the prime suspect in Akito's death doesn't *have* an alibi?"

"My guess is that Takaido will take care of ol' Charlie."

"That's what I was afraid you'd say. Okay, then, what happens if I tell Takaido *after* I lay the stuff out for Boyle?"

"Boyle will go to the grand jury. They'll indict Snow. Charlie will get snuffed the second he sticks his head out of the courthouse door."

"You really think Takaido would do that?"

"Easier for him than swatting a fly."

"What if I just tell him I've run into a brick wall?"

Rick removed his glasses to clean them with a corner of his shirt. "Let me tell you what a kindly sonovabitch that elderly fella signing your paychecks is. Japanese marine during the war, tough as nails. But he's no fanatic. He knows what side his corn bread is buttered on. Works for the American occupation after the war. Uses his connections to pull together a major black-market racket. Up the Yakuza ladder he goes, stepping on his rivals' heads, and takes over one of the biggest mobs in Sony land. Remember how he talked about harmony and all that?"

"He said harmony couldn't be restored until whoever killed Akito was found."

"Harmony's a big deal with the folks back home. What he

was talking about was his *gang's* harmony. The other gangs see his fair-haired boy knocked off, it's a sign of weakness, they're on him quicker'n ticks on a hound dog. He's got to save face by taking revenge. Then there's his *personal* harmony. Japanese don't like unpredictability. Goes against their grain."

"Akito's murder was about as unpredictable as it gets," I mused.

"My guess is Takaido's already got the wheels in motion. The old man is looking to do it right, though. He probably doesn't want any more surprises, like whacking the wrong guy, so he hires you."

I mulled an unpleasant possibility. "Just for chuckles, let's suppose Charlie *didn't* murder Akito."

Rick's quick dark eyes bore into me. "Thought you said his alibi was Swiss cheese."

"It is. All that means is that he was lying about his *alibi,* not necessarily about the murder."

"Doesn't make any difference. Somebody has to die. You going to eat your coleslaw?"

"Go ahead, I'm not hungry."

Rick took my platter and cleaned it. "You got an edge here," he said between bites. "Problem's to figure out how to use it."

"I don't get you. What *kind* of edge?"

"Takaido seems to think pretty highly of you."

"C'mon, Rick. Hell, he doesn't even *know* me. We talked on the TV."

"Don't get me wrong, all that mystical, romantic stuff the Yakuza likes to promote about itself is pure bullshit, but if anybody believes it, even a little, it's Takaido. He's old school. How many other Occidentals you figure he's given a peek of his garden? You sure he used that word? *Uchi?*"

"Positive."

"Well, it's like he said. 'Cause you're a fisherman, you are one with him in spirit."

"Hell, Rick, you're talking as if I'd been drafted by the Yakuza. I don't even like sushi."

"Neither do I. It's not like you got to quit your membership in the Elks or chop your little finger off if you screw up."

"I don't belong to the Elks," I said, rubbing my pinky.

"You know what I mean. It might be different if Takaido had done a big favor for you. Like Brando talking to the undertaker in *The Godfather.*" Rick chuckled at the thought. "You didn't ask Takaido to beat up anyone, did you?"

"No," I said without emphasis.

"Well, then . . ." Rick stopped laughing. "There something you haven't told me?"

What did Sam say when he told me the bill for the *Millie D.*'s work had practically evaporated?

Seems like someone had waved a magic wand over the whole thing.

I told Rick about the miracle boat repairs. How I had told Forbes the *Mildred D.* was going to need big-money work. How I'd even mentioned the name of the boatyard.

"*Damn,* that Takaido's a sly old fox." Rick flipped a french fry at a seagull, thereby starting a riot. "Fixing your boat was his way of establishing *on.* It means the gratitude you have when somebody does a real big favor."

"I never asked him to pay for the boat."

"Doesn't matter. Guy like Takaido does what he wants to do."

I stared off at the harbor, but its calendar-art picturesqueness was lost on me. "I'd say I'm in a bit of a pickle, Rick. Got any ideas?"

"The best thing I can figure is getting to the bottom of this. Find the real killer. Then work it from there."

"Doesn't seem like much of a plan."

"No, it doesn't, Soc, I'll be the first to admit that, but that's the only shtick I can think of right now."

"What if I go back to Forbes? Tell him I know what's going on?"

"Won't do any good. My guess, Forbes is nothing but a hired hand too."

Robin came back from the beach. She was using the front of her shirt as a basket to hold a bunch of shells she'd picked up.

"How was your walk?" I asked, happy for the chance to change the subject.

"It was fine." She appeared lost in thought.

"You okay, Robin?" Rick said.

"Yes, but I had a vision about your case."

"Hot damn," Rick said, although she had spoken more to me than to him. "What did I tell you, Soc? She's the real thing."

From her pile Robin pulled a scallop shell that had been bleached powder-white and held it between her pudgy fingers. "When I picked this up, I felt something." She closed her eyes. "I see water."

"You're thirsty again?" Rick said.

"No. Dark, cold water." Her brow furrowed. "Empty. Lonely. Death." She took my hand, talking faster. "There is danger there. Fish swimming. Some good, some bad. I can't tell which ones can harm you. Be careful." She blinked her eyes open. Her eyelids fluttered. "There's something else."

"What's that?" Rick said.

"Can we go back to the Kennedy compound?"

Rick drove me to my truck and gave me the name of the Hyannis motel he'd be staying in. He said he'd swing by and see if the Kennedys were home and drop Robin off to catch a bus back to Providence. I said I'd let him know if I turned up anything of importance. I looked at my watch. It was almost time for the tuna fishermen's protest rally.

Just before we parted, Rick said, "Hey, Soc, I've been wondering. You have an idea who recommended you for the job with Takaido?"

"Forbes wouldn't say. I've got a couple of possibilities I'm going to check on."

"One thing you *can* be certain of," Rick said with a shake of his head. "It wasn't a friend."

Sixteen

IN THE PARKING lot across from the federal building in Hyannis about fifty people were gathered around a man who stood in the back of a Chevy pickup truck bellowing through a portable public address system like Huey Long giving a stump speech in the bayou.

The summer heat of midday had lingered into the afternoon, and the man's fleshy face was boiled lobster red even though he had taken his suit jacket off and loosened his shirt collar. The hot air he was producing must have driven up the temperature another ten degrees.

"I will carry this issue to the halls of Congress, to the Supreme Court and the Oval Office if necessary," he thundered. I had the feeling he would have given the same speech if he'd been plunked down in front of a bunch of rutabaga farmers. I saw Powell near the edge of the crowd and went over to ask him who the speaker was.

"State rep from north of Boston who's running for reelection," Powell said with a grin. "North Shore tuna association sent him down here. Bet you didn't know the tuna quotas are nothing more than an all-out assault on motherhood, the flag, and apple pie."

"You learn something new every day."

The speaker would have kept going forever if a thick-set, dark-complected man hadn't climbed up beside him and gently muscled the microphone out of the pol's hand.

"That's Ron Rapoza, head of the tuna fishermen's association," Powell said.

"We'd like to thank the representative for taking the time from his busy schedule to attend this rally," Rapoza said. The rep made a halfhearted attempt to get the mike back. By then Rapoza had nudged him out of center stage, and hands were reaching up to help him down from the truck.

"The representative has done a great job of summing up what's at stake here," Rapoza went on. "As we all know, tuna-fishing isn't just a business, it's a way of life that's being threatened. Some people say we're millionaires. They're wrong. Some say we're greedy, and that we don't care about conservation. Wrong on both counts. We know damned well that if you take too many fish, there won't be any left for anyone. But don't take my word for it. I'm just a bureaucrat these days running back and forth to Washington. Our next speaker is a working fisherman. Excuse me, fisher*person*. And she's a hell of a lot prettier than me."

Rapoza leaned over and pulled a woman onto the truck. She had raven hair, cameo skin, and a litheness of movement I had seen and admired before.

Taking the mike, she said, "My name is Pam Snow. I came into the bluefin fishery the hard way, I *married* into it." She glanced at her feet where Charlie Snow stood beaming with pride.

Pam was a pro. She waited until the cheers and laughs faded. "When I was studying dramatics back at Wellesley, I couldn't have dreamed that one day I'd be crawling out of bed at the crack of dawn so I could go chase a fish ten times as big as I am. They never taught us how to run a boat or set up a harpoon. Most of all, they never taught me to how to deal with government scientists and bureaucrats."

102

She let the applause wash over her. Her voice was mellow and surprisingly strong from someone so willowy.

"The National Marine Fisheries Service in Miami says the tuna stocks are going down. But we know better, don't we?" Applause. "All those rich doctors and lawyers say *we're* ruining the stocks, not *them.* But we know better, don't we?" Louder applause and a few whistles. Stronger now. She was carrying on a singsong conversation with the crowd, like a preacher and the congregation in a Southern Baptist meetinghouse.

"Those people say they are recreational fishermen, but we know better, don't we? We know that the recreational fishery is a myth." She paused again and smiled impishly. "When was the last time you saw someone mount a twenty-thousand-dollar fish over their fireplace?"

That line brought the house down.

"Back in 1992, we saw the funny numbers out of Miami and knew they didn't make sense. And we're seeing them now. We heard about the tuna stocks going belly-up back then, and we're hearing the same thing now. We heard from the *recreational* fishermen how we were ruining the fishery, and we're hearing the same thing now. The pressure is on again. They want to cut the quotas in half. But what they *really* want is to keep us out of the business. How many of *them* are willing to cut their incomes by fifty percent?"

That one brought out the hoots and hollers.

"We've got a lot of people against us. The bureaucrats, the recreational fishermen, the seiners, the misguided scientists, other fishermen who should know better, and environmentalists who want to use the bluefin for their poster fish so they can gouge more money out of the public. They think they're going to drive us out of the business." She stopped and let the tension build up.

"But we *know* better, don't we?"

The crowd lost it. Applause was loud and prolonged.

Rapoza said, "Thanks for those inspiring words, Pam. This rally is proof that even ornery, independent characters like tuna fishermen can put aside their differences. The association has hired a professional to get the proof that the stocks are in great shape. We'll be sending someone up to take pictures of those big schools many of us have been seeing. Then we're going down to Washington with the evidence we need. We'll be looking for your support again. Thanks for coming. And good fishing."

Charlie Snow reached up and lifted Pam off the truck as if she were a feather. The crowd began to break up. Powell had disappeared. I saw Spinner Malloy making his way over.

"Hi, Soc," he said. "Fun party, huh?"

"I thought you stayed away from the crazy tuna fishermen."

He looked furtively around at the reminder. "The only reason I'm here is to go over my flight plan with the biologist type who's going to count tuna tushes."

"*You're* flying the survey run?"

"Yeah, the association's hired me to chauffeur the old drybones around in a couple of days. Just goes to show I'll do anything for money. Fishing hasn't been that great. I've got to check in with Rapoza about it as soon as he's through talking to that foxy lady. Hey, where're you going?"

I was going over to see the foxy lady. Sally greeted me with a smile. She introduced me to Rapoza, and I introduced her to Spinner, who had tailed after me.

"*Well,*" Spinner said. His eyes hungrily devoured Sally from head to toe. "I expected some old bearded guy in a white frock."

"Sorry to disappoint you, Mr. Malloy."

"No disappointment. And call me Spinner."

Sally smiled warmly and extended her hand. "Nice to meet you, Spinner. Please call me Sally. Do you have a minute so we can go over our schedule?"

"I have all the time in the world for you, Sally."

"Sally, I have to talk to Spinner, if you don't mind," I said, taking Spinner's arm.

"What's up, Soc?" Spinner said as he did a dreamy inspection of Sally's backside.

"Thought you might like to know. Miss Carlin is a good friend of mine. A *very* good friend."

"Huh?" The mouth dropped open. "Oh. You and Sally. Why, you old dog."

"An item. Off and on. But still an item."

"I get it. Hey, don't worry, Soc. She's in good hands."

Putting a hard edge in my voice, I said, "When you're up there, Spinner, I want you to take good care of Sally."

The message wasn't subtle. I didn't mean it to be. I knew Spinner could fly with his eyes closed. I just didn't want him to do it with Sally in the plane. He got the point.

"Hey, Soc, don't worry about the booze. I never drink when I fly. Man, I'm crazy but I'm not stupid."

In Spinner's case, crazy versus stupid wasn't a bad trade-off, and about as good as I'd get.

"Sally's pretty special to me. Keep her safe."

"Not to worry." He squeezed my cheek like an indulgent grandfather. "Talk to you later. Gotta go. It's impolite to keep a lady waiting."

Except for a dozen or people who stood around chatting in small groups, the rally was pretty much over. I saw Charlie and Pam Snow walking to their truck and wondered if this might be a good time to talk to him. It wasn't. As they went by a knot of fishermen, one of them called out, "Hey, Charlie, how come you're not with your bird people?"

Charlie put the brakes on and said, "You got a problem, Richie?"

"Yeah, Charlie. I got a problem with a fisherman who kisses ass with Audubon and the other environmento-jerks."

"And I got a problem with assholes who can't find a fish unless they've got the air force to help them," Charlie replied.

The other fishermen got into the act. Voices rose in anger.

Powell reappeared. "Sound familiar?"

"Déjà vu all over again."

"I'm just glad that you can see I'm not the only one Charlie has problems with. Those guys don't like the idea he's allied himself with the conservation groups over this plane thing."

"Charlie does seem to have a knack for attracting trouble."

The argument ended without violence when Pam once again took Charlie away. I wanted to talk to him but he didn't look in the mood to have a snoopy private eye ask him personal questions. I let my gaze drift lazily around the parking lot. My eye went past one point, stopped while my brain processed the data, and came back to focus on the dusky face of a big dark-haired man who was looking directly at me through mirrored sunglasses.

He turned abruptly and walked away, weaving through the maze of parked cars. I started after him. He had a lead of fifty yards at least and was moving fast with a shambling, ground-covering walk that I had seen before. He ducked around a corner. Moments later I plunged down the alley after him and broke out onto Hyannis's main drag.

The one-way street was heavy with traffic and the sidewalk crowded with pedestrians. A middle-aged couple were standing on the sidewalk eating Ben & Jerry's ice cream. It looked like my favorite, Cherry Garcia.

"Excuse me," I said. "I think I just saw an old friend. Did you see a tall man come through this alley? Black hair, big shoulders?"

"Nope," the husband said, and took a lick of his cone. "Can't say that I did."

"Of *course* you didn't," the woman scolded gently, "you were looking at those young cuties."

"Never saw them," he said with a guilty grin.

At another time I might have found the good-natured bantering of a long-married couple charming, but I was in a hurry.

"Wide face," I said, holding my hands a foot apart. "High cheekbones. Dark complexion. You might think he was an Indian."

"Oh, sure," the woman said. "He practically bowled us over, he was in such a rush. He crossed to that park over there." She pointed across the street.

I thanked them and dashed through the creeping traffic to the other side of the street, then jogged through the park in front of the big brick buildings that house the town offices. I didn't see what I wanted, so I trotted over to the municipal parking lot that borders the park.

It was packed solid with cars. No sign of my prey. I walked between the rows of autos and was about to give up when I caught a quick glimpse of black hair bobbing above the sea of cartops. I ran toward the far side of the lot and looked between rows. White backup lights blinked on. Then a dark blue Ford LTD eased out of a space. The driver dropped the transmission into low gear so the tires squealed. The car shot toward the exit, and without a second's delay it pulled into the traffic on South Street. By the time I got to the curb the LTD was out of sight.

I stood there catching my breath as sweat dripped down my face. I was wondering what my old pal John Flagg was doing at a tuna fishermen's rally. And why he had run away from me.

Seventeen

I BALANCED THE twelve-foot-long harpoon on my left hand, steadied the butt end of the shaft with my right, then whipped my cocked arm forward as if I were throwing a baseball. The target was a suit of red flannel long johns I'd filled with beach grass and propped up on some stakes like a scarecrow. The harpoon went off to one side and missed the long underwear by a yard.

Shorty was right. Throwing a harpoon took something of a knack.

On the way home from Hyannis I'd swung by the fish pier and borrowed the harpoon from a fisherman friend. He kept it on his boat in case he ran into Moby Tuna while he was out gillnetting for cod. I said I was thinking about trying my hand at bluefin, which wasn't exactly true. I didn't feel like telling him the real reason. I was curious how hard it would be to hit a human being.

The harpoon hasn't changed much from the design used on Capt. Ahab's good ship *Pequod* and dozens of other New England whaling ships that sailed out of Nantucket and New Bedford to bring home oil for lamps and stays for corsets. Instead of wood, though, the shaft is hollow aluminum. The rig was fairly heavy, eight to ten pounds. The dart screws into one end of the main shaft. The point is called the lily because of its shape, but it isn't like any flower you'd want delivered. It is razor sharp and toggled so that when the point goes into flesh, it stays in. A couple of lines are attached so you can retrieve the harpoon or the dart in the water. In the electrical harpoons the dart line is a plastic-covered wire cable connected to a battery.

That was pretty much it.

I went into the house and pulled out the copy of the medical examiner's report Leo had given me. The ME said the angle of penetration indicated the harpoon had been thrown from above and behind. Pretty much the way a harpoon goes into a tuna when thrown from a pulpit. I had been throwing on the flat. I wondered if height made any difference. I dragged a kitchen chair outside and stood on it to take another shot. This time I hit the long johns in the foot.

To hit a human, even a person with his back turned, the killer would have to have a sharp eye and a quick arm. Especially if the target was moving. In other words, we were talking about an experienced tuna harpooner. That narrowed it down. Only about a hundred and fifty guys between Cape Cod and Maine fit that description. Hell, the case was as good as solved.

I yanked the harpoon out of the grass, carefully wiped the dirt off the tip with a rag, and leaned it up against the house. I got a Rolling Rock from the fridge and went onto the deck. I sank into the sagging plastic webbing of a chaise longue and stared out over the sapphire water. The bay is my personal weather map. I've gotten so I can tell from its color, the way the way the wind ruffles the surface in little williwaws, or even the scent, what the weather is going to do.

The air was humid and heavy. Puffy, white cumulus clouds edged in indigo were building up into thunderheads beyond the barrier beach. A rainstorm was in the offing.

While I played Queequeg in the side yard, Kojak had sat a safe distance away. Satisfied that I hadn't lost my mind, he followed me onto the deck. I scratched his head. He closed his eyes in bliss. If he had any profound thoughts, he didn't share them. We sat there, man and cat, watching a black-feathered cormorant with a neck shaped like a question mark trying to catch a snack.

I wasn't happy. I was angry at myself for not listening to my gut. What had Takaido called it? "Haragei." The art of the belly. I didn't know what bothered me more, being a hired hand for the Japanese Mafia, or allowing myself be snookered into the job in the first place. It was probably a combination of both. Even now, I had trouble believing Rick's description of Takaido as a combo of Al Capone and Genghis Khan.

Rick. Now *there* was a piece of work. Rick said he'd done some work for the New York Police Department. That should be easy to verify. I could have taken him at his word. But if a bird can swim underwater like a fish, and a nice old guy could be a Yakuza don, maybe Rick wasn't what he seemed either.

Just to be on the safe side for a change, I called New York information and asked for the NYPD number. Rick said he'd worked with a homicide detective named Rosenweig. Rosenweig was out. I left a message saying I wanted to talk to him about Rick. Then I called Sam. Something else had been nagging at me.

"I've got a question for you, Sam. Say a guy owned a boat, named it after his wife, and kept it shipshape in Bristol fashion. Would a guy like that be likely to *scuttle* that boat?"

"You can never tell what people are going to do, Soc."

"I know, but even so, what are the chances of something like that happening?"

A sound like sandpaper on wood came over the phone. Sam was scratching his chin.

"When you name a boat after someone, it's partly to please the person, partly to please yourself," he said after a couple more scratches. "Maybe you think it will bring you luck. Mostly you do it because you know a boat's not just something to keep your feet dry when you're on the ocean. It's a *part* of you. Scuttle something like that? Can't see it, Soc. For most fishermen, it would be like cutting off an arm."

Millie overheard Sam talking and invited me over for dinner. Millie cooks like a dream. Earlier, I'd opened my refrigerator to get a beer and closed it before one of the strange purple-furred creatures on the shelves bit me. Now I said I'd bring the no-fat ice cream for dessert.

I hung up and turned my thoughts to John Flagg. Flagg is a Wampanoag Indian from Martha's Vineyard. We'd met in a Vietnam bar. I was in the Marines and he was former Airborne who'd gone over to the counterinsurgency group known as Operation Phoenix. After we'd mustered out, I went into police work and Flagg hooked up with a troubleshooting federal agency that's so secret it has a number instead of a name. I had a brief fling with his sister Annie, which ended up in the scrap heap like most of my romances. Flagg and I occasionally cross paths and we've worked on a few cases together. He was an odd duck, and I had long ago written off his eccentricities to too much Agent Orange in his blood, but this was the first time he'd treated me like Typhoid Mary.

While I waited for Rosenweig, I made a couple of calls. The first was to Ed Shaughnessy, a former Boston cop who runs a private detective agency in Beantown. I asked him if he'd recommended me to Forbes and Farnham. "Not a chance in hell," he said. "Closed shop. They've got their own investigative division." That was interesting. I called J. W. Jackson, the retired Boston cop over on the Vineyard, but nobody was home. He was probably fishing. He usually is.

The phone rang a few minutes later. I picked it up and heard someone mangle my last name practically beyond human recognition. He said he was Lieutenant Rosenweig calling from the NYPD. I told him I was a private detective and that I might be working on a case with Rick.

"The Kyoto cowboy? Hey, you see Rick, tell him to get back here in a hurry," Rosenweig growled in a voice scoured by too many butts smoked on too many stakeouts. "Homicide's softball team's got *tsuris,* big troubles, since he's been gone. The guy who took his place as shortstop catches grounders with his nose."

"I'll tell Rick you miss him, Lieutenant. I was wondering, how did he got hooked up with the NYPD?"

"Make a long story short, Rick's over at the UN, his job's

pretty routine, so he hangs out with our guys. One day he hears us busting our balls over the Asian gangs like the Ghost Shadows and Flying Dragons that come over from Taiwan. The Asian task force needs someone to go undercover. Our Chinese plainclothes are known. Rick volunteers."

"But he's not Chinese."

" 'Close enough,' he says. What do we know from Orientals? Kid's got chutzpah. He goes in, says he's a Japanese wiseguy who wants to do some business with the gangs. Score some dope. Illegal immigrants. Whatever. Chinese hate the Japs so much you can't imagine, stuff from the war and all that. But Rick talks big dough. They bite. We make a shitload of collars, break up the gangs. He's a hell of a cop even if his own meshuga people don't appreciate him."

"Rick said he had a problem with the Japanese National Police Agency. That's how he wound up at the UN."

"Yeah, he came over here to go to college and look into our police methods. The brass back in Tokyo said he'd turned into a cowboy. They put him on the shelf so to speak."

"Maybe his bosses didn't like red snakeskin boots."

Rosenweig broke into a coughing fit. "Hell," he said when he finally got it under control, "nearest Rick's been to a horse is a can of dog food maybe. His biggest problem is he's got *schpilkes.*"

"Pardon me?"

"*Ants* in his pants. He can't stay in one place. Kidding aside, lemme tell you something about the Karate Kid. To get to his level with the National Police, you've got to be some kind of supercop on top of kissing ass, which is the main qualification for promotion around here. They take tests like you wouldn't believe. College education. They have to study kendo stick-fighting and judo. You've got to stay in top shape. They speak English like natives. The only thing, there's not a lot of violent crime in Japan, so they don't have the street smarts an American cop has to have to stay alive."

"But Rick is streetwise?"

"This work you're doing, standard PI keyhole stuff or a heavy case?"

"Any heavier it would be in Weight Watchers."

"I got you. Then I'll put it this way. Our little pal may dress like Johnny Cash on a bad day, but you got some tough guys on your ass, you couldn't have a better buddy watching your back. He's a *macher,* kind of guy who makes the difference. It's like somebody sent you a guardian angel."

"That's good to know. Thanks for your help."

"No problem. *Mazel tov.*"

"*Mazel tov,* Lieutenant."

So Rick was the real McCoy. What's more, he was a good shortstop and a street-smart cop. I also learned something else about Rick from talking to Rosenweig. Where Rick had picked up his Yiddish.

The NYPD softball team wasn't the only one who had *tsuris.* My trouble cup still wasn't full yet, as I found out a few minutes later when the phone rang again.

It was my mother calling. I knew this because she said, "Aristotle, it's your mother."

I have given up trying to figure out the matriarch of the Socarides clan. Her roots go back to Crete, and she is as mysterious in many ways as the darkest cave in that island's highest mountain. She tends to communicate with a subtlety that is as sharp-edged as the daggers the old Cretan mountain fighters carried in their black cummerbunds. They didn't have to wave their knife under your nose to make a point. It was just there.

I could take her terse greeting a couple of ways. I could assume that she *really* thinks that her eldest child does not recognize her distinct accent and the velvet-lined steeliness of her delivery. Or more likely, that she is merely reminding me that I have not called or visited the family in such a long time that she must identify herself to me as a stranger would.

I said, "Hi, Ma," and waited for the other maternal shoe to drop, as it usually did, on my head.

Instead of a lecture heavily punctuated with sighs, she said simply, "One minute, Aristotle." A man's voice came on the phone.

"*Ari*stotle! *Yasou!*" the voice said, bursting with more exuberant energy than words could possibly accommodate. Only one person in the world says my given name as if it were a prelude to launching into a Greek wedding dance.

"Uncle Constantine! Is that *you?*"

"Of *course* it's me, Aristotle. How many Uncle Constantines you got?"

I had only one Uncle Constantine. I could not possibly imagine the world having room for more than two. My mother's brother lived in Tarpon Springs, where he'd been a top sponge diver. The gods despise hubris, and one day Poseidon rewarded his mortal effrontery with a case of the bends. Long before that, he and my aunt Thalia would come North once a year to visit the family. I remembered the strength that could lift me off the floor with a single sweep of a powerful arm, the uninhibited thirst for life and the incredible bedtime stories he made up. He stopped coming after Aunt Thalia died of cancer, and not long after that he had a heart attack. He hadn't come to Lowell in years.

I was suddenly struck by a guilt so heavy I could hardly breathe. Something terrible had happened and I was so far out of the family loop they'd forgotten to tell me.

"What are you doing in Lowell, Uncle Constantine?" I wasn't sure I wanted to hear the answer. "Is everything okay?"

"Sure, sure, Aristotle. *Kala, epharisto.* Everything fine, thank you. Except for your mother. She calls me last week. She says, 'I had a dream, Constantine. Someone died.' I say, 'Silly woman, ever' day someone dies.' She says, 'No, no, you must come to dinner. I cook your favorite, *skordalia,* moussaka, and baklava.' "

"You came North to have dinner because my mother had a dream?"

"*Neh,* yes, of course, Aristotle. Why else? I try to tell her I'm too busy. She says, 'What, busy being an old fool?' I say I'm too broke. She says she sends me a ticket. I should come before we die. I tell her she's crazy, always talking about death. For me, I still jump up and dance when the bouzouki plays." He laughed like a wicked old satyr, wheezing so hard he could barely get the words out. " '*Kala.* Good,' your mother says. 'You *jump* on a plane and *dance* to my house. So here I am, Aristotle. When you come to see me?"

114

"What if I come up the day after tomorrow?"

"Aristotle," he said, lowering his voice, "your mother is like the warden. She says don't do this, Constantine, don't do that. Go to bed early. The booze is bad for your heart. The cigarettes are bad for your heart. Playing *cards* is bad for your heart. Two more days and you come visit me in the cemetery."

"Hello, Aristotle," my mother said, breaking into the conversation. "Your uncle tells you all about all the good food I cook for him?" She knew damned well that's not what my uncle had been saying. She'd been listening in.

My uncle muttered something in Greek. I didn't catch it, but my mother's fine-tuned hearing did, and she didn't like what she heard. She launched into a nonstop stream of Hellenic invective, never raising her voice, but making it clear she wasn't pleased. My Greek is rusty, but I caught the gist and the oft-repeated word *stubborn*.

All at once she shifted gears abruptly back into English.

"Aristotle," she said sweetly. "You come for dinner with your uncle and family tomorrow?"

"I'm in the middle of a case, Ma. I'll have to come up later."

"You do what you have to do, Aristotle. Just remember, your uncle Constantine is getting older."

My uncle hates to be reminded of his age and she knew it. He cut in and started rattling like a machine gun. Again the word I heard repeated was *stubborn*. I held the phone away from my ear until he ran out of breath. Then my mother took a turn. My brother, sister, and father share the family penchant for hearty debate. It wouldn't be long before they'd be jumping in.

At one point my mother and my uncle paused for breath.

I said, "I'll call you tomorrow and let you know when I'm coming," and quickly hung up.

I don't know if they even heard me. I sat there staring into space, wondering if insanity was genetic, realizing that it was too late to have a DNA transplant. Lunacy has its advantages, I suppose. If I'd been sane, I wouldn't have do what I was about to do. I went through my telephone book, found the number I was looking for, and called Charlie Snow.

Eighteen

THE CURTAIN WAS about to rise on the storm brewing over the bay. The air was heavy with moisture, so soggy a good sneeze would have set off a deluge. Heat lightning glowed incandescently through the distant dark clouds. I sat in my truck at the edge of the harbor, listening to the distant grumble of thunder as I tried to build up my courage. The haunted-house atmosphere didn't help.

Time to fish or cut bait.

I got out of the truck and walked down the ramp to the boat slips. The harbor was as still as death. I plucked at my T-shirt in a lame attempt to cool my damp skin. It must have been the heat and humidity. Not the fact I was about to meet a suspected killer known for a hair-trigger temper.

The *Lady Pamela* was the only boat in the tuna fleet with cabin lights on. I stood behind the boat for a couple of seconds before I put my foot on the transom and vaulted lightly onto the deck. The wheelhouse door was open. I poked my head inside and called out, "Hallo. Anybody home?"

"Yeah. C'mon down," Charlie's voice rumbled from the cabin below.

I climbed down the companionway. The main cabin would have been roomy if Charlie hadn't taken up so much cubic footage. He sat on the edge of a bunk, drawing the edges of a harpoon point against a whetstone. He paused long enough to stick his hand out. It was like shaking hands with a lobster.

He said, "Sit down, Cap."

The first time I'd seen Charlie he was about to introduce Frank Powell to the finer points of assault and battery. But even at rest Charlie Snow reminded me of of a cement truck parked at the top of a hill. You know the brakes are on, but it still makes you nervous to walk in front of it.

"My friends call me Soc," I said.

Pam Snow was at the galley sink washing dishes. She wore a T-shirt and high-cut denim shorts that emphasized her long ballerina's legs.

She smiled and said, "Nice to meet you, Soc. I'm Pam, Charlie's wife."

Charlie gestured for me to sit down on the opposite bunk. He followed my every move with watchful gray eyes.

"You want a drink, Cap?"

"Beer would be fine if you've got one."

He nodded at Pam, who got two Bud Lights out of the fridge. Charlie sucked down half of his and went back to his sharpening.

The blade made a *whisk-whisk* sound as he drew it across the stone.

"Like I said over the phone, I don't have a site for you. It's just Pam and me."

When I called and asked if Charlie would talk to me, I said I was a fisherman, which was true, and that I was thinking of getting into the tuna fishery, which was not quite true.

"That's okay," I said. "I'm not looking for work. I already have a job, two of them actually. As I said on the phone I'm a fisherman. But I'm a private detective too." I showed him the PI license in my wallet.

"Thought there was something funny about you calling," he said. He stroked the whetstone a few more times, then inspected his work. The lily's razor-sharp edges glowed as if they were on

117

fire where the newly honed metal caught the light. "You here as a fisherman or a detective?"

"Fair question, Mr. Snow. Little of both."

He gave me a hard squint. "Maybe you got a story to tell me."

The portholes and door were open, but the cabin was close and the air was hot. I wiped the perspiration off my face with the back of my wrist. "Hope you've got plenty of beer," I said.

"Pam can go for more." She hesitated. Charlie put the whetstone and harpoon head into a metal box. "It's okay. I'll fill you in on what Cap here says."

After Pam left for the store, I chugged down the rest of the can. "Okay," I said, "this is the way it goes."

Starting with the Ansel Forbes interview, I told him how I'd been hired to look into Akito's murder. I left out a few names and conversations to save time and to keep something in reserve. Charlie listened calmly; his icy gaze never wavered. He sat stock-still until I came to the part about his alibi. When I told him I could prove that he no longer had one, he picked up the harpoon head.

Closely inspecting the edge, he said, "I told Gretchen she was wasting her time with a married man. Just 'cause my sister was out playing around doesn't mean I wasn't at her place all night."

"No, it doesn't, but it means nobody can account for you during that time. The only thing that's keeping the cops from pulling you in is your alibi. Without it you're dead meat."

Charlie thought about that. "You looking for some blackmail, mister, you've come to the wrong place. My lawyer's got all my money."

"Blackmail's not my line."

He stared impassively. "What *is* your line? You must be looking for *some*thing."

"You're right, I am."

He stroked the stone with the dart. Speaking quietly, just loud enough to be heard over the distant crump of thunder, he said, "Aren't you taking a big risk? If I'm the big bad killer they say I am"—*whisk-whisk*—"I could slit your gizzard with this thing here"—*whisk-whisk*—"dump you overboard before

118

Pam gets back with the beer, and nobody will ever hear what you found out." *Whisk-whisk.*

If Charlie was trying to intimidate me, he was doing a good job. "I don't think you'd do that," I said with forced casualness.

"Why not?"

"You'd have to drink all that beer by yourself."

"Hah. You've got brass balls, Cap. I'll say that for you."

Pam came back before long with the beer. She looked relieved to see that nothing was amiss. Charlie filled her in on what I'd told him.

"Charlie didn't kill that man," she said.

"I agree. He may be a lousy liar," I said, popping a fresh beer, "but I don't think he's the killer."

The harpoon point froze in midstroke. "Everybody *else* does. How come you're in the minority?"

I swept my hand in the air. "This boat speaks volumes in your defense."

"What are you talking about?"

"She's been around a few years, I'd guess, but there's not a square inch that hasn't been treated with loving care. The decks look like they've been scrubbed clean with a cotton swab. Every line is flaked down tight. The brightwork is so shiny you could shave in the reflection."

"That's just the way I do things."

"My guess is that you wouldn't put all that work into the *Lady Pamela* so you could bloody her decks and send her to the bottom. No matter how big the insurance settlement is."

"Sounds like you did some checking on me."

"I didn't have to. The cops had already talked to the insurance company and the bank."

Charlie snorted. "If they'd asked me, I woulda told them this boat is my whole life. That's why it's insured for so much. Besides, Pam here is the one who keeps the old tub shipshape."

"Soc is right. You're a terrible liar," Pam said. "He won't let a fish scale lie on the deck for more than five seconds," she said to me.

Charlie didn't comment. He got up and went over to the refrigerator. "Want another beer?" he said. My teeth were practically floating, but I said I'd have one. Charlie tossed a can over to me. He leaned up against a bulkhead and popped his beer.

"You still haven't told me what your stake in this mess is, Cap."

"Simple. I want to keep my professional reputation in one piece. And I want to keep us both alive."

"I don't get you."

"You will after you know more about Akito's family." I told him about Takaido being a mobster, how Akito was his heir apparent, about Takaido's need to avenge his family's honor.

Charlie put the harpoon head and whetstone back in the box and snapped the cover shut.

"I *knew* there was something about that little bastard. Didn't I tell you, Pam? He smelled like week-old haddock."

"Yes, Charlie," his wife replied with a tolerant smile, "you told me."

"He had the others around here fooled with his glad-handing, his big fish bucks, but not me." Charlie was working himself into a temper.

"I was told Akito got very upset after you called the fish company in Japan."

He pondered that. "It's funny. We'd had a couple of go-arounds before. When you're as big, loud, and ugly-looking as I am, you learn you can scare most people without raising a finger. Akito never backed down, I'll give him credit for that. But he kinda went to pieces after he heard I'd called the company, though. Almost as if he was scared."

"It doesn't figure. Akito was a Yakuza tough guy and his grandfather was head man. Why would he feel threatened by your telephone call?"

"You got me. Well, you tell Mr. Takaido I've never killed anyone in my life, not even in the army."

"I wish it would make a difference. He must know you called Golden Sun to complain about Akito. He knows you argued, that Akito's body was found on your boat, your harpoon in him. That makes you a prime suspect. My guess is you'd be in his sights despite anything I told him."

"Could be. That's my lookout. Still don't see why you have to worry about your hide."

"Once you're taken care of, he might decide that he didn't want anybody who could connect you to him. That means me."

Charlie grinned wolfishly. "Looks like we're in this fix together, Cap."

"Let's say we've got some mutual interests."

Pam said, "What can we do, Soc?"

"For a start, we can try to find out who killed Akito. Any ideas, Charlie?"

"Christ, all I know is somebody stole my boat and tried to sink it. Good thing she's built like a tank. That's how come she didn't have much damage after she hit the *Osprey.*"

"It might help if you filled me in on what happened after you had the argument with Akito."

"I came back to the boat and stewed about it. I'd let the fish rot first before I'd go crawling to him. I had the idea about selling it to the market in town. I called to see if they were interested, then I put it in the truck and hauled it over."

"What next?"

"Hell, Soc, what would *you* do if you'd just sold a five-thousand-dollar fish for pocket change? I went to the bar and got loaded. When they kicked me out, I went to my sister's place."

"Why didn't you go home?"

"I was too stinking drunk, that's why. Wanted to sober up first. My sister told me to sleep it off. I conked out on the couch. When I woke up, she was gone."

"That would have been after midnight."

"Not sure what time exactly, but that sounds right. I felt okay so I went home."

"Can Pam give you an alibi for the rest of the night?"

He gave her a funny look. "No, she wasn't home."

"If you don't mind my asking . . . ?" I said.

"Not at all," Pam said. "Charlie's sister called me and said he was at her place sleeping it off. I went to bed for a couple of hours. When I woke up, Charlie still wasn't home. I got worried.

I called Charlie's sister. Nobody answered. I drove to Gretchen's house. Nobody was there. I wondered if Charlie had gone to the boat. I swung by the harbor, but he wasn't there either."

"We must have just missed each other," Charlie said. "I got some things ready on the boat so we'd be ready to go fishing in the morning, then went home. Pam came in a while later. We caught a couple of hours' sleep, then got down to the harbor. That was around five. The boat was gone. I called the cops and raised hell. They called the Coast Guard. By then the boat was flying around the bay on its own."

I asked Charlie and Pam to go over their stories again to see if there were any inconsistencies. There weren't. I suggested we get together tomorrow to talk again.

"Can't," Charlie said. "Tuna day. Maybe the last for a while."

"I've got an idea," Pam said. "Why doesn't Soc come with us?"

"I was thinking the same thing. Ever throw a harpoon, Cap?"

I thought about my practice with the long underwear. "Couple of times. Nothing a fish would have to worry about."

"That's okay. It should be quite a show. You'll get to see what we're dealing with around here."

After thinking about his suggestion a minute, I said it might not be a bad idea. We shook hands and I thanked him for the beer. A few minutes later I was in my truck. I was halfway home, wondering what I had let myself in for, when the thundershowers began. Someone must have sneezed.

Nineteen

SHORTLY BEFORE DAWN the *Lady Pamela* steamed out of the harbor into Cape Cod Bay. Pam was at the helm, her slender fingers curled around the wheel. The sweet fragrance of fresh-brewed coffee rose from the galley. Charlie came up with three steaming mugs and toasted bagels that had at least a pound of cream cheese on each.

He cooled a sip of coffee with a noisy slurp and peered through the windshield. Sky and sea were still merged in the dusky gray that comes between night and day. "Keep 'er due north toward P'town, Pammy. We'll box the bay."

Charlie spread a chart out in front of him to show me our course. We would head toward the clenched fist at Province-town, then west about ten miles toward Plymouth on the main-land, south to the Cape Cod Canal, then make a final leg east to our home harbor, creating the four sides of a rectangle.

Talk settled down to the essentials after that. Mesmerized by the *shush-shush* of the hull through water, the steady grum-ble of the engine and the rhythmic up-and-down of the boat, we fell into the sleepwalker state that comes easily at sea. There was little talk in the wheelhouse. The coffee had yet to kick-start our biological engines, and we had the numbness of mind and tongue that goes with getting up before the sun no matter how often you do it. Having on board a stranger whose motives weren't entirely clear kept the conversation at a minimum.

When it became light enough to see the land as a thin, dark line, Charlie drained his coffee mug and said, "Stay on this heading, Pammy. I'm going up top."

Charlie climbed onto the wheelhouse roof and clambered like a rather large monkey to the spotting platform. Pam and I were alone.

The eastern sky went from gray to champagne pink. Our foamy wake caught the flecks of molten gold that dripped from the rising sun. The rosy fingers of the Homeric dawn reached out and stroked Pam's pale cheeks. She was a study in contrasts. Dark hair and white skin. Soft lips and a stubborn chin. Sad eyes and a mouth that always seemed on the verge of a smile.

The sky was clear except for a few whiskery cirrus clouds. Scrubbed of its moisture by the storm, the air was dry and crystalline. Pam pointed to a jagged and rusty hulk rising from the waters to our starboard.

"That's all that's left of the old ship the navy used for target practice. We'll be coming up on Billingsgate Shoal pretty soon. Charlie says there used to be a fishing village and a lighthouse out there before the island sank. Off that point over there was a shore whaling station back in the seventeen hundreds."

Her eyes danced with excitement and the breeze that tossed her hair seemed to pour new energy into her lithe body. It was clear Pam loved being where she was, skimming across the blue, satiny sea. She reminded me of a quote from a poet named George Serafides: "The daughters of the sea, Nereids, hurry to the radiance of the rising goddess."

"You like being out here, don't you?" I said.

"It can get wearisome as the season goes on. Home at one in the morning, get the boat fueled and iced, figure out where you're going to go next, out at dawn, commute three or four hours to your job. Then there are the periods in between when you wait for the government to tell you it's okay to fish. This has been a peculiar summer. There are fish everywhere because the bay is loaded with the sand eels they feed on. Lots of whales and dolphins for the same reason. It's been hit-or-miss in terms of quality. But yes, to answer your question, I *do* like it."

"How soon before we see some bluefin?"

"Bluefin rise to the surface during the day. If there are tuna, we'll find them. Charlie's got telescopic eyesight and X-ray vision. He can spot a fish when it's still twenty feet below the surface. I don't know how he does it. It's almost a special sense he's developed."

"Like one of those people who can find water with a forked stick."

"Yes, that's right. I never thought about it quite that way. Only he doesn't use a stick. Maybe he should get one. We fish mostly Cape Cod Bay out to Stellwagen Bank. The bay isn't what it used to be, Charlie says. The fish are small and hard to catch. They don't have the quality the market wants. Only problem now is that there's been a lot of fog offshore, so that's bringing more boats into the bay, putting pressure on the fishery. Did I hear you say you've thrown a harpoon?"

I told Pam about my target practice. She laughed and said, "That's been pretty much my experience. I've harpooned a couple of fish that we caught with rod and reel, but I didn't like it. There's a lot of pressure on the harpooner because so much is at stake. I'll leave the harpooning to Charlie. We work well as a team. I know his body language. He favors one side, so I compensate with my steering for his bad aim."

Before long the black spike on the horizon metamorphosed into the tall granite shaft of the monument marking the Pilgrims' first landfall in Provincetown. Sunlight reflected off the windows of the town nestled between the harbor and the high dunes beyond. As we neared the Wood End bell buoy, just south of the tip of the Cape, Charlie's voice crackled over the intercom.

"Take her due west, Pammy."

She eased the wheel over, watching the compass needle as the boat smoothly came about, then picked up the mike.

"See anything yet, Charlie?"

"Yep. Lots of company."

When we had first started off in the semidarkness, it was as if we were at the center of a great galaxy, surrounded by pinpoints of starlight. As the new day began, ghostly forms emerged from the gloom. Boats were everywhere. They looked like paper cutouts pasted onto blue cardboard.

Pam replaced the mike and turned, that almost-smile on her lips. "Soc, I just want you to know, I really appreciate your helping Charlie."

"I haven't done much beyond bust his alibi."

"Yes, you have. You've made Charlie aware that he's in more serious trouble than he thinks he is."

"I've found it's always easier to get into trouble than to get out of it."

"Especially for Charlie."

"You know him better than I do, Pam."

"I think I do. Most of the time, anyhow." She fiddled with a switch that didn't need adjustment. "I'm curious, Soc. What's your unbiased impression of Charlie?"

I took my time before I spoke, treading carefully.

"I think Charlie's a lot more subtle than he seems, for one thing."

"*Subtle* is the *last* word I might use to describe my husband. What do you mean?"

"The picture most people have of Charlie is a big scary guy with a loud voice. Once past all the noise and bluster you find somebody else."

"Who?"

I thought about it a moment. "Somebody it would be a mistake to underestimate."

"Hmm," she said, mulling over my pronouncement. "You're right about that. Charlie's a lot more complex than people realize. I think that's what caught my attention about him. How much he was like the moods of the sea. He could be stormy. Or as calm as the bay is today. But always mysterious."

"My impression is that his mood could be calculated. He said it the other night. When you're as big and loud as he is, you intimidate people."

"I think that's mostly true, that it's often something of an

act. But there are times when his anger gets away from him."
Her brow furrowed. "Like that argument with Frank."

"How well do you know Powell?"

"What do you mean?" she answered quickly, a startled look
in her eyes.

"Powell worked on your boat. You must have formed some
impression of him."

"Oh. Well, I agree with Charlie. Frank is only out for himself."

"Do you think Charlie would have taken Powell apart?"

"Yes. I do. That's why I intervened."

"I was there. You tamed Charlie like you've done that kind
of thing before."

"I'm used to it. Charlie was arguing with someone the day
we met."

"How *did* you two meet?"

"You mean, how did the young, college-educated girl hook
up with the grizzled old fisherman?"

"No, I meant what I said. How did you meet? Dating service? Singles bar? Blind date? Under a lemon-colored sky?"

Pam's cheeks flushed with embarrassment. "Sorry. I've been
asked the same question by people who wanted to use it as an opening to show their disapproval for a spring-autumn relationship."

"There's not a disapproving bone in my body."

"You'd never get along with my parents talking like that,"
she said, rolling her eyes. "My father was a musician, a compe-
tent but not imaginative symphony violinist. My mother was an
actor. I don't know if she was good enough to have a career at
it. But she often said she had the potential for greatness. How
she quit the theater to have me and my brother."

"Parents sometimes lay burdens on us that we don't deserve."

Pam nodded in agreement. "She and my father, to a certain
extent, pushed me to become the success she never was. I'm
afraid I disappointed them. I never wanted to study drama or
dance. I was one of those little girls who *liked* picking up bugs.
I was happier splashing around barefoot in the shallows looking for snails than doing an arabesque in a flouncy little tutu
and tights."

"When did you go from tutus to tuna?"

"Not right away. I finished college and did surprisingly well as a drama major."

"I'm not surprised. I caught your act at the fishermen's protest."

"Oh, you were there? Thank you. That was pretty easy with a friendly audience."

"Did you ever act professionally?"

"In a way." She laughed. "I got rave reviews for my imitation of someone pursuing a stage career. After college I bounced around. New York. L.A. Europe. Wherever I could find a party. My parents kept paying my bills. They thought I was working to break into the theater, and I'm afraid I encouraged them. Eventually they caught on. The checks stopped. I had to go to work."

"It happens to all of us."

"Luckily, a drama background is very good preparation for waitressing. I ended up at a restaurant on the Cape. Not very fancy. Charlie came in one night. I thought he was a jerk at first. Then I realized he was like nobody I'd ever met. Honest to a fault. Generous. Attentive. That was that. We lived together. Then we got married. My parents stopped talking to me years ago."

Heavy footsteps thumped on the wheelhouse roof. Charlie had climbed down from the tower. He was with us a second later.

"I just spotted some action to the north."

"Bluefin?" I asked.

The wolf grin crossed his windburned face. "Maybe," he said, eyes glittering. "Whyn't you go topside for a bit, Pam. It's real nice up there."

Pam put on a Shaker straw hat that tied under her chin and climbed to the tower. Charlie took the wheel and throttled up a couple of notches.

"You have a nice talk with Pammy?"

"She said you've got vision like Superman when it comes to spotting tuna."

"Better. What else did she say?"

128

"She asked what I thought of you."

"Oh, she did? The little devil. What did you tell her?"

"I said sometimes people have reason to be afraid of you and sometimes they don't."

"You musta guessed by now there are a lotta people around who don't like me."

"I haven't run into any Charlie Snow fan clubs, if that's what you mean."

He laughed. "You figure out why I've got enemies?"

"It might have something to do with your winning personality. But from what I hear, the fishermen who use spotter planes don't appreciate your efforts to ban them. They don't like you crawling into bed with the environmentalists and conservationists they see as the enemy. Some people felt you were getting a little pushy with the Japanese dealers, and that it might rub off on them. How's that for a start?"

"Not bad. You forgot one thing. Jealousy. I catch a lot of fish. The better you are, the more they hate you."

"You'll always find people who'll be jealous, Charlie. You can't change human nature."

"Naw, it goes beyond that. It's the way the whole business has changed," he said with disgust. "Years ago there were fish everywhere, but the price was pisspoor. They used to call these fish 'horse mackerel.' Weren't worth diddly-squat. They'd get into the weirs and tear the nets apart trying to get out. Price finally went up to where you could make a day's pay. I started in a small boat. Rigged a ladder onto the bow for a pulpit. Later we put up an itty-bitty tower. Fifty-five cents a pound was about average. If you got a dollar seventy-five, you think you'd died and gone to heaven. But I'd go out day after day, no matter what the price was. I still do. Some people don't like that."

"I thought fishermen are *supposed* to fish."

Charlie snorted. "You'd be in the minority with some of this gang. This business is different. You've got a card shark mentality in the fishery now. The harpooners get upset because I take big fish early in the season that aren't worth much money, but they put poundage on the quota. They'd rather I hold off until September. If I did what they wanted, we wouldn't catch anything. We don't have a plane. We have to *see* the fish to get it, and the fish don't come to the surface late in the season." His voice grew lower, more intense. "Some guys just see the dollar signs. They say I should wait till the price goes up. Hell, I look at the dollar signs too. It's what keeps the boat going."

"You're saying the big money changed the fishery?"

"Christ yes. Greed drives everything now. People want it all. It's not just Johnny-come-latelies like the *Bluesduster*. Guys I grew up with in this fishery have gone bonkers. They won't even talk with me anymore. You don't dare get into the pulpit with a harpoon till the last minute. If the other boats see you, they'll try to steal your fish. The whole fishery's become like the drug business was back in the seventies. They think they can go out, buy a boat and hit it big. Listen to this." He switched the radio on and fiddled with the channels until a quacking came out of the speaker. "Know what *that* is?"

"Donald Duck talking to Daisy?"

"Some of the hotshot fishermen use *scramblers* so people can't listen in on them, steal their fish. We never did anything like this in the old days. If you found a fish, you'd call the other fishermen in. There was cooperation when you got one seventy-five, two-fifty for a fish. Not like today. No one gives a shit for the other guy anymore. All that counts is bring in as many fish as you can."

"And the planes make that possible?"

"Right. You don't even have to *see* the fish. You can go out in six-foot seas, plane tells you where to go. Say you have a 'kill day.' Fish are all over the place, swimming on the surface. Spit anywhere and you'll hit one. Your plane goes out. Pilot gets a piece of the pie, twenty-five to thirty percent of the catch. He's working for two or three boats. He can get two to four fish a day. That's only one pilot. Christ, it's a bloody massacre."

"Okay, I understand why you don't like the planes, but what's your beef against the electric harpoon?"

"With a zapper, the fish rolls over, dead or stunned, second it's hit. Supposedly more humane."

"*Is* it more humane?"

"There might be something to that. The fish drowns with a regular harpoon because it can't draw water through its gills. All we do is slow the fish down so it suffocates. But those guys don't use the zapper because they don't want the fish to suffer. Main reason is, it keeps the fish from burning up that precious fat. My objection is that it's a tremendous poaching tool. In the general tuna category, you're allowed one fish per day per boat. We've seen guys stick a fish, throw the rig over, stick a fish, throw the rig over, another boat comes along and grabs the fish. Guy who originally caught the fish gets a cut."

"So money, planes, and zappers form the evil triangle?"

"Look, Soc, don't take my word for it. You could talk to a dozen guys who'd say I'm full of it, and they may be right. But I think that when you put the planes and the electric harpoons together, you're whacking the hell out of the fish. It's turned from a harpoon fishery into an airplane fishery. It's no different from hunting bears or wolves from a plane. They banned that because the critters didn't have a chance. Same with the bluefin."

"Frank Powell says the bad stuff was going on from the start. Bricks being dropped from airplanes, things like that."

"Hell, we've had cases where people have been rammed, pulpit snapped right off. I've been shot at out here, Soc. I'll take a brick over a bullet any day."

"Why would somebody shoot at you?"

"Guess they didn't like me using my video camera. I caught a bunch of the boys poaching. Sticking fish then giving it to another boat. Landing more than one fish per boat. I was going to turn it over to the feds, but I got sidetracked a while back."

"So people knew you had the video?"

"It's hard to keep secrets on the shore, you should know that, Soc."

Pam's voice cut in on the radio. "We're running into a little traffic, Charlie."

"Yeah, I can see it from down here. Okay, Pammy, you take over the steering from the tower." He handed me a pair of binoculars and pointed toward the dark dots wheeling against the blue sky. "Let's go see if we can catch a few buzzards." He gunned the throttle and the *Lady Pamela* surged ahead.

Twenty

SEVERAL SINGLE-ENGINED PLANES circled and dipped over a flotilla concentrated a couple of miles north of Provincetown near the edge of the great underwater bank called Stellwagen. Below the planes, the sun glinted off the metal pulpits and spotting towers of a dozen or more tunaboats.

Charlie spit over the side. "Got a little stick-boat convention going on. I see some trollers in there too. Day like today, with the fog offshore, you've got a lot of pressure on the bay. Planes coming out of Chatham, P'town, and Plymouth, all meeting in the middle."

"Tough neighborhood for a fish. I wouldn't want all those harpoons and hooks aimed in my direction," I said.

"Hell, Soc, this is nothing," Charlie snorted. "I count a dozen, fifteen boats today. Four planes. I've seen it when there's *twice* as many. Bloody mess. The plane sees a fish here, the harpoon boats are over there. Other guys are trolling in between. It's constant steaming, back and forth, back and forth. You'll hear hollering and screaming over the radio. People don't give a damn that all that activity drives the fish down. Sometimes troll boats will follow the planes. Or the planes will follow the troll boats. Harpooners come right in and stick a fish that's been following somebody's bait."

"Why not work an area away from the planes?"

"You ever go to a party and have some jerk with bad breath follow wherever you go, talking to your face? That's what it's like trying to get away from those bastards." He squinted at the sky and shook his head. "They say I want the planes out so I can have the bay all to myself. Hell, I just want to be able to do my thing without having some buzzard on my ass."

"Like what happened with Powell?"

Charlie snorted. "His pilot came in on me real low, around five hundred feet. Sonovabitch scared the fish I was chasing, drove it down with the plane's shadow and noise. The pilot musta had his scrambler off, 'cause I heard him calling the boat, saying, 'Get over here, I put the fish down three times.' Well, I put the fish down once and it *stayed* down." He shook his head. "What worries me, the whole situation is getting worse."

"In what way, Charlie?"

"It's crazy, Soc. The tuna fishermen go around yelling how the season should be longer, but those buzzards out there are why the quotas get filled up so fast. Now the troll boats are using them. That's only going to mean faster catches and quicker closings. With the planes, the harpoon-only boats are fishing even in the lousy weather, filling the quota quicker, which defeats the whole purpose of the allowing them to take more than one fish a day. Now *all* the harpoon boats use them. You can't compete in the fishery unless you have a plane, whether you like it or not."

"Then there are some who *don't* like it?"

"Shit yes. You've got a lot of harpooners who don't like the planes, but they're afraid to say so."

"Why?"

"Because if the government *doesn't* ban the planes, the pilots will just say, 'Screw you,' to the guys who spoke out, and they won't be able to get a plane when the next season rolls around."

"Why would a harpooner want to get rid of his plane if it makes him so much money?"

"Simple. The plane gets a thirty percent share right off the top. That's one-third of the catch and the quota going up into the sky."

"Sounds like catch-22."

"Hell, Soc, this is more like catch-222. Put yourself in the tunaman's place. He's only got a certain amount of days each year he can fish. He knows the quota is filling every day he goes out, but that if he doesn't get any fish, he can get shut off without making any money. Bang! The season is closed and he hasn't even covered his expenses. He sees that small group using the planes, and he feels he has to do the same. So he gets an airplane to bail him out."

"How long the planes been around, Charlie?"

"That's another crazy thing. They've hardly been around long at all. The harpooners started using them in the mid-1980s. By 1989 maybe, all the harpooners had them. They didn't start using them in the general category till about 1990. What happened, the planes closed down the harpoon category real quick, so the harpooners switched to boats in general category and brought their planes with them. Been hurting the shore support too. Guys who sell you the ice and fuel and gear don't do any business when the season's been closed early 'cause of the planes. Want to hear something else that pisses me off?"

I was going to hear it whether I wanted to or not. "What's that, Charlie?"

"Before I go after a fish, I've got to have all kinds of permits, depending on which kind of gear I use. Those planes up there are a kind of fishing gear in my view. Yet they don't have to have a permit. I could get in big trouble if I got caught taking more than one fish a day on my permit. Those sky jockeys can help land as many fish as they want."

"Frank Powell says the plane's nothing but a tool."

"Tool to *steal,* in my opinion. You've got a plane, it's easier to break the law, because the pilot can see enforcement coming miles off and tell the boat. Most every complaint you hear about in the fishery, whether it's multiple catches, passing off fish, and boats trying to ram each other, it involves the planes."

"If there are so many good reasons to get rid of the planes, why are they still flying?"

"Hah. Good question. I signed a petition back in 1988. Nearly five hundred of us wanted the National Marine Fisheries Service to restrict planes to everyone but the seiners. Not much happened. Then in 1994, you started seeing more planes in the general category, and you had a lot more complaints again. NMFS knew people were pissed, that the planes were going against attempts to control things. People like me have been speaking out at public hearings, writing letters. I've lost friends 'cause of my big mouth, but now they're coming around. Last year a *thousand* people petitioned for a ban."

Pam called down from the tower. "Charlie, what do you want to do?"

Charlie had worked himself up to a frenzy. I expected him to order ram speed.

Instead, he said, "Hell, Pam, let's have some fun."

He stripped off his T-shirt and scrambled out onto the pulpit, wearing his shorts and sneakers. He picked up a harpoon lashed to the metal railing and pointed into the water off to the right. Up in the tower, Pam cut the boat's speed to a walk and steered in the direction Charlie pointed.

I went to the bow and peered into the green water just ahead of the boat, looking for fins or ripples. Not even a clump of seaweed. The fish had to be deep down. Charlie must be using his X-ray vision.

"Where's the fish?" I called out to Charlie.

"Never mind the fish," he said over his shoulder. "You keep your eye on that plane over there to the east."

The plane had broken off from the swarm and was cutting tight circles over the bay between us and the tuna fleet. He was low, less than a thousand feet.

"Keep watching," Charlie said.

He pointed the harpoon to the left. Pam turned the boat left, then right again, zigzagging wherever the harpoon indicated. The plane widened the diameter of its circle. After a minute or so, the plane spun out of its orbit. The engine buzz grew louder as it headed directly toward the *Lady Pamela,* coming in low. The red-and-white Cessna made one overhead pass before it started a lazy circle with Charlie's boat at the center.

Charlie let the harpoon fly. It splashed into the water at a shallow angle. Pam stopped the boat. Charlie leaned over the pulpit, then pulled the harpoon in by the line attached to it. The pilot must have seen the move because the tight circle over the boat got even smaller.

"Charlie, we're going to have company," Pam called out. She was looking at the sky.

Another plane had broken away from the pack and was heading in our direction. Then another. Within minutes three planes buzzed overhead like gnats. Charlie ignored them. He lifted the harpoon, angling the point down, as if he were going to throw it again.

One plane swooped lower until he was around five hundred feet off the water. He came in over our stern and dipped his wings.

Not all the action was in the air. A couple of tunaboats had deserted the armada and were steaming in our direction. Charlie had been watching them. When the boats got close enough to satisfy Charlie, he secured the harpoon and came back to the wheelhouse. He picked up the radio mike.

"Come in *Bluesduster*. This is the *Lady Pamela*."

"*Bluesduster* to *Lady Pamela*, I read you." Powell's voice.

"Good," Charlie said. "Now read *this*. Tell your plane to stay off my ass."

"Don't know what you're talking about, Charlie."

"You're coming in on my fish. I've got a witness this time."

So *that's* why Charlie wanted me along.

"*Your* fish? C'mon, Charlie. You don't have your name on this guy. He's liable to pop up anywhere. If my plane sees him first, he's ours."

"You and your damned plane can go to hell."

"Competition is the name of the game, Charlie."

"Goddamnit, I don't need this kind of crap, Powell. You want this fish so bad you want to steal him, you can *have* him."

Charlie flicked the radio off. I expected him to be wild with anger. He laughed until tears came into his eyes.

"Let me guess," I said. "You never *did* see any tuna out there."

"Goddamn, Soc, you don't think I'd lead those boys on a wild fish chase, do you?" he said, mock distress in his voice.

"Of course not, Charlie. It would break your heart knowing they're wasting fuel and time chasing their tails."

He slapped me on the back without breaking any ribs. "Couldn't give him up too easy. Powell would have known something funny was going on."

As I'd told Pam, Charlie was rough around the edges, but only a fool would underestimate him. Charlie stepped out onto the deck and yelled up to his wife.

"Okay, Pammy, we don't need this crazy house. Point her due west and give her the gun. While Powell and his gang are out here looking for Tommy the Tuna, we're gonna find us a *real* bluefin."

The boat came around daintily, like the lady she was. Charlie climbed into the tower and took the wheel. As we skimmed over the flat surface of the water with the fresh air blowing in our faces, Charlie Snow's laughter echoed from one corner of Cape Cod Bay to the other.

Twenty-One

WITH CHARLIE RUNNING the boat from on high, Pam stayed in the wheelhouse. She settled into a chair, kept an ear half-cocked for the radio, and read a book of poetry. From time to time she checked the depth finder. I went below to take a nap. I'd hardly settled into the bunk when Charlie's voice boomed down from the tower.

"Fin fifty yards ahead."

Charlie was in the pulpit and Pam had taken his place in the tower by the time I got on deck. He leaned against the railing and watched the rounded crescent fin cut a ripple dead ahead. A minute later he came back off the pulpit without picking up a harpoon.

"Basking shark," he said with a shake of his head. "I thought that's what it was, but I couldn't be sure with the sun in my eyes. Some days you don't see any fish. Other days there'll be big slobs lying on the surface everywhere." He scanned the water. "I love fishing the bay. Guess Powell's right about one thing, I do kinda think of it like my own private pond. Wanta spell Pam in the tower?"

From the tower I had a wide view of the whole bay, the White Cliffs south of Plymouth, the Sagamore Bridge vaulting the canal, even the tops of the office buildings in Boston. I saw humpback whales, dolphins, and a dead ocean sunfish, but not one bluefin tuna.

The sun beat down on my head and shoulders. I was glad when Pam called up and said lunch was ready. She had made chicken-salad sandwiches with slices of apple. After lunch Charlie threw a trolling rig meant to look like a school of squid over the stern, in case the tuna were behind and not ahead of us. He dipped a thermometer into the water a couple of times, muttered to himself, and went back into the tower. Pam explained that you could pretty much tell where the fish might be by the water temperature.

"They get skittish when the temperature is high, like today," she said. "They come up but they won't stay on the surface."

I helped clean the galley, then chose a shady spot on the deck just forward of the wheelhouse where I could stretch out.

Apollo drove his fiery-wheeled chariot across the wide arc of the sky and descended toward the mainland. Still no tuna. The *Lady Pamela* made a jog off Duxbury and headed south, cutting a furrow through the bay past Plymouth Harbor toward the Cape Cod Canal.

Charlie's "box" was proving to be empty.

As the sun went down the sky, a puckering breeze came up. The coolness felt good against my face. Charlie came down a couple of times to use the head and take a drink of water.

Time passed. Just before six o'clock Charlie shouted from his perch.

"Look alive down there! Fin off the port side."

Pam stepped onto the deck with a pair of binoculars. I got stiffly to my feet. A bull's-eye ripple broke the mirrored surface off to the left. Charlie was down again.

"Soc, can you pull in that squid rig for me? Once you do that, stay put. The fish can get spooked by somebody walking around the deck. Be careful when we stick a fish. Everybody gets excited and forgets things; that's when accidents happen.

Pam, keep a light touch on that throttle." She smiled as if she'd heard it a thousand times before and saluted with the brim of her Shaker hat.

"Aye, aye, sir."

Charlie ran out to the end of the pulpit, grabbed a harpoon, and leaned over the rail, scanning the water.

About a hundred feet away a sickle-shaped fin broke the surface. A V-shaped ripple streamed behind it. Charlie pointed with the harpoon. The *Lady Pamela* moved at a crawl, the engine at near idle, trailing in the V's wake. This was not the kind of fishing I was used to, where you throw a bunch of baited hooks over and hauled them in. This was *hunting*.

The fish swam slowly along as if it didn't have a care in the world. Charlie's body was almost flat over the pulpit, parallel to the water. He pointed to the right. The boat followed, moving into a blinding sun sparkle. I lost sight of the fish, but Charlie brought the harpoon back over his shoulder and whipped it forward as if he were throwing a fastball.

Seconds later Pam called out, "You miss?"

"He was too far out." Charlie retrieved the harpoon. He squatted in the pulpit, his head moving slowly back and forth.

After a few minutes he said, "I've lost him. Keep going."

"Don't want to run over him."

Charlie and Pam kept up a steady conversation as the boat moved forward. They worked like a machine. He'd give her directions, she'd acknowledge them and make suggestions. About ten minutes after the first throw Charlie suddenly stood bolt upright and stared at an object gleaming in the water.

"Straight ahead." He pointed the harpoon like a javelin for emphasis.

The boat swung into the sparkle again. Pam shaded her eyes with her hand. "I don't see—"

The harpoon flew through the air.

"Miss again?"

"Yeah. Too far out again." Charlie retrieved the harpoon. He leaned over the pulpit to check the water. The fish was gone. Charlie shook his head. He put the harpoon aside and squatted.

Ten minutes passed before Charlie stood again. Pay dirt.

Four fins cut the water ahead. "Take the one on the left," he said. Pam kept the boat on a port heading.

Fifty feet.

The tuna turned to the right. The boat followed, closing on the V wake Charlie had picked.

Twenty-five feet.

He brought the harpoon up over his shoulder.

Ten feet.

The pulpit was almost directly over the V. Amazingly, the fish still hadn't sensed the sharp-edged disaster that loomed overhead.

Charlie leaned forward and sent the harpoon into the water on an almost vertical trajectory. There was an explosion of foam. A flash of blue and a silver-white belly. The other three fins disappeared as if on cue. Charlie turned and gave Pam the okay sign. She killed the throttle.

Charlie came off the pulpit. "Clean hit," he said. "That was the *easy* part."

The hard part was getting the fish aboard, he explained. Pam came down from the tower to help. Charlie got the fish alongside, using a long-handled gaff, and looped a line around the head. The fish didn't have much fight left in it. Still, it wasn't exactly like bringing in a minnow.

The tail line was attached to a boom that hung off the gin pole, which was basically a short mast with block and tackle. Charlie said he had been meaning to cut a hole in the transom so he could bring fish in from the stern, but hadn't gotten around to it. They would have to lift the tuna clear from the water, then swing it over the side and lower it to the deck.

I moved near the opposite rail to what I thought was a safe distance. The fish looked enormous as it came clear of the water. It was long as I am tall and more than twice as wide. The boat tipped to the starboard as the fish came clear and its full weight pulled against the boom.

"Looks like a seven- or eight-hundred-pounder," Charlie said with satisfaction.

The boat rocked as the dripping fish swung back and forth like a giant armored pendulum. Charlie waited for an inward swing, then moved the boom toward the boat with Pam using the gaff to try to keep the payload under control.

The fish swung in toward me. I expected it to sway back in the opposite direction, but the line snapped as the bluefin reached the end of its arc. The giant fish flew through the air, jerking the gaff from Pam's hand, and crashed to the deck. It skidded at me like a land missile. I did a quick two-step. Pure reflex. Otherwise I would have had a nearly half-ton tuna sitting on my lap, and we hadn't even been introduced.

The fish slammed hard into the side with a wet thud. Lucky Charlie's boat was built with thick timbers. I lost my balance and hit the deck.

Charlie moved fast. He wrapped new lines around the tail to keep the tuna from sliding.

Pam rushed over and helped me up. "Are you all right?"

"The only thing that hurts is my dignity." I rubbed my butt, looking at the fish. Dead or not, it could have crushed every bone in my body. Charlie went over and inspected the broken line. A second later the air crackled with curses.

"What's wrong?" I said.

"Look at this." He shoved the line under my nose. "This line was practically brand-new."

If the line had parted from wear and tear, all the strands would have been frayed and worn. At least half of them were even, like the tip of a brush. The rope had been working at half its capacity.

"Looks like it's been cut partway through," I said.

"Damned *right* it's been cut. Someone wanted us to have a mess of bad luck." Charlie angrily threw the lines down and stared at the bluefin. "Well, we can't worry about that now, we've got a hell of a nice fish and some hungry folks in Tokyo waiting for their supper."

He asked Pam to get on the cell phone and tell the dealer we were coming in. While she did that, Charlie got a sheet of bubble-wrap material to cover the fish so its scales and skin wouldn't dry out.

He gently touched the giant's scales. "Beautiful, isn't it? These fins pull back into the body, and the mouth is smooth, so nothing gets in the way when it's swimming fast. She's built for speed." He tucked the bubble wrap in like a blanket on a child. "I always feel a little sad when I kill one of these animals. I do it to live, not like some of those guys out there, who do it just for the bucks."

Charlie took the helm and sent the *Lady Pamela* steaming across the bay in a straight line that would take us to the harbor and the fish on the first leg of its long trip to Japan.

After a while Pam took over and Charlie went out to gut the fish. I stayed in the pilothouse, but we didn't talk much. I don't know what Pam had on her mind. But I was thinking about how close I'd come to what Charlie called a mess of bad luck. From what I had seen of the cut line, luck had nothing to do with it.

It was dark when I got back to the boathouse. I sensed something was out of place even before I flicked on the lights. The place had been tossed. Somebody had searched it, and they hadn't used a fine-tooth comb. Papers were scattered around the living room. Flour had been dumped onto the kitchen counter. The bedroom floor was covered with the contents from the dresser drawers. My place would never qualify for a spread in *House and Garden* magazine, but this looked as if a twister had gone through it.

I tensed at some rustling in a bedroom closet. Kojak poked his head out and yawned. Some watchdog! I was too tired to deal with the mess. I flopped into bed and went to sleep, finally, but it wasn't easy.

Twenty-Two

THE *MILLIE D.* PASSED her sea test the next morning with flying colors. Sam put the old girl through dizzying paces. High speed. Low speed. Big circles. Little circles. S curves and zeds. She danced through the waves like a young filly gamboling in a sea-green meadow. A flock of squalling gulls darted and swooped in our wake as if they were part of a trained bird act. The palsied vibration had vanished. The wide grin on Sam's burnished face showed his pleasure more than a thousand words. Which would have used up Sam's conversational quota for a week anyhow.

Sam's Yankee frugality eventually overcame his urge to play. "Guess we'd better get her home 'fore we waste a day's fuel," he said with regret. His callused hand swung the wheel over. The *Millie D.* cut a frothy swash through the ocean and strained at its harness toward the low-lying, tan dunes in the distance.

I leaned up beside Sam and cupped my ear. The engine purred like my cat after a tummy rub. "The boatyard did a ter-rific job," I said, watching the mainland draw closer.

"Finest kind," Sam replied. "She hasn't run this smooth in a long time. Really needed that tune-up."

"They did a *tune-up* too?"

Sam's brow furrowed. "Yup. Real funny though. Didn't see any engine work on the bill."

We had picked up the *Millie D.* at the boatyard earlier that day. I raised an eyebrow at the bill and jokingly asked the boatyard foreman if he had forgotten to add a zero to the bottom line.

Boat hardware costs big bucks. You practically have to get a bank loan to buy a marine screw that would cost pennies if you bought the same part for the house. The foreman simply shrugged. "Don't look a gift horse in the mouth," he said.

Some gift. Some horse.

More long-armed *largess* from Tokyo.

We were nearing the cut that offered passage through the barrier beach. The seas became higher and spaced closer together. The *Millie D.* jounced over the watery washboard and popped into the tranquil waters of the protected harbor. Sam cut speed to a few knots. We followed the channel markers to the fish pier with the swirl of gulls still looking futilely for fish leavings.

"Tomorrow okay for a fish day?" he said.

"Maybe not. I'm tied up in a case. I don't know how long it's going to take."

Sam and I have an understanding. The deal is, he gets someone to fill in on the boat when I'm busy chasing bad guys. He scratched his chin. "Maybe I'll wait. Boatyard offered to do some electrical work under the original billing, and it would be smart to take advantage of it."

I agreed. If I was going to be in hock to Takaido, I might as well do it big time.

Maybe I'd gotten as far as I could with Charlie Snow for now. Except for a few butt aches, the main thing I'd learned from my nautical adventure the day before was that bluefin fishing can be hazardous to your health. It also convinced me more than ever that Charlie was innocent. The accident that almost sent me to the happy tuna hunting grounds had been meant to happen to Charlie. Somebody wanted him out of the picture real bad and, when blackmail didn't work, resorted to less subtle ways.

145

At the same time, I realized a sabotaged lifting rope is indiscriminate. It could just as easily have been Pam in the path of a flying bluefin. She would have gotten out of the way with more grace than I did, but the possibilities were still chilling and unassailable. The person who cut the line didn't care *who* got hurt.

I still couldn't figure Pam Snow. She was as complicated as she was beautiful. She seemed to be the loving wife. But she was hiding something, I was convinced of it. And it had to do with Frank Powell. No surprise. Powell was young, rich, good-looking, and educated. Everything Charlie Snow was not.

A trawler was taking up our space in the little jog where the bulkhead angles in next to the fish pier. There's usually enough room for two or three boats. The trawler's skipper saw Sam maneuvering and called over that he'd be out in a couple of minutes. Sam hove to off the fish pier and waited.

I was readying the mooring lines and happened to glance up at the observation platform over the unloading dock. The town had built the platform years ago so the packers and tourists won't get in each other's hair. A handful of spectators leaned over the rail. One of them had a zoom lens as long as a cannon aimed right at me. It wasn't the first time someone's taken my picture. Most fishermen get a kick out of thinking their faces are in family vacation albums all over the world.

The man took his camera away from his eye. He stared impassively at me for a second. Another man stepped up to the railing beside him. They were dressed like twins, with tropical flower shirts, plaid shorts, and white baseball caps. The man with the camera saw me looking at him. He turned away and trained the camera on a hovering gull.

The whole thing only took a couple of seconds. But it was long enough to see that the men had Asian features. Japanese? Hell, tourists to the Cape come from all over the place. Coming home the night before to find my house searched had given me a case of the jitters.

"Look smart, Soc," Sam called out.

The other boat had moved, and Sam was bringing the *Millie D.* up to the bulkhead. I jumped ashore and cleated the mooring lines. We hadn't done any boat fishing, so it only took a few minutes to secure the boat.

As I walked to my truck, Lance the fish-packer yelled my name from the fish pier. I told Sam I'd call him later and headed over to the fish company office. Maybe Lance wanted to massage my eardrums again.

"Lady called yesterday afternoon and left a message." Lance handed me a piece of lined notepad paper with a ball-point scrawl on it.

The message was brief. *Call me tomorrow night.* It was signed Sally.

Maybe it was a mistake to read too much into four little words. Sally and I had been communicating on a subliminal basis of late, so it was nice for either one of us to be direct for a change. I remembered this was the day she was flying with Spinner.

Before I left the fish pier I climbed the stairs to the observation platform. I saw a handful of camera-toting tourists, but no Asian men in white baseball hats. I put it down to nerves. If I didn't get my imagination under control, I'd be seeing Fu Manchu's face in beer bubbles.

Back at the boathouse I changed from work clothes into more respectable khaki shorts, a clean T-shirt, and boat shoes. I dug out the name of the motel where Rick was staying. Kojak was sunning himself on the deck. I told him to take any telephone messages. He yawned. I guess that was something.

I could call ahead to see if Rick was in, I suppose, but I didn't have anything better to do. Sometimes I think better when I'm driving. St. Sherlock, the patron saint of consulting detectives, must have been on vacation. I wasn't any smarter when I arrived in Hyannis a half hour later.

Rick was staying in the cluster of motels that overlook Hyannis Harbor. He had a second-floor unit that must have given him a nice view of the waterfront. I knocked a couple of times. No answer. I didn't blame Rick for being out on a warm sunny day.

It was almost lunchtime. I walked across the street and had a grilled quarter-pounder and fries at a restaurant near the

Nantucket and Martha's Vineyard ferryboat dock. I finished my burger and strolled along the harborside walkway to a pretty little park next to the harbor. I sat on a bench and took in the sights, sounds, and smells. Tour boats, charterboats, fishing boats, pleasure boats, came and went. The total sensory experience. There's no better free show than a busy waterfront, if you like boats.

After a while I crossed the street to the motel. Rick had come back to his room. I could see him from the motel's front parking lot. He stood in the open doorway, leaning casually against the jamb.

Rick was a man of many surprises. It isn't every day you meet a Japanese, Yiddish-speaking detective who likes Garth Brooks. But I had to admit that Rick really had me flabbergasted this time. He was in deep conversation with the last person in the world I would have expected to see him talking to.

My elusive pal John Flagg.

Twenty-Three

FLAGG HAD HIS back to me, but I recognized him immediately. His body is shaped like the head of a wood maul, wide in the shoulders, narrow in the hips, and short in the legs. A young couple came out of a nearby unit. Flagg turned his head slightly and studied them until he was sure they were what they seemed. That's when I saw the profile that looked as if it had been carved on the side of a New Hampshire mountain.

When Flagg had run away from me at the protest rally, I was puzzled but not amazed. Flagg is a mysterious guy. He operates on his own planet, with its separate timetable and geometry. He can always be expected to do the unexpected. It is what has kept him alive in a dangerous business. "First thing you learn about being a troubleshooter," Flagg has said, "is that sometimes trouble shoots back."

I figured I'd run into him again sooner or later, but not this way.

I started toward the stairs that would take me up to the second-floor level. By the time I got to the deck that ran in front of the motel units, Flagg had disappeared. Maybe I'd appeared as a blip on his built-in radar. Some people have a sixth sense. Flagg has a seventh and maybe an eighth, and he moves with a pantherlike quickness you don't often see in big men.

I went to the door of Rick's unit and knocked.

The door practically flew open. Rick must have thought it was Flagg coming back. His jaw dropped down to the cranberry design on his Cape Cod T-shirt.

"Soc! Hey, good buddy."

"Can I come in?"

He gave me a grin that was as insincere as it was broad. "Sure. C'mon in."

Before he stepped back to let me into the room, he stuck his head outside and glanced around. It was a telling move. It told me I hadn't been imagining Flagg.

"Glad you-all dropped by." If his mouth got any wider in that cracker grin, the corners would meet at the back of his head. I planted myself in a chair. "Make yourself at home," Rick said when he saw I wasn't going away soon. "Want a beer?"

"Soda if you have it."

Rick got a couple of cans of Slice out of the fridge and tossed one over.

He settled into a sofa. "What brings you to the bright lights of the big city?"

Before I could answer, the door opened and Robin came in. She gave me that beautiful pearly smile. "Hi, Soc."

"Hi, Robin. I thought you were going back to Providence."

She beamed at Rick. "I thought so too, but Rick convinced me to stay. I'm glad he did."

If I didn't know better, I'd say Rick was blushing. "Robin," he said, "Soc and I have some private stuff to talk about . . ."

"That's okay," she said sweetly. "One of the shop owners is interested in buying my sculptures. He thinks he can sell them as Cape Cod harbor seals. I left my brochures here." Robin went into the bedroom and came out a minute later. "Bye, Soc. It was nice to see you again."

Rick walked her to the door. He held it open a moment, then came back to the couch.

150

He smiled wanly. "I'll tell you, it's handy having a psychic when you're picking a restaurant. She's a nice kid, don't you think?"

"Yeah, and I think there's a lot you're not telling me, Rick."

"Dunno what you mean, Soc," he said, shaking his head like a kid trying to explain away a jelly stain on his chin. "I've laid out the whole schmear."

Rick's cute little Brooklynese shtick was starting to annoy me. But then, *everything* was starting to annoy me.

I gave Rick the hairy eyeball. "Don't take me for a schlemiel, bubba. Your schmear was *dreck*. I saw you kibitzing with Flagg just before he schlepped off."

The lizardy grin vanished. Rick nervously rubbed his nose. "Sure you don't want a stronger drink?"

"This is strong enough."

"I could sure use one." He got up and mixed himself a vodka and tonic, came back to the couch, took a long swallow, and smacked his lips.

"Sure beats sake." He swirled the drink so that the ice made a tinkling sound. He may have been hoping I'd go away if he delayed long enough. I didn't.

"Tell me what John Flagg was doing here."

"Business."

"What *kind* of business?"

"Cop business."

"Let me ask you something that's *not* cop business. Why didn't you tell me you knew Flagg?"

"Flagg asked me not to."

"How come?"

"Business."

My patience was running out like air from a flat tire.

I sighed. "Okay, Rick, I can keep asking questions and you can keep coming up with cute little answers that tell me nothing. Or I can finish my can of Slice. Then I can call the Japanese embassy in Washington. I can tell them that a cowboy cop they assigned to a UN detail is out riding the range. That he's meeting a secret agent of the U.S. government in a Hyannis motel room. That he's been doing undercover work for the NYPD. You'll be back walking the beat in a Kyoto suburb, which might not be so bad."

Rick's eyebrows lifted. "*Wow,* that's pretty good. I'd be worried if I had something to worry about."

"Thanks." I shrugged. "Best I could do on the spur of the moment."

"I'm not kidding. The Kyoto part was a great touch. Really. I'd be filling my britches if it wasn't for one thing."

"What's that, Rick?"

"My government knows all about what I'm doing. In fact they *instructed* me to do it."

I stared at him for a few seconds. "You got any beer?"

"In the fridge. Grab those Cheez-Its too, if you don't mind. God, I love those things."

I popped an Amstel Light and we chewed on crackers for a while. I hadn't really expected my bluff to work. I'd figured Rick to be as hard as a horseshoe-crab shell behind that smarmy smile, and in a way I was glad to know I was right.

"Rick, I've decided to go easy on you," I said when he passed the box over. "Tell me what you know and I won't eat all your Cheez-Its."

He thought about it a minute. "Now *there's* a threat that makes me shake in my boots."

"We professional tough guys know how to play on a man's most basic fear. Yours is fear of losing tasty goodies."

I flipped a cracker in the air and caught it with my chin. I must have seen Richard Widmark do it with a peanut, but the effect wasn't the same. It was enough to impress Rick though.

"Okay, you got me. I can only deal a few cards, *comprenez?*"

I handed the box of crackers back. "Even a pair of jacks would be fine for openers."

"I'll do better than that, Soc. Fact is, I was sent here to baby-sit for you. I was supposed to protect your backside."

"Protect it from *whom?*"

"Anybody who got too close."

"You said your government sent you?"

"Uh-huh. Goes back about a month. A guy on our UN

staff asked me to meet with someone from the National Security Council. Name's not important. He says there's something real heavy going down between your country and ours. That it involved Akito's killing and you might be in the middle of it. They wanted me around in case you got into trouble."

"What kind of trouble?"

"He'd only say it had something to do with the Akito case. They wanted me to look into that too. So I came here and set myself up where I could keep an eye on you, which isn't easy by the way because you're always on the water."

"Where does Flagg come into this?"

"He called me before I left New York. Filled me in on your background, said this was a special case. He called again this morning, said he wanted to see me for an update. He wanted to make sure I was on the job."

Rick grabbed another handful of Cheez-Its and stuffed them into his mouth.

I sat back in the chair. "The whole thing's crazy."

Rick said something that sounded like *mmbrl.* I took it to mean he agreed with me.

"What else can you tell me?" I said.

"That's all I know. Anything else, you've got to talk to John Flagg."

I had an old number for Flagg back at the boathouse. The way he moved around it was probably out-of-date the minute he gave it to me.

"Any idea how to reach him?"

"Just happens that I do." Rick seemed relieved at being able to pass the buck. He went to his dresser and got a business card out of his wallet. The company on the card was named Wilmington Export-Import, Inc. It was registered in Delaware. My guess was that the only thing you'd find at that address was an empty rented office. I copied the number down and asked Rick if I could use his phone. Without waiting for an answer I dialed the number on the business card.

A New Age concerto of beeps and boops serenaded me as the call was patched through.

"Wilmington Export-Import," a deep voice said.

"Hello, John. It's your old pal."

Pause.

"How'd you get this number?"

"You gave it to the baby-sitter. I'm calling from his motel room."

Another pause. Longer.

"You get around, don't you, Soc?"

"Same goes for you, Flagg. I missed you at the fish rally. Then again here at the motel. You move too fast."

"Not fast enough."

"We've got to talk, Flagg."

"Yeah." He didn't sound overjoyed at the prospect, but that was too bad.

"Where are you?"

"In my car heading to Boston. I'm a few minutes from the Cape Cod Canal bridge. Pick a spot."

I thought about it a second and said, "There's a public parking lot east of the Canal Electric Plant. See you there in twenty minutes." I hung up before he could give me an argument.

I stood and said, "Thanks for the beer and snacks, Rick," and headed for the door.

"Hey, waitaminute, what about me?"

"What *about* you?"

He thumped his chest. "Remember? The baby-sitter."

"You've just been fired."

"Aw, Christ, you can't fire me. You didn't hire me."

He had a point there. "Look, Rick, you're a fine fellow and I really appreciate your concern. But to be perfectly honest, I can't have you dogging my ass. I work alone."

Before I got to the door I stopped and turned. "Hey, Rick, are you the *only* baby-sitter they sent over?"

He frowned. "Yeah. All I know of. Why do you ask?"

I was thinking about the Asian guy taking pictures of me from the fish pier platform.

"No reason."

Rick was no dummy. I could tell the mental wheels were spinning from the intense expression on his face. My question had told him a lot more than I'd intended. And probably a lot more than he wanted to hear.

"You're not talking about a couple of guys in white ball caps?"

"How'd you know that?"

"They're out there in the parking lot. I saw them when I was talking to Flagg and again when I went to the door with Robin. They were taking pictures of the motel. I thought, why would somebody take pictures of a motel?"

I didn't answer. I walked out onto the deck and scanned the parking lot. Rick was right. There were the same guys in the white caps. And they had their cameras pointed toward the motel. That is, until they saw me. Then they started shooting photos of seagulls. They must have had a lot of bird pictures by now. I went back inside.

"You have any idea who they are?"

"Never seen them before."

"How'd Flagg get out of here without being seen?"

"Not hard. He walked down the end of the deck, then through a hallway that comes out on the backside of the motel. His car was parked there."

"I'll do the same thing. My truck is out back. You keep an eye on those guys and we'll talk about them later."

I grabbed a plastic bucket and sauntered along the extended deck as if I were headed for the ice machine. I turned into the short hallway and came out onto a deck at the backside of the motel. Stairs led down to the parking lot. Moments later I was in my truck, headed toward the Cape Cod Canal and my rendez-vous with Flagg.

Twenty-Four

FLAGG WAS SITTING at the top of the stone riprap banking that sloped down to the canal. He was facing toward the water watching a fisherman pull in a wad of seaweed when I came up behind him. He turned while I was still a few yards away and nodded, his face impassive.

I sat down beside him. We shook hands. "How long has it been?" I said.

"Year, maybe. Time flies when you're havin' fun."

Flagg didn't look much different from the last time I saw him. He never seemed to change. The mocha skin was as unwrinkled as the day I'd met him in the noncommissioned officers' club at the MACV compound behind the walls of the Quang Tri City compound. The black, wavy hair worn long and combed back from the broad forehead didn't have a single strand of silver. He had on Southern-sheriff sunglasses whose mirrored lenses hid eyes that I knew were dark, almond-shaped, and flat.

"You're looking good," I said.

"Easy living. Government work."

Flagg was wearing a light gray suit and white shirt, his standard summer uniform. He wore a navy blue suit in the winter.

When I'd first met Flagg, he had been rediscovering his Indian roots with the irritating fervor that sometimes afflicts the born-again. After a few years in a job putting out brushfires around the world, he discovered that victimhood was not the sole property of the Native American. He had tempered that passion with a sardonic sense of humor. I noticed, though, that he still wore a turquoise tie clip with a Thunderbird on it.

The narrow paved lane that skirts the edge of the canal was busy with bikers and hikers.

"It's a little crowded here," I said. "Let's take a walk."

We set off along the bike path in the direction of the Cape Cod Bay entrance to the canal.

Flagg got right to the point. "You talked to Rick. What'd he tell you?"

"He said he'd been asked by his government to baby-sit me, and that you were checking on him today to make sure he was doing his job."

"Huh. You know the whole thing then. Don't know why you need me."

"That's right. I know the answer, but not the question. It's like that game. *Jeopardy!*"

"I don't play games. I hate sticking to the rules."

"Give it a try, for old times' sake. What's the question that goes with this answer? He's the godfather type of the Japanese mob. Runs a gang called the Red Dragons."

"No-brainer. Who is Takaido?"

"Not bad. Try this. He's Takaido's nephew and heir apparent. Now deceased."

"Who is Akito?"

"*Very* good. Try this one. He's a PI who was conned into working for Takaido and the Japanese mob."

Flagg glanced at me, a smile playing around his thin lips. "Who is A. Socarides?"

"Congratulations. That was a tough one."

"Not for me. I advised Takaido to hire you."

My heels practically skidded to a smoking stop like a character in a Looney Tunes cartoon. I looked hard into the mirrored shades.

157

"What? *You* hooked me up with Takaido's gang?"

Flagg shifted his gaze out over the canal where tidal rips were cutting sharp creases in the water. "Y'know, this is one hell of a ditch," he said as if he were looking at it for the first time. He started walking again.

I caught up with him. "Yeah, Flagg, it's the widest man-made waterway in the world."

"Do tell."

Flagg settled into a bench next to the bike path and I sat next to him. He watched a big sailboat making its way through the canal under power. "Hope you're not pissed at me for getting you into this," he said finally.

"Of course not," I said pleasantly, "that's what friends are for. Mind telling me exactly *what* you got me into?"

Flagg nodded. "You remember those crazies who killed a bunch of people with poison gas in the Japanese subway couple of years ago?"

"Sure. Sarin nerve gas. It was a big story. They were following the orders of a charismatic cult leader."

"You've got it. They arrested the head crazy and a bunch of the gang. Only problem, they didn't get everyone. Some of the folks got away and formed a splinter group. Which was bad enough, but they took some of their killing hardware with them."

"There's a lot of that kind of thing going around these days."

"Good thing. Job security for me. Japanese government sees it different, though."

"You still haven't explained where I come into this."

"This thing is really bigger than the Panama Canal?"

Flagg was stalling but I held my temper. "That's what they say."

He frowned as if I had told him the world was balanced on the back of a giant tortoise, then went on.

"Folks in Japan have a love-hate thing with the Yakuza. Mob's always operated half in the open. When they had that big quake in Kobe, the gangs ran a better rescue operation than the government. Cops haven't bothered them so long as they didn't hassle law-abiding citizens or leave bodies all over the Ginza. Last few years, though, the gangs have gotten out of control. They almost torpedoed the banking system with bad loans. They called it the Yakuza recession over there. They used to break up corporate board meetings unless they got paid off, but now they're killing CEOs. Been shooting it up in turf wars, innocent people getting killed. So the cops have been cracking down big time. Takaido's got a lot of influence. Cops figure if they can get the Red Dragons pacified, the others will calm down. Takaido tells the government he'll go one better. He'll clean up the rest of the cult crazies as a goodwill gesture."

"That shows how you can be wrong about people. I didn't figure Takaido for a public-spirited citizen."

"He isn't. Turns out the Red Dragons did some business with the crazies, setting them up with weapons and chemical sets."

"Let me guess. Takaido knows that if people find out the Yakuza was involved, the government might have to change its mind about working with the mob."

"Uh-huh. Takaido's all set to move on the cult, get rid of that little embarrassment. Before he can do that, Akito is killed. That changes the whole program. The other mobs figure one of Takaido's enemies did it. He's got to act, show who's boss of bosses, or the guys inside and outside his organization will think he's weak. Only problem, if he starts cleaning house the old-fashioned samurai way, government's going to crack down."

"I think it's called between a rock and a hard place."

"Something like that. So Takaido says to the government if they won't let him do it his way, they've got to serve the killer up on a platter or he'll pull out of the program. No peacemaking. No cleaning up the cult. He'll have to take his chances. Japanese police say Akito's killed in the States, that's out of their jurisdiction. Takaido says, '*Make* it your jurisdiction.' See where I'm heading, Soc?"

"Of course. How could I be so dense? I should have known that the problems of the Japanese government, the Yakuza, and a crazy murder cult would wind up dumped in my lap."

159

"Glad you're not being sarcastic the way you get sometimes."

"I'm *beyond* sarcasm. Where does John Flagg come into this made-for-TV movie?"

"Usual way. Buck gets passed. The Japanese government gets in touch with the State Department. State turns it over to the boys who do the dirty work in the cellar. That's us. The brass says find out who did Takaido's nephew in. Akito's killed on Cape Cod. This is my ol' pal Soc's territory, so I put in a word, say you're the man for the job. Figure we can subcontract your services."

"Takaido knew a lot about me. Was that your doing?"

"He asked a lot of questions."

"Why didn't you just call your ol' pal Soc and ask if he *wanted* the job?"

"That was my plan originally. Takaido's still dragging ass, so I talk to him. Old guy's a hard case, says no middleman. Wheels were already in motion. Figured it wouldn't be a big deal to make an adjustment."

"Except that you started to worry. So you brought in Rick."

"You know how I operate. Can't have too much insurance."

"Why didn't you tell me at that point what was going down?"

"Bad call on my part. Didn't want you to get nervous and mess things up."

"Well, that's really considerate. But if it's no big deal, I don't have anything to get nervous about, do I?"

"Things have a way of getting more complicated than you want them to."

"*How* complicated?"

Flagg shifted his weight uneasily. "Here's how it goes. If Takaido doesn't get to the bottom of Akito's murder, he won't help the government go after the terrorists, the gang wars will start up again, the Japanese government takes a nosedive. New guys will come in who'll be more hard-assed on trade agreements. Down in the District of Columbia, heads will roll."

"*Man.* When will you damn spooks learn to leave things alone?"

Flagg didn't answer.

"What now?"

"Rick says you got the killer. A tuna fisherman."

"Rick's wrong."

"Huh," he grunted. "That could be a problem."

"That's only *part* of your problem. I'm helping the guy who's accused. Charlie Snow."

Flagg frowned. Then grinned. "Heh-heh. Shoulda known better than to use you as a bird dog. You don't come when someone calls."

"Damned right I don't." I got off the bench and started to walk back to my truck.

"Where are you going?"

"If I stay here, I'll push you into that damned canal, Flagg."

Given Flagg's weight and physique, it was a highly unlikely scenario, but he got the point. "Hey," he called, "let's talk about this."

"Maybe after you get those guys in the white ball caps off my ass."

"What are you talking about?"

"Screw you!"

I'd always counted on Flagg as my best friend. He could use all the semantic sophistry he liked, but he'd set me up. I got into my truck. I was still seething. I barely remember the ride back. I didn't want to go home so I stopped at the 'Hole, a local bar I sometimes frequent, drank myself drunk and sober again. In between extremes I remembered vaguely that I had to call Sally. I never got around to it. Some nice people from Poughkeepsie thought I was local color and kept buying me drinks.

The phone was ringing when I got back to the boathouse. It was Charlie Snow.

"What's up, Charlie?" I growled.

"You heard about the spotter plane, Soc?"

My mind was fuzzier than an old tennis ball. I thought he was talking about the fishing trip of the day before.

"What plane? One of those guys who chased your boat yesterday?"

"That's right. Pilot's name was Spinner."

"What about him?"

"His plane crashed in the bay this afternoon."

An icy hand grabbed at my heart.

"There was someone with him," I said. "A woman."

"Yeah, I know. She was doing a survey for the tunaboat association."

"Her name was Sally Carlin."

"Sounds right. Did you know her?"

"She's a friend of mine. Spinner too. Any word on them?"

"Goddamnit, Soc. I'm sorry. From what I hear, nobody survived."

Twenty-Five

"FROM WHAT WE know, sir," said the young coastguardsman, "the plane went down here yesterday afternoon." He tapped the chart on the wall with his fingertip.

"There's no mistake?" I said, knowing the answer, but still hopeful.

"No, sir. There were dozens of eyewitnesses on a whale-watch boat coming back to Barnstable Harbor. The skipper steamed over as fast as he could to look for survivors. He was on site within minutes. Got a GPS fix right here." He penciled an X on the chart in the southwest corner of Cape Cod Bay.

"Any trace of wreckage?"

"We've had two boats on the scene. There was nothing except a fuel slick."

"What did the witnesses say?"

"Everyone we talked to had pretty much the same story. They said the plane passed overhead a couple of times, flying at a fairly low altitude. At one point it flew upside down."

"Upside *down?*"

"I had the same reaction, sir. They said the plane was doing crazy things. Loops. Circles. It buzzed the boat several times, flew wheels-up at one point just skimming the water. When it turned rightside up again, one of the wings hit the water and it cartwheeled."

It didn't make sense. Why would Spinner fly like a barn-stormer? Sally would never let him get away with it. She has low tolerance for fools. She would have grabbed the wheel, kicked Spinner out, and flown the plane home herself if she had to. And why was the plane miles from Stellwagen Bank? I stared at the X on the chart until the grids and depth lines blurred.

"Did you know the pilot, sir?" the coastguardsman was asking. He was a clean-cut kid around twenty.

"Yes. The passenger too."

"I'm sorry, sir."

My eyes came back to the wall chart. The depth in the area was sixty to eighty-five feet.

"How soon can you get someone out there for a recovery operation?"

"Not for a few days."

"Why so long?"

"Congress has cut our funding," said the station chief, an older man who had been sitting at his desk listening to our conversation. "We have to beg divers from the other services. That takes time. The navy divers we'd normally use have been tied up with other projects. We'll get the divers, but it could take a few days. We'll let you know when we hear for sure."

"Thanks, I appreciate that."

I copied the position coordinates from the chart, folded the piece of paper, and tucked it in my wallet. Numbers and letters. Squiggles and lines. All I had left to tie me to Sally and Spinner.

On the drive home I thought about what the plane was doing just before it crashed. I had known Spinner a long time. I'd seen him get so out of it he couldn't walk. But when he told me at the protest rally, "I may be crazy but I'm not dumb," I believed him. Spinner never had a death wish that would make him mix booze or drugs and flying. He got too much fun out of life.

Back home, I went out on the deck and gazed at the island where Sally and I had had a picnic the summer before after a

164

wind-spanked sail across the bay. It all seemed like a dream. After a few minutes some internal survival mechanism kicked in. This way lies madness, it warned. Keep moving. *Do* something. I went back inside and cleaned up some of the mess. That's when I saw the message Lance had taken from Sally on the kitchen table where I had left it.

Call me tomorrow night.

The numbing persistence of memory: hot summer nights, drinking wine coolers and listening to the june bugs scratch at the screen door. Raw spring mornings when we had awakened, bodies warm and intertwined. There were other recollections too. Of time wasted. Hard feelings. Words spoken in anger, or even worse, thoughts left unsaid.

My face grew hot with anger. Damned if I'd let my friends sit on the bottom of the bay while the bureaucracy spun its wheels. I grabbed the phone and pulled a chair to the table. A minute later I was talking to the chief at the Coast Guard station.

"Would there be any problem with you folks if I dove on the plane?"

"You *sure* you want to do that?" the chief said. "Could be pretty rough for you."

"These are my friends. I owe it to them."

"Don't see why not. Just don't touch anything the FAA might be interested in."

"That's no problem. I used to be a cop."

"Well, good luck. We'll keep a boat on call in case you find something."

I thanked him and hung up. Then I took a deep breath, called Sam, and asked if he had heard about the plane accident in the bay.

"Sure, Soc, it was all over the radio. Two people killed, they say."

There was no easy way to break the news. "Sally was on the plane."

"Oh, *no.* You *sure* about that, Soc?"

"I just got through talking to the Coast Guard."

Sam keeps his emotions under lock and key, but he couldn't

prevent sadness from creeping into his voice. "I'm awful sorry. You know how we loved that girl. Don't know how I'm going to tell Millie. She'll be crushed." He paused and said, "You going to be okay?"

"Thanks, I'll be all right. Sam, I've got a big favor to ask." I told him what I wanted.

Sam said there'd be no problem using the *Millie D.* as a dive boat. He appreciated my asking him. Sam could handle the wheel. I needed an experienced dive tender I could trust.

I made another call, this one to Lowell. Uncle Constantine answered the phone. The family was all at the bakery, he said. "Your mother says, 'Come see the new dough-maker, it has a brain.' 'Maria,' I tell her, 'I wish my brain told me to stay in Tarpon Springs.' So now she's mad at me." He brightened. "Aristotle, you coming to see me?"

"That's why I called, Uncle Constantine. I've got a big favor to ask. Would you be my dive tender?"

"Of course! I come now. *Hopa!* I get out of jail at last!"

"Wait a minute, Uncle Constantine. We've got to do this right. You know how Ma worries."

"Hoosh. Sure I do," he said soberly. "Stubborn as hell."

"Get your stuff ready. I'll call Ma at the bakery. I'll say I can't come to Lowell, but I want you to visit me so we can do some fishing. I'll arrange for you to get a ride to the bus station in Boston. I'll pick you up down in Hyannis."

"Okay, okay. But hurry. She's like a fox that old woman."

I hung up, called the bakery, and told my mother I wanted Uncle Constantine to visit me.

"Good idea, Aristotle," she said without a fight. "I send your brother, George, to give Constantine a ride. And Aristotle . . ."

"Yes, Ma?"

"Don't let your uncle lift anything heavy," she sternly warned me. "No smoking. No drinking. His heart . . ."

"I promise I'll take good care of him, Ma."

I called Uncle Constantine and said George would be there within minutes. He said he was already packed.

I had a boat and a crew. I spread my dive gear on the bed and checked each piece of equipment. Then I went to the dive

166

shop, got my air tanks refilled, and picked the brains of a couple of guys who had dived the bay. I was back at the boathouse going over a chart when I heard the crunch of tires on the clamshell driveway. I looked out the window and saw a white Lincoln Continental. The word PIZZA was on license plate. My brother, George, isn't shy about letting the world know he's worked hard to make Parthenon Pizza, the family's frozen-pizza company, the success it is.

I outside went to greet them. George leaned from the car window and smiled. "Special delivery."

The door on the passenger side burst open and Uncle Constantine hobbled over. He's had a bad leg from a case of the bends. He wrapped his long, muscular arms around me in a rib-crushing bear hug and thumped my back like a tom-tom.

"Thanks for coming down, Uncle Constantine."

"*Ohi*, no, Aristotle. I thank *you*." He disengaged and went over to a low bluff that overlooks the bay and threw his arms in the air. *"Eleftheros!"* he shouted to the winds. Freedom.

"Amazing," George said, looking on in wonderment "You'd think he just got out of a Turkish prison."

"From his point of view the Turks would have been preferable. Sorry Ma made you come all this way."

"Hell no. I had to get out of the bakery. She was driving me crazy."

"What was the problem?"

"What *isn't* the problem? She was redesigning the whole plant. You gotta stand back or get run over when she gets going." George shook his head. "You know how God created the world in six days? Ma could have done it in *three*." He lowered his voice. "I think our uncle over there has been getting on her nerves."

"I had the same feeling. Want to come in?"

George whines a lot about running the family business and says he envies my beachcomber lifestyle, but he reaps the benefits. My whole house would fit into his hot tub. It's all I've got, but it must look like a sharecropper's shack to him.

"Thanks," he said, with an involuntary wrinkle of his nose, "I've got to get home. Kids, you know."

Minutes later George pounded out of the driveway in his land boat.

Uncle Constantine took a lungful of fresh air and let it out like the escape valve on a steam engine.

"You know, Aristotle, it's a terrible thing when a man can't breathe."

He put his arm around my shoulders and squeezed hard enough to prove his point.

Later in the day I took Uncle Constantine over to introduce him to Sam. Millie asked us to stay for dinner. She was making burger and potato puffs. Uncle Constantine got into Mildred's kitchen and showed her how to make the burgers Greek style with mint, oregano, and garlic. Sam is a plain meat-and-potatoes man; I couldn't tell if he liked Constantine's recipe or not. "That's what I call interesting," he said thoughtfully after a mouthful of burger. Sam is one of the last of the gentlemen fishermen.

After dinner I laid out the whole story about Sally and Spinner, as much as I knew it. Sam said again how sorry he was. Uncle Constantine listened quietly. Millie fussed over me and refused any help with the dishes. Sam told us to turn in early because it was going to be a long trip and we'd have to be under way well before dawn.

We said our good-nights and drove home. We were barely back at the boathouse a minute before Uncle Constantine said, "You got any ouzo, Aristotle?"

"Yeah, I think so." I pulled a bottle out of the cupboard.

He filled two substantial glassfuls and we went out on the deck. Uncle Constantine produced a crooked cigarette from a crumpled pack of Luckies he'd been hiding from my mother. We sat in the quiet of the late-summer evening listening to the insect chorus at the edge of the huge puddle of darkness that was the nighttime bay. Yellow pinpoints of light glowed in camps on the distant barrier beach.

"It's crazy, the whole thing," he said finally.

"What's that, Uncle Constantine?"

"Life. When I'm married, I always think I'm going to die first, before your aunt Thalia. Diving for the sponges. Maybe too much of this," he said, raising his glass. "Or this." He elevated the cigarette. "When your aunt died, I got mad. I went to the priest. I said I wanted to punch God in the nose. *Poom!*" He swung his fist to make his point.

"What did the priest say to that?"

Uncle Constantine came out with a barking laugh. "Father Demetrious says he doesn't blame me. Sometimes he wants to give God a big kick in the pants. But then he says, okay, Constantine, maybe God's doing you a favor. He took your wife away before she got all dried up, no teeth and big warts on her chin. Now she won't have to visit you in the nursing home where your head is so old you don't know who she is. She'll always be a young girl. When you see her again, she'll be like the first time you saw her at the feast of the Epiphany, beautiful and smelling of flowers.

"I guess what bothers me is that I could have spent more time with Sally, but I didn't."

"Did you and your woman ever sit here and watch the stars?"

"Yes. We did. Many times."

"So, Aristotle! No problem. Even if you only watch *one* night together, it's better than *no* night. Your woman will always be beautiful. Maybe like the priest said, God did you a favor."

"I'm sorry, but I don't believe that, Uncle Constantine."

"Hah! Me neither." He slugged his drink down as if it were springwater. "The priest has to do his job. But we've got to live like men. You got some more ouzo?"

What little family currency I still had would have vanished if my mother could see Constantine smoking and drinking in strict disobedience of her orders. I poured him another glass and said we should be turning in soon because we had to get up early.

"Go to bed, Aristotle. I finish my drink. Then I come too."

I got the coffeepot ready and set the alarm clock for 3 A.M. I told Uncle Constantine to use my bed; I'd stretch out on the sofa. After tossing and turning for a while, I finally fell asleep.

The clatter of Uncle Constantine in the kitchen woke me up. We poured the stiff brew he'd made into a couple of travel cups and drove to the fish pier. Sam had the boat engine warming when we arrived. Within minutes, we had cast off the mooring and slid into the channel. The wet, guttural growl of the *Mildred D.*'s exhaust echoed off the cottage where I'd had my interview with Takaido. Right now he was far from my mind.

The good weather of the past couple of days was holding. The seas were mild going through the cut-through into the Atlantic. Sam kept the *Mildred D.* at a speed of about 14 knots. I set a course north, then west, following the long curve of the Cape. Sam and Uncle Constantine were both in their seventies, but I couldn't have asked for a better crew. They hit it off immediately, the taciturn Yankee and the garrulous Greek, swapping sea stories, comparing the waters of New England and Florida. I wished I could have concentrated on the wealth of their combined experience, but I was already looking toward the task ahead.

The high dunes of Wellfleet and Truro were gold in the slanting rays of the new-born sun. Highland Light blinked as it had for more than a hundred years. By the time we got to Peaked Hill Bar it was daylight and we had started on the westerly turn that would take us past Race Point, then south into Cape Cod Bay in a great spiral.

Around four hours after we started out, I checked the Global Positioning Readings readings against the coordinates the Coast Guard had given me. I told Sam to head west. After a few minutes I drew my finger across my throat. He cut the engine to an idle, and we rocked gently in the ocean. It looked like any other stretch of water. Jade green seas running one to two feet with little rills of froth on them. But this was different. Somewhere down there were Sally and Spinner and the tomb that held them.

Twenty-Six

THE WHALEBOAT SKIPPER who'd seen the plane go down had taken a GPS reading, but he had eyeballed the crash site from a mile away, which meant the position fix he made when he got there was an educated guess.

At least it was a start.

When you're working on the featureless surface of the sea, you have to create your own road map from scratch. I tossed a weighted buoy over the side. The bobbing white plastic globe would be the center of the search. I did some quick figuring on a calculator and told Sam to proceed north from the buoy for three minutes at five knots. This would give us a half-mile run. At the end of the run I threw another buoy in the water.

We steamed back to the center-point buoy and repeated the procedure for the other three cardinal compass points. Soon we had marked out a square mile of ocean.

With the grid staked out, the next step was to use electronic eyes to see what lay under it. For that we had the equipment from my last dive job. It was a state-of-the-art seafloor imaging system developed by Datasonics, one of the high-tech marine outfits near Woods Hole.

I gave Uncle Constantine a run-through on what the equipment did. The system had three parts: a black box that held the electronic guts, the big-screen monitor, and the "fish," a torpedo-shaped probe that was towed behind the boat at the end of a cable.

Uncle Constantine ran his hand lovingly over the boxes. He might not have understood their internal workings—I certainly didn't—but he appreciated their craftsmanship. And their utility.

"You know, Aristotle, this beats dragging a hook on the bottom."

"It's not all push-button, Uncle Constantine. That probe weighs three hundred pounds and we've got to get it into the water."

"Edaxi," he said. Okay. Within minutes he had rigged the trawl-line hauler to take the probe. We hoisted the probe off the deck and through the aluminum trawl chute on the stern. I kept a sharp eye to make sure he didn't lift anything heavy. I don't ignore *every*thing my mother tells me.

Two separate horizontal bands appeared on the monitor screen. The lower one could tell me what was under the ocean bottom. I was more interested in the upper band, which painted a picture of what was on *top* of the ocean floor.

I drew a diagram on a piece of paper, showed it to Sam, and asked him to make a series of slow, side-by-side parallel runs within the square we'd marked out. The side-scan was set so the probe would look at the ocean bottom for a hundred meters on either side of our track, which gave us a total swath of more than six hundred feet.

With the fish in tow, the *Millie D.* made its first run at three knots. At the end of the run Sam swung the boat around in a U-turn that would have done a Boston cabdriver proud. Then he started on a parallel line in the other direction. Back and forth.

Sam can't read a newspaper headline without his glasses, but his practiced eye and steady hand kept the runs as straight as if he were following lines drawn on the water. The bottom flowed across the screen in a steady ribbon, with the seafloor showing as a blackish green. Contours and objects came up lime-toned. Sam finished his last run.

Negative.

I slashed the rectangle with diagonal lines and drew another mile square on the diagram north of the area we'd looked at. Uncle Constantine limped around the deck flipping the buoys over with pinpoint precision.

Sam started his runs in the new square. The probe danced in our wake, scanning each square inch of the ocean bottom rolling under our hull. If anything was down there, we'd see it.

Again the results were negative.

With growing anger I drew more diagonal lines and laid out another rectangle to the west. We had the routine down pat. The deck crew was ready with the buoys. Sam's boat paced off the distance like a soldier walking sentry duty. Up to now, I had shoved my feelings aside to make room for the job at hand. With nothing to show for my work, the personal thoughts were were starting to creep in. If they took over completely, I'd be paralyzed.

Nothing.

We flipped the square over to the south. Again with no results.

Sam cut back on the throttle. "What now?" he asked.

I squinted against the sea sparkle, trying to read the featureless surface. I was frustrated. This wasn't a job that could be done in hours. It could take days, even weeks. The plane could be only yards from our search pattern. I remembered what the people on the whaleboat had said about the crash.

"The plane was flying low, guys, so low that it caught a wingtip and cartwheeled. The bay was pretty calm, like today. The plane might have skipped along the top of the water like a stone before it went down, then would have sunk at an angle."

"Y'know, Soc," said Sam, scratching the white stubble on his chin, "might help if we knew the plane's heading. Anyone see which way it was flying?"

"Maybe," I said. I got on the radio and called the Provincetown Coast Guard station. The young coastguardsman I'd talked to earlier was on duty. He asked if I'd had any luck finding the plane.

"Not yet," I said. "I was wondering, did anyone see which way the plane was heading when it hit the water?"

"I'll check." He came back a few minutes later. "Nothing in the report."

"Damn."

"But I just called the whaleboat skipper. He saw the plane seconds before it went down. He was heading south, back to the harbor. The plane crossed his bow coming in from the right."

West to east.

"Thanks," I said. "You've been a big help."

I went back to the grid I'd drawn and sketched out another two-mile rectangle to its west. Sam got the boat under way. We still had several hours of daylight, but with each minute that passed, a cold hand clawed away another piece of my stomach. I was afraid that if we didn't find something soon, I'd lose courage completely. I'd go back home, drown myself in a bottle, and leave the dirty work to others.

I increased the scanning range to five hundred feet. That would give us a swath of a thousand feet with each run. The *Millie D.* made its runs, back and forth. We were pacing our third quadrant when I heard a sharp intake of breath.

"*Look,* Aristotle." Uncle Constantine pointed to the monitor.

"Hold it right there," I said to Sam.

He throttled the boat down to a crawl, just fast enough to keep the tension on the probe's tow cable.

Uncle Constantine had his fingertip next to a sharp angle of light green barely visible at the edge of the band. It was shaped like the point of a pencil and was sharply defined, indicating something solid.

"Okay, Sam, do another run outside the square," I said. He brought the boat around and steamed back at three knots. All three of us had our eyes glued to the monitor. Swatches of pale green rolled by. Then a couple of rocks.

Then the ghostly image of a plane suddenly popped into view. One of the wings appeared to be missing.

"Hold it, Sam."

The *Millie D.* slowed to a slight wallow and dropped anchor. All the buoys were in the water. I grabbed one of the Clorox bottles we keep around to use as makeshift floats, tied a line and weight onto it, and threw the assembly over the side. I marked an X on the diagram, then went back and studied the screen. Depth was fifty-seven feet. Not a deep dive.

Uncle Constantine was in motion from the second we saw the plane. He had laid out my wet suit, hood and gloves, weight-belt, fins, mask, and the buoyancy compensator, the inflatable vest that holds the air tank. He helped me get dressed and ran me through a check. I pulled on my fins and straddled the rail with one leg dangling on either side while I put some air into the BC.

"We're practically right above it. I'll follow the anchor line down, then let the current drift me over."

Uncle Constantine's brow was furrowed. He tapped his forehead with his finger. "Remember, Aristotle, stay with the dive."

I knew what he meant. Stay focused on the job. The dead were dead. Nothing I could do would bring them back. Don't join them. Down there I was on my own. There was simply no room for grief. That could wait until I got back on the boat.

I nodded, gave him a hug, and set the dial on my dive watch. I pulled my mask down and held it tight to my face, the air hoses close to my chest. I got the other leg over, perched on the rail for a second, then jumped in. There was usual wild explosion of bubbles and momentary shock of cold water before it warmed to skin temperature. I bobbed to the surface. Holding on to the anchor line, I tested my regulator underwater and rubbed spit in the mask to keep the lens from fogging.

Sam and Uncle Constantine were leaning over the rail.

"The *dive,* Aristotle. Remember the dive."

"Good luck, Soc," Sam said.

I gave them a thumbs-up, held the BC hose above my head. As I hit the deflate button, Robin's warning came back to me.

Be careful. Dark, cold water. Empty. Lonely. Death.

I began my slow descent into the unknown.

Twenty-Seven

AT THIRTY FEET, the halfway point in the dive, I stopped and hung on to the anchor line. Above me the *Mildred D.*'s long silhouette looked like a whale floating on the shimmering surface. Below was a spinachy gloom. I squeezed my nose to equalize the pressure in my ears and continued down. The wet suit's insulation was slow to work. Icy chills ran little footraces up and down my spine, and I chided myself for not going with a dry suit. The sea seemed to close in on me, its suffocating weight pressed against my ribs. I had trouble breathing. My lungs couldn't draw air in fast enough.

Christ, what the hell was wrong? I'd checked my gear twice. The regulator was working fine a few minutes ago. I removed the plastic mouthpiece and pressed the release valve. Air burbled out in a hissing explosion. Nothing wrong with the equipment. It was me, I realized. I'd been sucking down air like a sump pump. I should have been taking slow, measured breaths.

Stay with the dive, Aristotle.

Uncle Constantine's reassuring voice whispered in my ear. I slowed my breathing. Soon the exhalations that sent clouds of bubbles past my face mask were regular again. With each breath the tide of dread that had swept over me ebbed. The mind-numbing claws of panic that had threatened to pull me into a dangerous pit of confusion released their grasp. I jack-knifed my body, angled it down along the anchor line, and swam with slow, powerful strokes of my fins.

Minutes later I was on the bottom. I looked at the depth gauge. Fifty-five feet. There was virtually no current. Visibility was fair, thirty feet maybe. I hovered vertically a few feet off the sandy sea floor and pivoted 360 degrees, scanning the murky blue-green.

No sign of the plane. Not even any fish.

I looked at my compass and drew a mental Etch-A-Sketch picture. The *Mildred D.* was almost directly overhead. Using the anchor buried in the sand as a point of reference, I moved north, stopping every twenty feet or so. After about sixty feet without success, I headed east for three minutes. Still nothing.

I backtracked along the top of the T for six minutes and stopped again for a look around. An amorphous, pale green smudge loomed from the murk almost out of my range of visibility. It could be only one thing. I swam closer, covering the distance quickly. The vagueness formed into definite lines and patterns of white and red. It was the Cessna that had buzzed Charlie's boat. *Spinner's* plane. As I approached the plane from almost directly behind, I saw that it was upside down. One wing was missing and the other was dug into the sandy sea bottom.

The plane lay at a crazy angle, with the pilot's side lower than the other and scrunched against the bottom. I swam around to the passenger side, paused for a second over the jagged stub of the wing to unsnap a halogen light from my weightbelt, then moved in closer to the darkened cockpit window.

This was the moment I had feared. Had the dive been a mistake? The officer at the Coast Guard station had warned me it would be tough. I pushed away visions of Sally's dead white face behind the darkened Plexiglas window. My God! What if her eyes are open? My heart was pounding. I wanted to bolt for the surface. Light and air. My hand went to the inflate button on my BC. With one squeeze air from my tank would hiss into my vest, and the positive buoyancy would rocket me to the surface. Then what? It wouldn't be the first time I'd pulled back from Sally, fearful of being too close to her. I was failing her once more.

Stay with the dive, Aristotle.

Damnit, Uncle Constantine, where the hell did *you* come from? The sea plays funny tricks on your senses. It distorts your hearing and sight and, if you let it, will warp your mind. Get a grip on yourself, Soc. Sally would have wanted you to be the first to come to her. Give her *that,* for godsakes!

I bit down on the regulator mouthpiece, pointed the light into the cockpit, and squeezed the switch on the trigger grip. An intense white beam stabbed the darkness and threw back a reflection that blinded me. I blinked the glare from my eyes and peered in. Then blinked again.

The passenger seat was empty.

I moved my face closer so that it was inches from the window. No mistake. The seat was *empty!* Crazy thoughts raced through my head. Maybe this wasn't the right plane. Maybe Sally's body had been jarred loose and thrown into the backseat. Except for one thing. The seat belt was buckled snugly as if it had never been used.

The cockpit wasn't entirely empty, though. A man was slumped against the window on the pilot's side. His back was to me so I couldn't see his face. Spinner? I tried to open the door, but the water pressure kept me from moving it more than a couple of inches. I put my feet against the fuselage for leverage and tried again, using all the strength I could muster in my back and legs. The door opened. I stuck the front half of my body inside the plane. Making sure once more that the backseat was empty, I reached in and pulled the man by his shirt and shoulder until his head came around.

I stared dumbly, trying to comprehend. What was going on? Spinner's hair wasn't black, it was dark red going gray. And Spinner didn't have a beard! The man's weight pulled against my fingers and I let him go. I backed slowly out of the cockpit and let the door close. I swam around the plane one more time to imprint its image on my mind. There wasn't much more I could do.

I pushed the inflate button on the BC and began a slow, controlled rise to the surface. Soon, the spectral outline of the plane merged with the dark water.

I came up around fifty feet from the *Mildred D.* Through the water-streaked lens of my face mask I saw Uncle Constantine leaning over the rail. Like any good dive tender, he'd been watching my bubbles and knew exactly where I'd surface. He waved. I waved back.

I pulled my mask under my chin and shouted, "She's not there!"

Uncle Constantine held his hand to his ear and scowled in concentration. "What you say?"

I swam closer. "Sally. She's not on the plane."

Sam came over and stood next to my uncle. "What's going on, Soc?"

"The *plane.* Sally's not on it."

They looked at each other. "It's *empty?*" Sam said.

"No, there's a pilot, but it's not Spinner. I don't know who the hell he is."

The puzzled exchange again.

"What?" Sam said.

It was a waste of time shouting across the water. I breast-stroked over to the boat and grabbed on to the ladder. I handed up my weight belt, tank, and fins and climbed onto the deck. When I got my breath, I explained what I had found below, and what I *hadn't* found.

Sam pursed his lips, let out a long whistle, and headed for the radio.

"I think I'd better call the Coast Guard," he said.

I looked out over the bay. I wanted to shout for joy, but my impulse was tempered by a big question.

If Sally and Spinner weren't on the plane, where in God's name *were* they?

Twenty-Eight

OFF THE AEGEAN island of Kalimnos is a narrow passage where boats must pass between a gigantic whirlpool and a six-headed monster who lives high on a cliff and snacks on passing sailors. I know this is true because Uncle Constantine told me so when I was young. Other kids got Winnie-the-Pooh and Mother Goose bedtime stories. I got sponge-diving terror-of-the-deep tales.

They were pretty much all the same formula. Diver meets unfriendly critter. Critter tries to have diver on toast. Diver escapes by the skin of his teeth. The only thing that varied was the species of critter. When Uncle Constantine ran out of giant octopi, clams, and squid, he'd breed hybrids. Things like the fearsome clamtopus and the dreaded octoquid. All described with fiendish delight.

"*Six* men I lose. Like this. Chomp. Chomp. Chomp . . . The monster sucked the marrow out of the poor devils and their bones cracked like straw, Aristotle." The stories were invariably accompanied by gnashing teeth and horrible wet chewing sounds. Sometimes he brought in props like pretzels and crunched them gleefully.

The scene that followed was always pretty much the same too. I screamed in fright. My mother would rush in and yell at Uncle Constantine. I had delicious nightmares. I'd beg him to tell me even scarier stories the next night. Which he always did. Bad-tempered one-eyed giants. Witches who turned men into pigs. There seemed to be no end to his tales.

Years later I read about the six-headed monster called Scylla and the whirlpool named Charybdis and came across a few other familiar faces in a little book called the *Odyssey*. Uncle Constantine's plagiarism didn't bother me. I'll bet Homer never chewed pretzels for effect!

The story came back to me on the drive home from the fish pier. Like Odysseus, Uncle Constantine told his men they had two choices. They could skirt the rock and lose six of the crew; or they could brave the vortex and lose ship and all. I empathized with their decision. On one side I had the monstrous possibility that Sally and Spinner were dead in a plane crash. On the other hand uncertainties and unanswered questions whirled around in a dangerous funnel of black water.

Uncle Constantine snuffled in my ear like a rooting pig. He had dozed off against my shoulder within minutes of saying good-bye to Sam at the fish pier. The pickup's worn shock absorbers clunked in the potholes that pock my driveway, but my uncle's eyes didn't blink open until we stopped in front of the boathouse.

"Ah, we're home," he grunted wearily. "Long day, Aristotle."

"A *very* long day, Uncle Constantine."

The Coast Guard patrol boat from the canal station had arrived on site about an hour after we radioed in. I told them what I'd found and they called for divers and salvage boats, but nobody would be able to do anything until the next day. They threw a radar-reflecting buoy into the water over the plane wreck. We started the trek around Provincetown then south along the slender arm of the Cape.

The fish pier was silent when we arrived late that night under a sky filled with burning stars. As we trudged to our trucks, Sam said to call him in the morning and we'd figure out what we'd do next.

181

Back at the boathouse, I insisted that Constantine take my bed again. He was too tired to argue. He yawned, said, "*Kalinichta,* Aristotle," *good night,* and disappeared into the bedroom. I was thirsty and went into the kitchen for a drink of water. I was getting some ice cubes out of the fridge when I saw the bottle of champagne. A red ribbon and a card were attached to the neck. I took the bottle over to the table and read the card.

Dear Soc, Thought we could share this tomorrow night, after I get back from flying, to celebrate my first "real" job as a fisheries scientist. Love, Sally. She had written "7:15 P.M." in the corner of the note.

I hadn't looked in the refrigerator the night before because we had had dinner at Sam and Mildred's house. Uncle Constantine had gotten the ice cubes out for the ouzo. I poked my head in the bedroom and asked him if he'd noticed a bottle with a ribbon on it.

"*Neh,* Aristotle," he said sleepily. "Sure I notice the bottle."

I back-pedaled in time. I had looked in the fridge the morning before I went to Hyannis to see Rick. There was no champagne then. Sally must have come by the boathouse the night *before* she planned to fly. It was the same night someone searched my house. I was drinking at the 'Hole. Sally obviously expected to fly the next day. Yet she didn't. She expected to come back to the boathouse after the flight. She didn't do that, either.

I stretched out on the couch and tried to assemble the pieces of the puzzle. Before long the cumulative effects of sun, fresh air, and underwater exertion overcame the worrisome thoughts. I slipped into a fitful sleep.

The morning sunlight streamed through the window. I resisted its efforts to pull me fully awake. Then the phone rang. It was my mother checking on Uncle Constantine.

"Aristotle, I call last night and you and your uncle, you're not home."

Yeah, Ma, I wanted to say, Uncle Constantine and I were out drinking and chasing women till all hours. Trouble was, she would have believed it. The truth wasn't any better. I couldn't tell her I'd worked Uncle Constantine into exhaustion without any regard to his health. Instead, I picked a middle course between the maternal monster and the whirlpool of lies.

"We went out fishing, Ma. Sometimes you have to wait for the tide to be just right."

My mother waits for neither time nor tide. Natural forces are simply irritating obstacles that must be brushed out of the way. She accepted my excuse, though.

"The fishing, it was good?"

"So-so. Not great."

Uncle Constantine emerged from the bedroom. I mouthed the word *Ma* and pointed to the phone. He made a face, but came over anyway.

"*Kalimera,* Maria. *Neh, neh,* I'm fine. Aristotle is a good boy. We go out yesterday and catch many big fish." My mother is too sharp not to have caught the difference in our fish stories. She must have mentioned the discrepancy, because Uncle Constantine gave me a puzzled look. Understanding dawned in his face. "Oh, sure, Aristotle is right," he said, talking in a stage whisper. "But I don't want him to feel bad. So I say we catch *lots* of fish."

They talked a few minutes longer. Rather, my *mother* talked and Uncle Constantine nodded his head. Finally he straight-armed the phone to me. His eyes were glazed.

"Aristotle," my mother came on again. "I'm sending your brother to get your uncle tomorrow. You take good care of him. No smoking, no drinking, no running around." I heard some rattling in the kitchen. Uncle Constantine came out with a cigarette hanging from his lips.

"I'll take good care of him," I said, glancing at the bottle of ouzo in his hand. She told me again what a good boy I was and hung up.

Uncle Constantine had poured a shot of ouzo into his coffee. He saw me staring at him and thumped his chest. "Heart medicine."

It would have been interesting to hear how ninety-proof hooch is good for anything beyond a buzz and a headache, but the telephone interrupted our discussion. I picked it up, expecting it was my mother calling back.

"Soc," a whispered voice said, like someone with a bad cold.

"Who's this?"

"It's me. Spinner."

In a way I wasn't surprised. Especially after I hadn't found his body in the plane. I'd seen Spinner come back from the dead before; it seemed something he would do. I figured he'd turn up somewhere. It didn't make me any less angry at him for not calling me before this.

"Where the hell have you been?"

"Jeez, Soc, I thought you'd be glad to find out what happened to me."

"I'm deliriously happy. Where's Sally?"

"Huh? Sally? I don't know. She didn't fly?"

"I dove on the plane yesterday. She wasn't in it."

"My God, that's a relief."

"*You* weren't in it either, Spinner. What gives? The pilot was a guy with a beard."

"I know, man. That's Franco Guzman."

"Franco *who?*"

"Guz— Aw, hell, Soc, it's a long story."

"I want to hear every word of it. Where are you?"

"At a pay phone."

"How far are you from the boathouse?"

"Maybe twenty minutes."

"Come over now. I'll wait for you."

"Yeah. Okay. Damn. Franco. Sally. Goddamn."

"*Now,* Spinner." I hung up.

Spinner had an unruly two-days' growth of beard stubbling his chin. Dark half-moons outlined his eyes. He looked and smelled as if he'd slept in his clothes. I sat him down at the kitchen table and poured him a cup of black coffee.

"Okay, pal," I said. *"Talk."*

He glugged down some coffee. "Whole thing started when I got paid half in advance for the flying job, was what happened," Spinner said sadly.

184

"So Tony the bartender opened a new line of credit for you."

"Yeah. How'd you know?"

"Just a long shot, Spinner."

"Anyhow, I got drunk. *Monumentally* drunk. And I met this woman. She was drunk too."

Uncle Constantine, who was sitting across from Spinner, nodded sympathetically and said, *"Big* trouble."

I gave my uncle a look that told him we didn't need a Greek chorus. He rolled his eyes innocently up to the ceiling.

"Go on. What happened next?" I said.

"I woke up the next morning about an hour before I was supposed to show at the airport. I was still trashed. My God, you could have launched a rocket with my breath. There was no freaking *way* I could have flown. Hell, I couldn't even see the steering wheel of the car. I never fly when I'm that buzzed. Malloy's golden rule."

"So you got Franco what's-his-name to fly for you."

"Yeah, that's right. I knew Franco from a long time ago. Down in Florida. We used to fly . . . Never mind." Spinner took another gulp of coffee. "I told him I'd pay him half what I got for doing the flight. He shook his head. Thieving bastard wanted the whole thing."

"What about Sally?"

"She was supposed to meet me at the airport. I assumed she went up with Franco."

"When did you find out about the plane crash?"

"Next day. I went into the bar for a little hair from the dog. Tony looks at me like I was a zombie. 'I thought you were *dead,*' he says. 'I wish I were,' I answered. 'No kidding,' Tony says, 'I just heard about that plane of yours on the radio. Crashed. You and some woman. I was seriously thinking of putting your picture up in with our other dead patrons.' They got pictures of guys crashed in their Harleys."

"That's touching. Why didn't you tell someone right away that you didn't fly?"

"I was too fucked up for one thing. I needed time to clear my head. Plane was leased in my name, for starters. I had to come

185

up with something to tell the tunaboat association. They're the ones who hired me for the photo run. I didn't want to say I got loaded on their money and couldn't fly. Hell, Soc, I promised you I'd take good care of Sally." He scratched his greasy scalp. "Must have been karma, Franco crashing and not me."

"It was more than that, Spinner. The witnesses who saw the plane crash said it was acting wacky. Flying upside down and so damn low that it caught a wing. What was *that* all about?"

"Franco's a hell of a pilot, but—"

"But *what,* Spinner. Spill it."

"It's like this, Soc. When Franco was flying cargo in Florida, he had too much of his own product. Lost a few brain cells, if you know what I mean."

"You were going to send Sally up with a junkie who's burned out half his brain?"

"He's a hell of a pilot, Soc. You've gotta look at the bright side—Sally never flew with the guy."

"No thanks to you, Spinner. We'll talk about that later. They're going to try to raise the plane in the next couple of days."

Spinner leaned back in his chair and grinned. "Everything's cool, then."

"You're going to make it cool. Get on the phone. Tell cops you're still alive, for now anyhow. Then call the Coast Guard. Make it quick. When you're through talking to them, we've got a big job to do."

"What's that, Soc?"

"We're going to find Sally."

Twenty-Nine

SPINNER SLAMMED THE phone down. "Migod," he said with indignation, "you'd think *not* being dead is a bloody *crime!*"

I held my nose and pointed to the bathroom door. "Smelling like a toxic waste dump *is* a crime. The shower's right through there."

Uncle Constantine watched me get some clothes out and toss them into the bathroom.

"You know this crazy man a long time, Aristotle?"

"From the war."

"Ah," he said, as if it explained everything, which, in a way, it did. "I go make breakfast."

While Spinner scrubbed the grit off his body and Uncle Constantine fussed around in the kitchen, I went out on the deck with the telephone. I called Sally's apartment and left a message on her answering machine. I didn't expect her to be there, but I was covering all the bases. Her voice haunted me again when I called her phone at the aquarium and left the same instructions.

I called Provincetown Airport next. They had seen Spinner's plane take off, but nobody remembered a woman answering Sally's description. Sally wasn't the kind of woman people forget. That meant she never showed at the airport. Spinner's pal Franco must simply have decided to go for a joyride alone.

Uncle Constantine brought out a plate of tomato patties fried in olive oil and sprinkled with oregano, three feta-cheese omelettes, and Pepperidge Farm raisin toast.

Spinner emerged from the bathroom rubbing his hair dry with a towel. My borrowed shorts and T-shirt were a little big, but otherwise they didn't look bad on him. We ate on the deck, hungrily devouring breakfast. Spinner helped clean up in the kitchen and I picked up the phone to make more calls. It rang in my hand.

"Soc," Charlie Snow said. "Tried to get you yesterday."

"I was out on the water, Charlie, sorry I didn't get back to you." I told him about my dive, Spinner's miraculous resurrection and Sally's disappearance.

"My *God,*" he said. "Do you need any help finding your girlfriend?"

"I might, Charlie. I'll let you know. Anything new with you?"

"That's what I called for. I thought you might want to know about a couple of guys who came by the harbor yesterday. They were taking pictures and asking people questions."

"This is tourist season. What's unusual about that?"

"They were Japanese."

"You're *sure?*"

"Yeah. Some of the guys talked to them."

"Charlie, was one of them short and heavy and the other guy kind of tall and skinny? White baseball caps."

"Yeah, that's right. Real Mutt and Jeff. Caps too. Hey, do you know these guys?"

"They were at the fish pier the other day taking pictures of me. Did anybody get their names?"

"No, but Pam got their license number. You talk to her."

Pam came on the phone. I jotted down the number she gave me and said I'd get back to her and Charlie.

"Soc," she said. "Those men. Is there any reason to worry about them?" She sounded nervous.

"There might be. I want you and Charlie to lie low for a few days. Stay out of sight. Don't be paranoid, but keep watching over your shoulder. And let me know immediately about anything that doesn't sound or look right."

I hung up, rang Leo Boyle, and asked him to run a registry trace on the license plate. No problem. He called back a few minutes later.

"Alamo rental car," he said. "Name on the Visa card is Tashio Hakira, East-West Trading Company. What the hell's going on?"

"I don't know."

"Tell me another one, Socarides."

"Okay, I'm not telling you everything, but I've only got part of the story. I'll fill you in as soon as I have some answers."

"Talk to me sooner than that if you get in over your head."

"Don't worry. I'll call you before it gets to my chin."

I hung up and punched the number of Rick's motel room. No one answered. I tried Sam's house. Mildred said he'd gone to the fish pier. I told Uncle Constantine and Spinner to find something to do and drove to the pier. Sam arrived a few minutes later. I thanked him again for the use of his boat.

"Any word on Sally yet?" he said.

"I'm working on it, Sam."

He put his hand on my shoulder. "Don't you worry, she'll turn up and she'll be fine."

"I know she will, Sam."

I said I would call him later. I was walking past the packing company office when Lance stuck his head out the door. "How was the fishing yesterday? I went home before you came in."

"It was okay, Lance."

"That's good. Say, you know that lady who called the other day and left a message?"

That lady would have been Sally. "I remember."

"Well, I wrote the message on a piece of paper. Do you still have it?"

"Yes. Why?"

"Real fox came by the fish pier the other day," he said dreamily. "Says she just *loves* fishermen. I wrote her number

189

down. It was on the piece of paper I ripped out of the notebook and gave to you."

I pulled Sally's note out of my wallet. I read off the telephone number on the back to Lance. "Never let it be said that I stood in the way of true lust."

"Thanks, man. I appreciate it. Hey, you ought to make your driveway bigger with all the traffic you get."

Outside of the possums and the squirrels, the only traffic I get is me. I asked Lance what he was talking about.

"I was in the neighborhood so I dropped by your house a few nights ago to see if I could get the number. Coupla cars were coming out."

"About what time was that, Lance?"

"Around seven or eight, I think."

I was still at the 'Hole.

"What kind of cars?"

"White one was a Continental, I think. Then there was a red Honda."

Sally drove a red Honda. I kept a lid on my excitement.

"Did you see who was in the cars?"

"Naw. I was too busy backing up to the cranberry bog where the drive gets wider."

I asked him a few more questions. The big car had at least two people in it. He hadn't seen their faces. I told him to let me know if he thought of anything else, which was probably unlikely given the state of his frustrated libido.

I went back to the boathouse. Uncle Constantine and Spinner were involved a noisy game of backgammon. Constantine was winning. I supposed I should have warned Spinner that Uncle Constantine is the reigning backgammon champion of the Tarpon Springs sponge fleet. I called Boyle and asked him if he could check on the make and color of the rental car. Then I tried Rick's motel room again. This time he answered. He said he'd had a hankering for eggs and grits. The best he could do was fish cakes, which wasn't too bad by the way. Robin was at the pool.

He asked rather tentatively, "Did you talk to Flagg?"

"He filled me in, Rick. Now I need some info. You ever hear of a guy named Tashio Hakira?"

"Doesn't ring a bell."

"What about the East-West Trading Company?"

"That's a front for a Red Dragon operation. How'd you know about them?"

"I'll tell you when you get here. Looks like I might need a baby-sitter after all." I gave him directions to the boathouse.

Boyle called back a few minutes later to tell me the rental car was a white Continental.

I left the deck and walked down to a small beach near the boathouse and sat on the sand with my back to my overturned skiff. I needed a quiet place to think while I tried to connect the dots. This was the picture as I saw it. Takaido sends a couple of his thugs over to watch me. They search my house. Sally shows up with the champagne and catches them in the act. They all leave together. Which is when Lance sees them.

In a way, I owed these guys. If Sally had flown the next day as planned, she'd be in a Cessna sitting on the bottom of the bay with a guy named Franco. I'd have to remember to thank them when I found her. *If* I found her.

It would not be easy. On any given summer's day the population of Cape Cod swells to more than half a million people. The happy-go-lucky vacationers who make up this throng are strung out along a seventy-mile peninsula that varies from a half mile to five miles in width. They stay in hundreds of motels, B and B's, hotels, and rented cottages. There was no guarantee Sally and her new friends were still on the Cape. There was another possibility, but I quickly pushed it out of my mind.

I needed a bird dog with a good nose. Preferably a purebred.

I walked back to the boathouse just in time to hear Spinner's anguished yell at losing another game. I grabbed the phone again and dialed a number.

"Ansel Forbes," a voice answered.

"Hello, Ansel. It's your fisherman friend."

"*Soc.* How are you?" There was talking and laughter in the background.

191

"Am I interrupting a party?"

"Oh, no, I'm at the Four Seasons for lunch. You got me on my cell phone. Is everything okay?"

"I need to ask you a few questions. Can you find someplace to talk?"

"Sure." He put me on hold. A minute later he came on the phone again. "I'm in the men's room. Don't worry. Nobody's here, I checked the stalls. Are all private detectives this cautious?"

"The healthy ones are. I need a big favor from you, Ansel. I want you to tell me where I can find a guy named Tashio Hakira."

"I don't know what you're talking about, Soc."

"Look, Ansel, I'm not in the mood to play lawyer games. You can help me out or I can tell the whole world, starting with the bar association, how F 'n' F does the dirty work for the boss of one of the biggest organized crime gangs in Japan."

There was a silence.

"Mind if I take a leak?" Ansel said.

"Go right ahead."

A moment later I heard a toilet being flushed. Ansel came back on the line. "I needed time to think. How'd you find out about Takaido and his, uh, business connections?"

"Long story. We don't have time. After you find Tashio for me, we'll talk about it."

"What makes you think I'd know something like that?"

"You told me F 'n' F represents Takaido's interests in this country. If he were sending over a couple of company representatives, they would need someone to take care of car and hotel arrangements for them."

Ansel chuckled evilly. "You know, I'm the *last* one you should threaten. I really don't give a damn about this firm. It would be fun to see some of the pompous types around here squirm in front of a grand jury."

"Then here's something for you to chew over. First of all, there is no doubt in my mind that F 'n' F would hang you out to dry along with its dirty linen. Second, Takaido's men are holding a very good friend of mine prisoner. And third, if

192

something happens to her, I will wipe up the floor with what is left with you."

Pause. "Do you really think your friend is in danger?"

"Sorry to spoil your lunch, but do you know anything about the Red Dragons?"

"Yes. I'll see what I can do. Are you at home?"

I gave him my phone number and waited. I stared out longingly at the sails gliding across the blue waters of the bay, too worried about Sally to appreciate the beauty of the living calendar art.

Ansel was true to his word.

"God," he said when he called, "it's worse than the CIA. Luckily I used to date someone in accounting." He gave me the same information Boyle had about the car. Ansel said it was the best he could do for now, but he would keep trying. I believed him and said to call if he heard anything else.

I went back to staring at the bay, wishing I could recruit Flagg, knowing I wouldn't because I didn't trust him. Flagg and his born-again Indian mysticism. What had he told me many times? Don't be so damned logical, Soc. The world doesn't operate on logic. Don't think. Let your mind float like a hungry marsh hawk. I closed my eyes and let my mind drift back to the call from Ansel Forbes. Thoughts tumbled over themselves in a senseless confusion. Damn. Maybe you had to be an Indian to make it work.

Try again. I concentrated on Akito, extracting from my memory everything everyone had told me about him. I was listening to Takaido, then to Boyle pontificating in his office, then I was gliding toward the harbor. I flew on, but something pulled me back like the rustling of a mouse. I hovered over the assistant harbormaster washing down his boat, the spray making a rainbow in the sun, Brad talking about Akito's love for Big Macs, *Gilligan's Island,* saying how Akito sometimes stayed near the harbor in a place he rented.

A place he rented.

I called Ansel Forbes again. "Akito used to rent a place on the Cape. Can you find out where it was?"

"I don't—let me check."

Ansel got back to me a few minutes later. "*Jackpot!* My friend in accounting handled the rent bills. Get this. F 'n' F *owns* the house. We rented it to Golden Sun." He gave me an address and said, "That was the good news. The bad news is that you were wrong. We handled travel arrangements for *four* East-West employes, not two."

"That *is* bad news."

"It gets even worse, I'm afraid. Two more people are on the way from Japan."

"When do they arrive?"

"Tomorrow morning."

"I appreciate the tip." I thanked him again for his trouble and went inside to break up the backgammon game.

Thirty

THE BIG WHITE house sprawled along a low hill overlooking Cape Cod Bay to the west of the tunaboat harbor. It was enclosed on three sides by pretty fencerows of hedge, hydrangeas, and lavender that complemented each other and hid unfriendly coils of razor-sharp ribbon wire. Several acres of sweeping green lawns separating the house from its neighbors covered built-in sprinklers and a state-of-the-art alarm system that would do everything except read a trespasser his Miranda rights.

I knew all this because Forbes had told me about it. Guilt is a wonderful thing. He was bending over so far backward to help that he must be looking at his heels. He knew about the alarm system, and even better, he had plans for it.

Before F 'n' F acquired the house it had been owned by a minor movie star who had been convinced the world would be knocking at his front door so often he wouldn't have time to admire himself in the mirror. He was wrong, of course. This being New England, *no*body recognized him, not even when he identified himself to the regulars at the coffee shop or general store. He went back to California where he could be assured of being annoyed by the public. F 'n' F took over the house in lieu of the substantial legal fees he owed them.

I arranged for Forbes to fax the security system plans to me through a local print shop. Back at the boathouse Rick and I pored over the diagrams probing for weak points. Our unhappy conclusion: a frontal assault on the land side was out of the question. There was no way to get past the wide-open spaces to the house without tripping an alarm or being seen by an infra-red surveillance camera.

There was more than one way to skin a polecat, Rick re-minded me, using one of his Appalachian aphorisms. I never knew whether Rick was going to come across like Myron Cohen or the Dukes of Hazzard. Since we couldn't go in by land, maybe we could go in from the sea, he suggested. I had my doubts.

"You don't lock the farmhouse windows and leave the barn door open," I said.

"True," Rick countered, "but a swarm of bees in May is worth a load of hay."

"What the hell does *that* mean?"

He scratched his head. "Damned if I know. Think I read it in the *Old Farmer's Almanac.*"

While Rick pondered country wisdom, I called Charlie Snow and asked if he could round up a small boat with an out-board. He said he had a Zodiac inflatable with a thirty-horsepower Johnson. I said that was perfect.

Forty-five minutes later I met him at the harbor. He'd thrown a couple of fishing rods in as I had asked. We buzzed out of the harbor, then headed west along the bay shoreline for several minutes until we were about a half mile due north of the house. We got out the fishing rods, cast our lines over the side, and began a slow, easy troll in toward shore.

A couple of hundred yards from the beach I asked Charlie to turn the Zodiac around and head slowly out again. Using his body as a shield, I studied the back of the house through my binoculars, going from the deserted beach with its no-trespassing signs to the wooden staircase that ran up the fifty-foot banking to a sundeck as long as the house was wide.

I wondered if I was being overly cautious hiding behind

Charlie until I focused in on a man who was standing on the deck. He was looking at us through binoculars. It was clear that the house was just as well guarded on the water side. My guess was that the staircase was wired with an alarm like everything else. We headed back to the harbor.

When I told Rick that we'd have *six* Yakuza heavies to worry about tomorrow, he groaned.

"Damned Japanese," he said with a shake of his head. "They always have to do things in groups."

"How much of a problem are the four Yakuza thugs we've got now going to be?"

"You don't want to know."

"I guess that says it all."

"Not by a long sight. Each one of these guys is probably a killer. He's sworn absolute loyalty to his boss. He puts the organization before his own life. Which means he doesn't care diddly-squat about anybody else's."

"What about calling the cops, letting them do the dirty work?"

"Your townie cops got a SWAT team or two?"

"I see what you mean. There's the Staties, but they spend most of their time working the Dunkin' Donuts detail. Guess it's up to us."

Rick spread his hands.

"From what you're saying, six would be a disaster," I said. "If we make a move, it would have to be tonight while it's still four to four."

I was playing fast and loose with the odds-making. My team consisted of Uncle Constantine, Spinner, and Rick. An over-the-hill sponge diver with a bad heart; a pilot who'd lost too many brain cells to booze, dope, and high living; and a Japanese detective who was just, well, weird. Then there was me, a cut-rate private eye. Not exactly the Dirty Dozen, but it was the best I had. Back home, I gathered my troops together.

"Here's the situation," I said. "We're going to have to go in tonight or not at all." I laid out the details of the security system and told them about the two additional Yakuza guys due in tomorrow.

"Aristotle," Uncle Constantine said, "how come you don't go to the police?"

Rick answered before I could. "Not a good idea. These guys would rather go down shooting than let the cops come in. Someone might get hurt."

"Someone like Sally," I added.

"Too bad I couldn't dig up a fully armed Huey," Spinner said wistfully.

"Sure," I said, "if we had a gunship, we could strafe the place and lob in a few air-to-ground missiles. A precise surgical operation. Anybody else got a bright idea?"

We all looked at each other, except for Uncle Constantine, who took a last puff of the cigarette stub he'd been smoking and ground the ashes into a sea-clam shell.

"Sure, I got an idea," Uncle Constantine said almost nonchalantly.

We all looked at him.

"Trojan horse," he said, beaming as if we would immediately know what he was talking about.

We looked at each other again.

"Maybe you should tell us what you have in mind," I said.

Uncle Constantine gave a condensed version that put the Trojan War in its simplest terms:

"Turkish man comes to visit a Greek. The Greek gives him food and drink, but the Turk wants *every*thing. He runs away with Helen, the Greek's beautiful wife. The husband goes crazy. He gets the other Greeks and they go to Turkey to get Helen back. The Turks fight dirty. Then *all* the Greeks go crazy. They build a wooden horse, fill it with soldiers. The Turks take it inside their city. Poom! No more city. No more Turks."

Uncle Constantine smiled at the thought. He is a friendly guy and he'd probably buy a Turk a drink if he met one. But people from his part of the world tend to think in terms of feuds that go back thousands of years.

"I'm not sure I understand, Uncle Constantine."

He outlined his plan. It was built on a shaky foundation of assumptions, guesses, suppositions, and just plain luck. But it was the only plan we had, and no nuttier than building a wooden horse. After some discussion, we decided to push ahead with it.

We spent another hour drawing diagrams and going over who would be doing what. As soon as night fell, we set out from the boathouse in the pickup truck and Rick's Mustang. Spinner and my uncle waited with the pickup a mile down the road where they were out of sight. I got behind the wheel of the Mustang.

"Be danged careful with this car," Rick's muffled voice came from the trunk. "It's a rental."

"I will."

"Hey, Soc," the voice came through again. "I just thought of something real funny. What if your lady isn't here? What if it's just a meeting of the Japanese-American Cultural Society?"

"We'll know in a minute," I said, and put the Mustang into gear.

The driveway stopped at a steel-framed gate and a gatehouse. My headlights caught the figure of a man leaning against the gate. The night was warm but he wore a black, lightweight leather jacket and a white baseball cap on his head. He looked like the shorter guy I had seen taking pictures of me at the fish pier. It was hard to tell how old he was. A small, wiry man, he could have been mistaken for a boy from a distance.

He walked over to the car, a cigarette dangling from his thin lips. Up close his face looked hard enough to chip flint on.

Rick had warned me not to do anything sudden or to say anything or make any move that could be taken as hostile. "These are Red Dragon. Killing's easy as spittin' for these boys." Keeping my hands on the wheel where the gatekeeper could see them, I grinned and said, "Good evening."

A taller man with a long horse face came out of the gatehouse and sauntered around to the other side of the car. It was the other observer from the fish pier. They would know who I was. They eyed me suspiciously, not saying a word.

"Nice night." I was grinning so hard my cheeks hurt.

The man nearest me said something in Japanese. Horse-face answered him, also in Japanese. Their voices were low and wary. At least they hadn't pulled out any hardware.

That situation changed a moment later,

"You don't suppose you could open up so I could go inside, now do you?" I lifted one hand off the wheel and gestured toward the gate.

Two hands reached under the jackets. Two hands came out filled with shiny black semiautomatics.

"I guess not," I said hoarsely, picturing the bullets meeting head-on between my ears. Maybe company solidarity would work.

"Look, guys, you probably don't know this, but we both work for the same outfit, same boss."

Not a single muscle twitched in their tough faces.

"You know who I mean," I said, "Hashimoto *Takaido*."

It was as if I had pushed a starter button. Both men started to talk at the same time, fast. Takaido's name came up several times. They yapped a few minutes, then the one on my side went into the gatehouse. I could see him talking on the phone. Horse-face kept his gun leveled, clutching it with both hands as if it were getting heavy. His pal came back and opened the Mustang door, gesturing with the gun. I guessed he wanted me to get out, because that's what I did and he didn't shoot me.

I kept my hands high while he frisked me for weapons and didn't find anything more lethal than a Swiss army knife. He put it in his pocket and pointed back into the car. I got behind the steering wheel again. While he went back into the gatehouse and pressed the switch that opened the gate, Horseface slid into the passenger seat.

He gestured at the open gate and stuck the gun barrel in my ribs so hard it hurt.

I clenched my teeth, put the car into drive, and pressed the accelerator.

A second later we were within the gates of Troy.

Thirty-One

PHASE TWO OF Operation Trojan Horse was about to kick into action. I hoped.

When I had said we would need a diversion at the gate, Spinner had jumped right in to volunteer. "Connie and I can drive up and pretend that we're a couple of drunks." He had seen it done in a movie whose name he couldn't remember.

He and my uncle would give the guy at the gate a hard time. Not *too* hard a time, Rick warned; the Yakuza might be edgy. Then they'd disengage and stand by for further orders. I agreed reluctantly. If my uncle got hurt, my mother would kill me even if the Yakuza didn't. But I *had* to have the gatekeeper diverted so he wouldn't notice me stopping halfway between the house and the gate. Which was what I was doing now.

I touched the brakes and slowed to a stop.

"Got something to show you," I said. I got out of the car, trying to keep my movements slow and deliberate. The hair prickled on the back of my neck. This could be dicey. I didn't *think* the guy would shoot me unless I threatened him. Or he *thought* I was threatening him. I counted on his being a professional hoodlum. He'd be less apt to have the nervous trigger finger of an amateur and be more inclined to obey the orders of his boss. I assumed those orders were to bring me up to the house in one piece.

He got out of the car, barked in Japanese, and waved the cannon at me. I kept my hands in the stratosphere and walked slowly around to the back of the car.

The stupid grin was still pasted onto my face. It would take a week for my mouth muscles to relax.

"It's in there," I said with a jerk of my chin. "Big surprise."

He glanced with narrow eyes at the trunk. Then he stepped back and held the gun in both hands, still pointed at me. He said something that I took to mean "Open it."

I bent over and fiddled with the lock, stood up, shrugged, and stepped back. He stiffened, eyes darting back and forth from me to the trunk. Timing was crucial here. I wanted to catch his attention.

So I said, "Takaido."

During the moment that followed, several things happened.

He looked at me.

The truck lid flipped open.

His eyes shifted back to the trunk.

The extended barrel of a pistol with a silencer pointed at him.

Thut!

The muzzle blossomed hot red and white. Rick vaulted out of the trunk as if he'd been catapulted. He landed on his feet before Horseface hit the ground, snapped into a bent-knee shooting position, and followed the man's head with his pistol, ready for another shot if needed. He could have saved his energy. Horseface clutched his arm and writhed in pain. He moaned even more when we rolled him over and removed his jacket. Rick's transformation was scary. The little guy with the unlikely accents had disappeared. In his place was a coolly efficient assault machine.

Rick was a good shot too. The wound was right above the elbow. It had hit neither bone nor artery. Rick took a colored bandanna from around his neck and folded it into a makeshift compress. He used a strip of duct tape to attach it, then more tape to make sure the man couldn't move or talk. We put him in the trunk and locked it.

Rick slipped into the leather jacket. It wasn't a bad fit. He stuck the guy's cap on and pulled it low over his eyes. We got back in the car and I drove up to the front of the house. It was a square-built, white-shingled house of two stories, with guest wings on either side of the Georgian-style main building. Parked in front were two white Lincoln Continentals and Sally's red Honda.

The front door was under a square portico supported by four slender columns. The light over the door was on.

"Looks like they're expecting company," Rick said.

"You bring a house gift?"

"Yeah. This." He waved the pistol around.

We weren't trying to impress each other with our cute tough-guy repartee. We both knew Uncle Constantine's scheme looked a lot easier on paper. As Rick soberly pointed out, we weren't dealing with choirboys. We needed a lot of luck. From now on we were making it up as we went along. We didn't know what we'd find on the other side of the door. Only that whoever opened it wouldn't be glad to see us. What really worried me was Sally. Where would she be if bullets started flying?

We started toward the front door, Rick holding the gun on me. I had my hands in the air.

"Ready?" I said, when we got to the door.

The more we delayed, the more dangerous it was for everybody. We were easy shots in the illumination from the overhead light.

Rick pulled the cap even lower over his eyes.

"*Do* it," he grunted.

I punched the doorbell.

The man who opened the door had a gun pointed at my belly. He stepped back to let me into a big central front hallway. He looked at Rick's shadowed face, then at the hole burned in the leather jacket sleeve. His mouth curled in a frown. I took a leaf from the Book of Rick's chapter on preemptive strikes. While he was diverted by Rick, I stuffed my elbow into the side of the man's head. Rick nailed him on the way down with the barrel of his gun, although it was totally unnecessary.

"Japan has strict gun control," Rick said. He pulled the gun from the guy's hand and passed it over to me. It was a Colt Python .357 with a six-inch barrel. It had been a long time since I'd held a gun in my hand, and it felt heavier and more cumbersome than I remembered. I didn't have time to give it further thought.

The fourth Yakuza man stepped into the hallway from a lighted doorway, he saw us and stopped. You could almost hear his heels making skid marks on the polished floor.

Rick smiled.

The man understood the unspoken language of Rick's gun. He grabbed for air. We frisked him but he wasn't carrying.

Low, murmuring voices were coming through the portal that led to a big wing I'd noticed on the drive up to the house. Talking low, Rick said something in Japanese and jerked his gun toward the door. The Yakuza man bowed politely, then led the way into the room. My stomach muscled tensed. I prayed that I would be smart and fast enough to do what had to be done.

With the Yakuza in front of him, Rick moved forward, me following practically in his shoes. We stepped into a brightly-lit oversize living room. At its center, facing each other, were two plush sofas. Sally was sitting in one of them sipping tea. She didn't look scared or worried. She had a look of astonishment on her face. I'm sure it was nothing compared to mine.

Because sprawled comfortably in the other sofa, looking equally surprised, was John Flagg.

Sally sprang from her seat and was across the room in an instant. She threw her arms around me and burrowed into my shoulder. I held her as if she were a bird that might fly away.

"Are you all right?" I said, my eyes still glued to Flagg.

She held me tighter. "I couldn't be better."

Flagg stared, first at Rick, then at me again. His mouth widened in a grin. He started to chuckle. The chuckle changed to a deep laugh.

Tears streamed down his wide cheeks. "The guy down at the

gate called and, heh-heh, said there was a crazy gaijin, heh-heh, trying to crash our party. Shoulda known. Hi, Rick. Doing a good job baby-sitting, I see. You can put your guns away. Folks here are friends of mine."

I didn't see anything funny. My heart had been pounding since I pulled up to the front gate. My shirt was soaked with nervous sweat. And I still didn't know what the hell was going on.

I said, "Don't you know this guy is Yakuza, Flagg?"

Flagg nodded. "Guess I got some explaining to do."

"Guess you do, Flagg."

Rick said, "Before you and Soc have a nozzle, we ought to clean up that little mess we made coming in." Rick told Flagg about the wounded man in the car trunk and the guy sleeping in the hall.

Flagg grimaced, pulled a cell phone from his shirt pocket, and punched out a number. He talked quietly to somebody and hung up. "Housecleaners are on the way. We'd better get the guy out of the trunk."

He looked worried. I smiled. It was nice to see Flagg's life get complicated for a change.

Thirty-Two

AFTER WE'D EMPTIED the Mustang's trunk, Flagg and I drove to the front gate, where I learned the second phase of Trojan Horse hadn't gone off *exactly* as planned. Spinner had driven up to the gate with Uncle Constantine as we'd worked out. They made sure their arrival was well advertised; they laughed and shouted raucously while still hundreds of feet from the gate. The guard signaled for them to stop. They were supposed to ask directions, say, "Guess we're lost," then turn around and leave.

What *hadn't* gone as planned was the guard's reaction. We assumed he'd simply pass them off as noisy but harmless inebriates and would order them to turn around and get lost. Maybe I had made him suspicious earlier. Or maybe it was Uncle Constantine's idea to offer him a swig from his ouzo bottle. Whatever the reason, instead of sending them on their merry way, he had pulled his gun and ordered them out of the truck. That was his first mistake.

The second mistake was keeping an eye on Spinner rather than my uncle. He probably thought Spinner, the younger man, was the more threatening of the two, although it was hard to see why. Spinner was so taken with his role as a drunk that he could hardly stand. His wobbly legs crashed under him. While the guard was trying to figure out Spinner, Uncle Constantine gave him the slug of ouzo without taking it out of the bottle first.

Or, as Constantine put it, "Poom!"

We rigged up a makeshift infirmary in one of the bedrooms. Flagg and Rick administered first aid. Flagg's housekeepers showed up before long. My guess was that Flagg was keeping them nearby. Insurance, as Flagg would say. Four grim-faced men in dark blue suits took away the guy with the bullet hole in his arm, the gatekeeper who'd run into the Dynamic Duo, and the one who'd been introduced to my elbow at the front door. They collected a small arsenal and took that with them too.

I had to say this about Yakuza hoodlums, they didn't hold a grudge. Not even the guy we'd stuffed in the trunk. He smiled and bowed before they took him off for a blood transfusion.

We were all gathered in the big living room. Spinner had passed out in a corner. Uncle Constantine was nodding off. Flagg sat in a chair. And Sally and I were on the sofa. Rick, ever the cop, was keeping a wary eye on the sole Yakuza survivor, who was serving tea and doing it quite nicely.

Flagg and the tea boy exchanged a few words in Japanese. The Yakuza laughed and went off to the kitchen to make another pot of tea.

"What was so funny?" I asked.

Flagg translated. "He said it was a good thing they'd been drinking sake all night or you'd all be dead instead of drinking tea. No disrespect for your assault team," he said.

"Your ninja guys weren't so tough," I said defensively.

Flagg laughed. "Funny thing about it is that Takaido sent these guys over to back you up, case you needed any help."

"Why, it all makes perfect sense. That's why they tossed my house and kidnapped Sally."

"Something got lost in the translation. They followed you and saw you talking to Rick. They didn't know what to make of it, so they decided to talk to you personally. The guy you coldcocked in the hall speaks some English. While they were waiting, they searched your house. Sally showed up, so naturally they took her along."

"Naturally. I wouldn't have expected them to do anything else. How did you get into the picture?"

"They got word back to their bosses. The bosses called me. I came over as soon as I could. Sally could have left anytime after that, but the Yakuza boys were real apologetic, wanted her to have some tea."

Sally sensed a confrontation and tried to head it off. "John arrived about an hour before you did," she said. "He was explaining this to me when you arrived. They've treated me very well, Soc."

"Hell, Flagg, you know me," I said. "I always overreact when somebody breaks into my house and trashes it, drags my friends away, and sticks a cannon in my eye."

"We still got a little problem," Flagg said.

"*We,* white man?"

"Funny," he said, unsmiling. "Fella here must keep you in stitches all the time." Flagg had misjudged Sally's attempt at mediation as siding with him. She set him straight on that score.

"You have to admit, John, that Soc has a right to be suspicious," she said pointedly. "*You* suggested that he be hired for this job. How is it *his* problem?"

"What Flagg is saying is that until we find Akito's killer, no one is going to be happy," I explained. "Isn't that right?"

Flagg nodded. "You got it."

"And Takaido's sending two more tea boys to replace some of those your friends just took away."

Flagg's eyebrows rose. "*Two* more? How'd you know that?"

I smiled, gently took Sally by the wrist and stood to leave.

Rick had been been listening to our conversation through the half-lidded eyes of a Mississippi riverboat gambler. "Flagg's got a point, Soc. Things could still get messy around here."

"It's not my mess."

"Yeah, but Charlie Snow is," Rick said.

I sat down.

"Fact is," Rick went on, "Takaido's not going to call his troops home till the killer is found. He's still got problems with the other gangs, and he's going to have to show he isn't getting soft. Like I said before, he might decide to settle for the most likely suspect. That's good ol' Charlie. It's a matter of honor, nothing personal. Japanese thing. Even I can't explain it."

I leaned back in the sofa and gazed at Sally. She had circles under her eyes and looked tired. The Yakuza boy brought in a fresh pot of tea and poured it all around. I took a sip. It burned my tongue, but my brain cells started working again.

"Okay," I said wearily, "let's start at the beginning, with Akito's murder."

Sally looked around. "This seems like a golden opportunity. Akito spent time in this house as I understand it. Maybe he left something of his life here."

"Smart lady," Flagg said. He was already out of his chair. In short time we found Akito's office. He had a desk near a window with a bay view. The desk drawers were thick with folders. We switched on his computer. It was loaded with files. I glanced at the screen, then at the material in the desk, and wearily shook my head.

"I wouldn't recognize a smoking gun if it were pointed right at me, Flagg. Can you have this stuff boxed and shipped to my place? I'll look at it in the morning."

Flagg said he'd get the paperwork over to me right away. The computer files would take a little longer. We loaded Spinner and Uncle Constantine into Rick's car. He said he'd drop them off at my house and tuck them into bed.

I drove Sally to her apartment over an old carriage house north of Hyannis on the bay side. We left a trail of clothes from the living room to the bedroom. A funny thing happened on the way to an intimate encounter: we talked a long, long while. We told each other things we'd never said before. And after a while, we stopped talking.

Thirty-Three

A NOTE WAS lying on the kitchen table when I got home from Sally's place late the next morning:

Went out with Uncle C. Want to let world know I'm not dead.
It was signed, *The Spin-Man.*

The house was blissfully quiet. With Kojak padding softly behind, I strolled from room to room, onto the deck, and back inside the boathouse again savoring the peace.

Flagg was true to his promise. Next to Spinner's note were two cardboard boxes sealed with tape. I mixed some lemonade, cut the boxes open, and started going through Akito's papers. I found it hard to concentrate. My thoughts kept drifting to Sally. Another problem was that half the records were in Japanese.

Someone must have worked hard through the night. One box contained computer printouts and a note saying more would be on the way. I did a preliminary run-through, placing the contents of the first box into two piles, one English, the other Japanese. Then I called Rick. Robin answered.

"Oh, hello, Soc, how are you?"

"I'm fine, Robin, but I'm afraid I'm going to steal Rick away from you once again."

"That's all right. I have to go back to Providence anyway. Rick's putting me on the bus in a little while."

"It was nice to meet you. Thanks for the psychic reading. You were right about the water part."

"That's good. I knew it would turn out okay."

"Any other advice?"

She thought about it for a minute. "This sounds dumb, but—remember that things aren't always what they seem to be."

"That's not dumb at all. It's good advice to keep in mind. Thanks."

"Thank you for taking me to the Kennedy compound. Here's Rick. Bye."

Rick said he'd come over as soon as he saw Robin off. In the meantime I dug into the English pile. Most of the computer printouts were records of money Golden Sun had paid out to tuna fishermen. Akito did business with a couple of dozen fishermen and dealers between Cape Cod and Maine, making dock payments that totaled in the hundreds of thousands of dollars.

What became quickly apparent was that Powell was selling three times as many fish as the other fishermen. I couldn't figure it. He had two fast boats and a plane. But other fishermen had fast boats and planes as well. Maybe he was just lucky. Some fishermen are.

Rick arrived. I got him set up with a tall, cold glass of lemonade and a pile of Japanese records. The kitchen table was soon covered with papers and we spread onto any flat surface. Kojak came in a couple of times and tried to curl up on the records, but I shooed him out. I think he was feeling neglected.

Before long, Rick held up a sheet of paper. "This is interesting. It's a fax from Golden Sun. They want Akito to finish up his business in the U.S. and come home immediately."

"When was it dated?"

"End of July."

I took the paper out of his hand and examined the intricate characters as if I knew what I was reading. "This doesn't make sense. The season was just starting for the high-paying tuna. Why would they want Akito to come home before the best fish started coming in?"

While Rick chewed that over, I went to the fridge for more lemonade. When I came back, I said, "You told me the day I met you that Akito got banished to the U.S. for getting in trouble. What *kind* of trouble?"

"The worst kind. He wasted a guy from a rival gang in a fight over a woman."

"How did Takaido feel about his heir apparent brawling over a geisha?"

"Takaido never said much about it, which is no surprise. The Japanese don't show their feelings in public. Just remember what I told you, though, that the gang boss is called the *oyabun*. What it means, closest I can translate, is 'parent status.' That's Takaido. Then you've got your *kobun,* which means 'child status.' That's Akito."

"I remember something Takaido said about Akito scaring the fish in the garden when he was a kid. I guess he was precocious even back then."

"The way it works in Japan, it's opposite how it is in the West. Over here, kid's expected to behave, but the older he gets the more freedom he has. Back home a naughty kid can get away with murder, but later on he's going to have to toe the mark or get hammered down, like that nail I told you about."

"Akito was a nail, in other words."

"Worse than that. The word *samurai* means 'servitor.' Loyalty is a prime virtue. You gotta show gratitude. It's not considered cool in Japan to lose self-control. It means loss of face, big-time, when you shame your family."

"Which is what he did when he shot that guy."

"Uh-huh. Someone who brings dishonor to the family is supposed to feel a sense of shame. Trouble is, Akito was shameless. The old man never lets on what he's thinking, but my guess is that he was pissed because Akito showed no shame."

"That guess have anything to do with Akito's missing pinky? The coroner's report said it was a fairly recent thing."

Rick smiled. "What I heard, Takaido demanded the chopchop. It was more than the shooting, though. Akito was acting like the old man had already retired. Takaido wanted to remind his boy who was still the biggest rooster in the barnyard."

"Akito couldn't have been happy about being put in his place. Or losing his pinky."

"He wasn't. I've been hearing rumors of a rumble."

"Something here doesn't fit. Akito was a hothead. On top of that he was getting too big for his britches. Yet Takaido told me he still considered Akito to be his successor."

"Takaido *had* to say that for public consumption. Akito had been making a lot of promises to people about what he was going to do when he was top dog. If they knew Takaido had changed his mind about turning the Red Dragons over to Akito, they could cause problems for the old man. Akito and his boys might attempt a takeover. Hold on a second."

Rick rummaged through the pile of paper. "This is what I was looking for. It's a copy of Akito's letter back to Golden Sun. Says he'd love to come home, but he can't 'cause the tuna season has been extended and he's getting in some great fish."

I handed Rick some telephone bills "These numbers mean anything to you?"

Rick scanned the bills and compared the numbers to the one on the Golden Sun letterhead. "Lotsa little stuff to the company. Faxes probably. He really started using the phone after he got the billet-doux from the home office." Rick sat back and locked his hands behind his head. "Want my finger in the pie?"

"You can put your whole hand in."

"Akito was suspicious about being called home. He knew the old man better than anybody, so he stalls. Then Charlie Snow calls the home office to complain that he's been cheated. Akito knew that would give Golden Sun the perfect excuse for a recall. They'd say he was bringing dishonor on the company. *That's* why Akito went over to try to put things right with Charlie Snow. What does that tell you?"

"He didn't *want* to go home," I said, "because . . ."

"Because he was afraid," Rick said.

"Maybe we've got this all backward. We thought Takaido was all broken up over Akito's murder and wanted the killer caught. Hell, maybe he *wanted* Akito out of the way. Permanently."

We dug through the paperwork again. Rick pulled out a note. "This is interesting. It's written to Akito, routine thing, but it's in Japanese, and it's signed by an American. Guy named Powell. You know him?"

"Yeah, he's a hotshot tuna fisherman. Learned Japanese at MIT. Said he planned to go into high tech. Real knowledgeable about Japan. Wait—"

"What's wrong?"

"I just remembered. One of his crewman said Powell went to the Golden Sun office in Tokyo."

"That so?" Rick said. "Let's go over this again. Takaido's got problems with guys in his own gang who think he's getting over the hill. Akito is breathing down his neck. Takaido can't get rid of Akito outright 'cause it would stir up a mess. When Akito kills that guy, the old man sees his chance. He gets Akito out of the way while he lines his ducks in a row. Then he tells Akito to come home."

"Where a 'warm' reception awaits?"

"It fits."

"Yeah, but I can't figure it. I know we were talking from thousands of miles apart, but Takaido wasn't faking that sadness. I could feel it. How could he knock off his own flesh and blood?"

"He *was* sad. Getting rid of Akito went against the respect the boss guy is supposed to have for his family members. But what he's really looking at is the welfare of the *tribe*. Akito was endangering the stability of the gang by messing around. He had to go. Akito figures he'll be samurai shit the second he steps off the plane, so he plays for time. Now what would you do if you were in Takaido's place?"

"Easy. I'd get someone to take care of him."

"You saw the guys he sent over to watch you. One-man crime waves back home, but in this country they're fish out of water. So who else is he going to get? A hit man from the Sicilian Mafia? Someone from a *Soldier of Fortune* classified ad? Takaido doesn't like not having complete control."

"How about somebody with a lot to lose?" I said.

"Got somebody in mind?"

214

"Yeah, according to these records, Powell is making a bundle selling tons of fish through Akito. Charlie Snow told me he could prove Powell was poaching bluefin. Powell starts to worry when it looks like his money machine will go back to Tokyo with Akito. Powell goes to Golden Sun to see if he can work out a new deal. Takaido knows Powell's history, that he'll do anything to keep the money coming."

Rick reached for the receipts and started going through them. "Powell was getting the big bucks even *after* Akito died. What's that tell you?"

"Powell's payoff for doing a *big* favor for Takaido. Only thing I can't figure out, if Takaido set his nephew up for a hit, why did he turn around and hire me to find the killer? There was always the chance I might figure out Powell did it."

"The inscrutable oriental mind at work. You've got to look at this through Yakuza eyes. The other clans would think Akito was a gang hit. I did for a while. Takaido would look weak if he didn't do something. Takaido *wanted* you to find out it was Powell, that it was outside the gangs, Powell icing Akito over a personal thing. Then his boys would take care of Powell. No loose ends. If you didn't get to Powell on your own, he'd lead you there by the nose."

"Powell doesn't know Takaido will be gunning for him. He's simply covering his own ass," I added. "He tries to frame Charlie Snow. With Snow getting the blame, Powell could get rid of a real pain in the butt *and* any worry he'd be nailed for the murder."

I thought of another reason Powell might want Charlie out of the way. Pam. I went to the cupboard and came back with a box of Cheez-Its. "You deserve a treat. Sorry if they're a little stale."

While Rick got his fingers cheesy orange, I called Charlie at home. Looking back at it later, I should have broken the news to him bit by bit, in person. When he heard about Powell's sales receipts, he did his usual imitation of Mt. Vesuvius.

"Sonofabitch! I *told* everybody Powell was poaching the goddamn ocean dry."

"That's only part of it, Charlie."

215

I filled him in on what Rick and I had concluded about Akito's death. The heat from his reaction came over the phone line.

"So Akito and Powell were in it together. Powell was trying to drive me out of business. When that didn't work, he tried to sink my boat and set me up at the same time."

"Looks that way, Charlie."

"Wait'll I get my hands on that weasel. He's dead meat."

"Take it easy, Charlie."

"*You* take it easy, Cap. I'm not somebody who lets another man steal what's his."

"You don't want to do prison time just because somebody stole your boat."

"I'm not *talking* about my boat."

The line went dead. I called back and Pam answered. She sounded breathless.

"Soc. What did you just say to Charlie?"

"I told him that Powell killed Akito."

"*Migod!* That can't be true."

"That's the way it looks now. Could you put Charlie back on the line?"

"He just rushed out the door. He didn't say where he was going."

I felt as if I'd pushed the go button on an ICBM, and I knew exactly where it would land.

I told Pam I'd try to stop Charlie. I slammed the phone down, grabbed Rick by the arm, and pulled him toward the front door.

"Where we going, man?" he said, clutching his box of crackers.

"We're going to try to prevent another murder."

Thirty-Four

CHARLIE WAS A walking volcano. I knew that. But I'd been so eager to show how smart Rick and I were when I spilled the whole story about Powell I'd forgotten that a big mouth can be a dangerous thing. Now Pam was about to pay for my case of the dumbs.

Traffic was slow and it took a half hour to get to the harbor. Plenty of time for Charlie to get into trouble. We skidded to a stop next to Charlie's truck and Pam's car, ejected from my pickup, and raced down the boat ramp toward the tunaboats.

It was déjà vu in reverse. This time, Frank Powell stood in the stern of his boat. Charlie and Pam were on the pier. From what I could see, Charlie had made a big mistake. He should simply have walked up to Powell and given him a knuckle sandwich to chew on. My guess was that I wasn't the only one who couldn't resist shooting off his mouth. I based this assumption on the fact that Powell had time to fetch the gun that was leveled at Charlie.

As we approached, the barrel swung in our direction.

"Stay out of this!" Powell ordered. We stopped a couple of dozen feet away. The confrontation must have just started because it hadn't attracted any attention. It was just the five of us. Charlie tried to take advantage of Powell's momentary distraction. He took a step toward the boat.

Powell brought the gun barrel around. Charlie froze.

"Frank, don't," Pam cried out.

Powell laughed. "Sure, anything for ol' slam-bang, thank-you Pam."

You would think that by this time Powell would have learned that it didn't take much to set Charlie off once he was primed. Maybe he just didn't care. Maybe he *wanted* Charlie to come at him. If that's the case, he got his wish. Charlie started for him again, ignoring the black, ugly muzzle pointed in his direction. Pam saw what was happening and stepped in front of her husband. Powell had an instant when he could have growled a warning, waved the gun, or given Charlie the chance to push Pam out of the way, which is what would have happened. Instead, his eyes went flat and his grip tightened.

The gun's crack echoed around the harbor. The bullet caught Pam high and right. She spun around and her hand clutched her shoulder as she fell to the deck. Charlie forgot Powell and knelt down to catch Pam in his arms. Powell cast off the mooring lines, then waved the gun before he ducked into the *Bluesduster*'s pilothouse. He could have saved his energy. Rick and Charlie were busy with Pam. I sprinted for the harbormaster's shack and shouted for someone to call the rescue squad.

When I got back to the tuna dock, Pam's head had been propped up on a boat cushion. Rick had folded his cranberry T-shirt into a neat compress and was keeping it tight to the wound. The bandage was already soaked with blood. Pam's face was even paler than usual. Charlie was kneeling by her side. He shouted her name in the kind of voice people say can wake the dead.

The eyelids fluttered. Her eyes focused on Charlie and there was recognition in them.

Heavy footsteps thumped along the dock. Two EMTs from the Rescue Squad had arrived with their rescue kit. I learned later that they'd been at the beach around the corner when they got the emergency call, stitching up a kid who'd cut his foot on a shell. They gently pushed Charlie back so they could work and snapped an oxygen cup on Pam's mouth and nose. A faint pink flush crept into her face. They opened her shirt and checked her wound.

"She's lost blood, but it's not in a vital spot," one of the EMTs said. "Whoever put this compress on did a good job."

Rick grinned. "Thanks. Tokyo cop training."

They quickly redressed Pam's wound, then got her onto a stretcher and carried it toward the ambulance. Charlie followed, with Rick and me just behind. I expected Charlie to get into the ambulance, but he stopped and looked back to Powell's empty slip. The *Bluesduster* had slipped out of its mooring during all the confusion.

Charlie's neck and arm muscles seem to double in size.

"Powell," he snarled, his nostrils flaring. "*He* did this."

I followed his gaze and glimpsed a spotting tower through the forest of masts. It was moving toward the harbor entrance.

Charlie glanced at Pam once more, then strode toward his truck. I went after him and got there just in time for him to slam the door in my face. The truck's wheels dug a shower of dirt and gravel. Rick and I jumped into my pickup and tried to follow Charlie's fish-tailing Chevy as it blasted out of the parking lot. A truck that was backing up a boat trailer to the launching ramp pulled in front of me. I hit the brakes and swerved.

Rick had seen Charlie's truck turn down the marina road. By the time we got there, Charlie was standing at the top of a banking that sloped down to the channel. He was watching the *Bluesduster* approach the harbor entrance. Powell was ignoring the 5 mph "no-wake" speed limit. The washboard ripples set every boat in the harbor to rocking.

Another minute and Powell would be through the entrance and into the bay.

As we approached, Charlie did a curious thing. He reached into a nearby rubbish barrel and pulled out what looked like an empty fifth of vodka. He disappeared over the top of the banking. By the time we got there he was below us, standing on the fuel deck. I peeked into the trash barrel as if it could tell me what he was up to.

Rick was way ahead of me. "*Uh*-oh," he said.

Charlie had grabbed the hose from a fuel pump. He kneeled on the dock and was filling the bottle with gasoline.

"Goddamn," I said. "Is he doing what I *think* he's doing?"

"Dude's making a Molotov cocktail, Soc."

It wasn't hard to see what Charlie had in mind. The channel between the fuel dock and the opposite side was only about fifty feet across. Powell would have to come right past Charlie on his way out of the harbor.

I yelled, "Let him go, Charlie. We'll get him later."

Charlie turned and gave me that scary smile. Then he stepped to the edge of the fuel dock, took the bandanna from around his neck, and stuck it in the mouth of the bottle. He calmly waited, granite still, holding the makeshift firebomb behind his back.

Something went *pop-pop,* over the sound of the boat's engine.

Wood splinters exploded on the fuel dock a few feet from where Charlie stood. Powell was shooting at Charlie through an open window in the wheelhouse.

The second shot shattered the glass covering the fuel pump gauge. Charlie didn't flinch. Rick and I hit the dirt, which was totally unnecessary because Charlie was the intended target.

Powell gunned his engine and moved the *Bluesduster* closer to the opposite shore to where the beach ended and the riprap boulders began. A small sailboat on its way in passed between the fuel dock and the *Bluesduster.* The sailboat tossed in the tunaboat's wake and its boom whipped back and forth.

Charlie coolly waited until the *Bluesduster* was in the clear. Then he brought out the bottle and touched a match to the gas-soaked bandanna. He held the blazing bottle over his head for a second, then whipped it across the channel with his harpoon arm.

The bottle hurtled like a rocket toward the *Bluesduster* in a near-flat trajectory that left a fiery trail through the air. An instant later, the firebomb smashed against the side of the wheelhouse in a tinkle of glass.

Whoof!

There was an explosion of yellow and red. Flaming gas spread onto the deck. Powell burst from the wheelhouse and scrambled up the ladder to the spotting platform. In those few seconds with nobody at the wheel, the *Bluesduster* veered to the right and slammed into the beach.

Through the black, greasy smoke I saw Powell climb onto the rail at the top of the tower. He paused, but he didn't have much choice. He jumped into the channel, barely clearing the rail, and hit the water with a belly flop that must have hurt.

He tried to swim toward the shore on the far side of the channel. The current pushed him toward the riprap on our side.

Charlie was at the water's edge waiting for Powell. He reached down and dragged him by the collar onto the boulders just as Rick and I got there.

"That's enough, Charlie," I said. "We'll take it from here."

Charlie grabbed a fistful of wet hair and lifted Powell's head. I don't know if he would have slammed Powell's face into the rock. I didn't give him the chance. I put my hand on his shoulder.

"Charlie," I said, sharper this time. "Pam *needs* you."

Powell lay there panting, all the fight gone out of him.

"Looks like a drowned possum," Rick commented.

Charlie must have seen the resemblance too. He lowered Powell's face gently to the rock.

"Pitiful" was all he said.

"We'll take care of him," I said.

"I don't give a rat's ass *what* you do with him," Charlie said, moving off. "I'm going to see my wife."

He climbed the rocks in the direction of the parking lot. Rick and I let out the breath we'd been holding.

Rick glanced at the blazing boat and the black cloud over the harbor, then back at Powell. "You know something, Soc, this place is crazy. I can't wait to get back to the peace and quiet in the Big Apple."

In the distance, sirens wailed.

221

Thirty-Five

THE MIDDLE-AGED LADY volunteer working the hospital's reception desk said Pam Snow was out of the intensive care unit and gave me her new room number. Pam smiled when I poked my head in the room, especially after she saw the dozen red roses in my hand.

"Oh, my," she said, looking at the bouquets that filled every level space. "You may have to ask the nurse for a vase. A lot of the fishermen sent me flowers. I think Charlie bought out the florist. That's his vase over there." She pointed to a flower burst that dwarfed all the others.

The duty nurse found a vase and my posies joined the rest.

Pam was still on IV and connected by cables and wires to various monitors. Her arm and shoulder were bandaged, but she looked well.

"I'm going to be sore for a while. Good thing the tuna season is about over."

"I just saw Charlie at the harbor. He says he'll come by later. He's helping clear away what's left of the *Bluesduster*. Says he feels guilty about blocking the channel."

"Will he have any problem with the police?"

I shook my head. "He was trying to stop a fleeing felon. A firebomb might be considered excessive, but Powell's going to be too busy with other legal matters to sue Charlie for damages."

Charlie told me what had happened before Rick and I arrived. It was pretty much as I figured. Charlie had gone to the harbor to turn Powell inside out. Instead of simply decking Powell, Charlie had to gloat first. That gave Powell the opportunity to get his gun. Then Pam showed up.

"Frank was going to kill Charlie, I was sure of it," Pam said. "He was trying to goad him with his nasty little nickname for me. He hated Charlie." She closed her eyes and her voice lowered to a whisper. "But I never thought Frank would shoot me."

"Powell won't be shooting anyone for a while," I said.

I told Pam about my conversation with Boyle. Powell laid out the story on a plea-bargain offer. Powell said he and Akito had an "arrangement." He brought in fish he caught illegally. Akito bought them for top dollar and doctored the records so everything was legal on paper. Powell gave Akito a kickback for his trouble.

The night Akito was killed, he'd come by the harbor looking for Charlie. He was afraid of being recalled to Japan, so he was going to offer Charlie a deal. Charlie would call Golden Sun and say he was mistaken complaining about Akito. In return, Akito would buy Charlie's fish at better-than-average prices. He wouldn't even ask for a cut of the action.

Charlie was sleeping his binge off at Gretchen's. Akito ran into Powell. *Caught* Powell, actually, on Charlie's boat. Frank was searching for that video of him poaching. Akito told him their deal was off, and that Charlie was climbing aboard the gravy wagon in his place. Powell threatened to tell Golden Sun. Akito said go ahead, he had all the records of the illegal fish Powell had sold him. It was bad timing, given Powell's state of mind and the deal Takaido offered him if he got Akito out of the way.

Akito went back to his car to get some paper so he could leave a note on Charlie's boat. Powell was waiting to nail Akito with a harpoon. Afterward, he took the *Lady Pamela* to the mouth of the harbor, locked the steering, then jumped off and swam to the beach.

Pam had listened quietly as I talked. Now she impaled me with a level gaze. "You knew how it was between Frank and me that day we went fishing, didn't you?"

"I suspected earlier than that."

"How? Was it something I said or did?"

"Just a feeling."

Her mouth widened in a sad smile. "It's amazing. The human capacity for self-delusion is endless. Frank and I got to know each other when he fished with us. He came along at a bad time in my life. He seemed like a breath of fresh air. Charlie can be grim at times."

"You don't have to explain."

"I want to. I have to tell *somebody* for godsakes."

"Okay, it's your call."

"We broke off after he quit. I thought that was the end of it. Then we started up again. Frank was always something of a snake, I'll have to admit, but a charming snake. He'd changed. He'd become colder. Or maybe it was me, realizing how unfair I was being to Charlie. I pulled away. Frank wanted to see me again the night Akito was killed. I was with him when Charlie came home from his sister's house. I told Frank we were through for good. He was furious. Maybe that's what sent him over the edge."

"Frank had gone over the edge a long time ago."

"You may be right," she said doubtfully.

"You have to remember Frank wasn't a pro at this. Killing Akito was almost an accident. He was *primed* to do it but hadn't worked up the courage. Once you *think* something is possible, it becomes easier to do it. Akito said he was ending their deal. That was the real push that sent Powell through the window of opportunity. Giving Akito's body a boat ride was a crude attempt to link Charlie with the crime. Later on he even sabotaged his own electrical harpoon to divert attention."

"I've been wondering about something else. The line being cut on our boat."

"Just a quick swipe with a knife. *That* was calculated. Powell *wanted* Charlie to catch a bluefin in the face. I happened to be the one who almost got squashed."

"I don't understand. If he wanted to frame Charlie, why would he try to get rid of him?"

"As far as Frank knew, Charlie had a solid alibi and a sharp lawyer. Looked as if he'd walk."

"I worked on that boat too. I could just as easily have been the one hurt or killed by what Frank did."

"No doubt about it."

"He didn't really care about me, did he?" she said in a dull-edged tone.

"You've got your answer under that bandage."

"I suppose I do." She stared off into space and sighed heavily.

"Tell me, do you think Charlie knew about us all along?"

"He knows Powell had the keys to your boat. He might wonder how Powell got them."

"*Migod!* Frank must have stole them from me. Of *course* Charlie would know."

"Has he mentioned anything to you?"

"Never." She seemed to wilt. "I don't know what to do now."

"That's easy. Get well. Then do nothing. Charlie doesn't want to hear any confessions. Pick up your life where it left off. Charlie loves you. That's all you have to know."

She thought about it a minute.

"You're right. Thank you for making it so clear. You should go into the advice-for-the-lovelorn business."

I could have told Pam that I was better at solving other people's problems than my own. I didn't. Instead I kissed her on the forehead and wished her and Charlie well.

It had been a busy morning.

Flagg had come by first thing. We'd sat out on the deck with our coffee. Flagg eventually got around in his usual elliptical fashion to what he intended to say. He talked about the weather, politics, the attempts of his tribe on Martha's Vineyard to build a gambling casino, narrowing the conversational circles until just the two of us were at the center.

225

"I did a lousy thing to an old friend of mine," he said, inching a millimeter closer to the subject at hand.

"Well, I wouldn't worry too much about it, Flagg. The *Mildred D.* runs like new, I've got some yen in the bank for a change. I had an excellent adventure with a crazed uncle and a maniac pilot and the opportunity to meet fascinating people from different cultures."

"Huh. Guess maybe you should thank *me.*"

"Guess maybe you shouldn't push it, pal. Besides, you know how we always seem one up on each other. I owe you a favor similar to the one you bestowed on me."

"Maybe we should call it even," he said, heaving his bulk out of the chair. "Got to get back to D.C. to make sure the Republic is safe."

"Before you do that, we've still got a problem with Takaido. I wouldn't want Powell to find a homemade knife in his ribs, courtesy of the Red Dragons, while he's taking in the sun in the prison exercise yard."

"No problem. I already talked to Takaido about that. Suggested he wouldn't want it to get around that he had set his nephew up. He agreed maybe he'd let the American authorities take care of Powell."

"Nice of him. He'll never be called to accounts on Akito's murder, will he?"

"His kind never are. He never actually hired Powell to get rid of the ungrateful nephew. He merely suggested that it might be to Powell's benefit if Akito were no longer in the picture. It wasn't even a question of right or wrong. Akito would have taken the gang back to the strong-arm stuff. Takaido was acting for the good of the group."

"A Japanese thing."

"That's right."

"Charming. I hope you gave him my regards."

"Didn't have to. He said to give you his thanks. Says I'm a fine judge of men with honor. What do you think about that?"

I had a flashback to swimming goldfish and a beatific grandfatherly smile.

"I think I won't be turning on any television sets very soon."

After Flagg left, I gave Uncle Constantine a ride to Hyannis and put him on a bus that would get him back to Lowell. He and Rick bade an almost tearful good-bye at the boathouse and vowed to hitch up again when they were both in Florida. Ouzo makes brothers of all men I guess.

Uncle Constantine seemed ten years younger. He thumped my back hard enough to hurt, kissed me on the cheeks, then practically danced up the steps into the bus.

Before he left I said, "Remember, Uncle Constantine, if my mother asks, we went fishing every day and caught lots of fish."

He held his finger up to his lips in the universal sign of conspiracy. "You come down to Tarpon Springs soon, Aristotle. You show me a good time here. Next it's *my* turn."

"I can hardly wait, Uncle Constantine."

Spinner turned to me after the bus drove out of sight.

"I'm going to miss that crazy old Greek."

"Just think of the fun you'll have at your reunion."

"No hard feelings about the thing with Franco flying my plane?" he said warily.

"How could I be angry at an old comrade in arms who saved my butt back in Nam?"

"Aw, hell, Soc, I was afraid you might still be mad at me."

"I *will* be mad if you don't take it easy with Uncle Constantine. He's got a bad heart, you know." I was beginning to sound like my mother.

"Are you kidding? Your crazy uncle will kill *me* before I kill him. Do you know where we ended up the other day?"

"The less I know the better."

I had two more stops to make after leaving the hospital.

The first was at Rick's motel. He and Robin were packing to leave. She had decided to stay another night. She gave me a hug and said that the waters were no longer dangerous and fishing would be good. Rick pulled me into the kitchen.

"Got some news for you. Robin and I are going to be an item. She's thinking about moving to New York. She can do her walrus sculptures anywhere."

"Congratulations. Let me know if you set a date."

"You bet." He handed me a big box of Cheez-Its. *"Mazel tov,"* he said with a grin.

"Mazel tov."

As I left Rick's motel, I remembered what Sophocles had said: that sometimes we ignore the good in our hands until we've lost it. Smart guy, Sophocles. I thought I'd lost something good the day I dove on Spinner's plane. And I wasn't going to ignore it any longer.

I got in my truck, joined the parade of hot and happy people clogging the roads in search of the perfect Cape Cod vacation, and headed over to Oceanus where Sally was waiting.